TIM WAGGONER

THE MOUTH
OF THE DARK

This is a **FLAME TREE PRESS** book

Text copyright © 2018 Tim Waggoner

FLAME TREE PRESS
6 Melbray Mews, London, SW6 3NS, UK
flametreepress.com

Distribution and warehouse:
Baker & Taylor Publisher Services (BTPS)
30 Amberwood Parkway, Ashland, OH 44805
btpubservices.com

Thanks to the Flame Tree Press team, including:
Taylor Bentley, Frances Bodiam, Federica Ciaravella, Don D'Auria,
Chris Herbert, Matteo Middlemiss, Josie Mitchell, Mike Spender,
Cat Taylor, Maria Tissot, Nick Wells, Gillian Whitaker.

The cover is created by Flame Tree Studio with
thanks to Nik Keevil and Shutterstock.com.
The font families used are Avenir and Bembo.

Flame Tree Press is an imprint of Flame Tree Publishing Ltd
flametreepublishing.com

A copy of the CIP data for this book is available from the British Library
and the Library of Congress.

HB ISBN: 978-1-78758-013-8
PB ISBN: 978-1-78758-011-4
ebook ISBN: 978-1-78758-014-5
Also available in FLAME TREE AUDIO

Printed in the US at Bookmasters, Ashland, Ohio

TIM WAGGONER

THE MOUTH
OF THE DARK

FLAME TREE PRESS
London & New York

PROLOGUE

It's dark, the air hot, thick, and heavy. She's naked, skin coated with a layer of slime that makes her itch all over. She wants to scratch – God, how she wants to – but she can't move. She's held fast, like an insect trapped in tree sap, her back, arms, and legs pressed into some kind of sticky substance, leaving only her head free. She faces downward, head hanging. She's too weak to lift it, and since she can't see anything, why bother?

She's not alone. She can hear others breathing. Sometimes she hears them moan softly, but she never hears them speak. She figures they're not strong enough to talk. She knows she isn't. She senses that they're stuck in the same whatever-it-is as she, but she has no real way of knowing. They just *feel* close to her.

There are still others here, wherever here is. These others are not constrained, and they move around freely. They aren't here often, coming and going as they please, and they never speak. At least, she's never heard them do so. They move almost silently, but she's been hanging here long enough that she's learned to detect the subtle sounds that they make. The rustle of cloth, the soft padding of rubber-soled shoes.... Most times they go past her without stopping, and she's very grateful when this happens. Other times they do stop, and then....

She doesn't like to think about what happens then.

She sleeps much of the time. At least, she thinks she does. How can she tell when it's always dark and quiet and time has no meaning? She can't remember the last time she ate or drank. She's not hungry or thirsty, though. She thinks the slime that coats her flesh might be feeding her somehow, but it's only a guess. It could just as easily be killing her. How would she know?

Time passes – she doesn't know how much – and eventually she hears the distinct rustle of cloth. Although it's pitch-black, she closes her eyes, the way a very young child might do in the hope that if she can't see anything then she can't be seen either. She wills the Other to pass her by. She doesn't bother praying. She may not know much about this dark place, but she knows this much: prayers don't work here.

The rustling grows louder, closer, and then it stops. She hears faint breathing – shallow and even – and she senses a presence close by. She squeezes her eyes shut tighter, as if by doing so she can banish the Other standing beneath her. She struggles to speak, to say *No, please don't,* but the most she can do is let out a near-silent exhalation of breath as she mouths the words. It doesn't matter. Even if she could scream the words, she knows her plea would be ignored.

She hears another rustle of cloth and feels something cold and hard press against her bare abdomen. It's rounded and solid, metal of some kind, she thinks. She imagines it's the end of some kind of staff. She can feel weight behind it, as if someone's pressing it against her flesh. The slime retreats from the spot where the metal touches, as if to make sure not to interfere with what is to come next. Or maybe it fears the metal's touch as much as she does.

The metal begins to grow warmer the longer it's pressed against her, and the heat quickly becomes uncomfortable, then painful, then agonizing, until finally it becomes excruciating. There's light, too, and she can see it blaze even through her closed lids. Tears pour from her eyes and she grits her teeth so hard she wouldn't be surprised if they shattered. It's at this point that she always wishes she will pass out from the pain, but she never does. She thinks it's because the Others don't want her to.

Then, when it feels as if the metal is molten-hot and will burn a hole all the way through her to the spine, the rod is removed, and she hears the Other step back several feet. Even though the metal is no longer in contact with her body, her abdomen still burns. She feels the warmth inside her now, feeding on her, growing stronger, becoming...something. Her abdomen swells rapidly, as if she's experiencing a hyper-fast pregnancy. Her flesh grows tighter, harder, until finally it splits down the middle and something slides out of her with a wet sucking sound. It hits the floor with a heavy *smack* and just lies there.

The pain is beyond anything she's ever felt before being brought to this place, beyond anything she's ever imagined was possible for a human body to experience, let alone endure. She hopes the pain will kill her this time. At least then she won't have to go through this anymore. But then the Other steps forward and touches the staff to her abdomen again. This time the metal's touch is cool and soothing, and she feels the terrible injury that's been done to her start to heal.

No, she thinks. *Please, let me bleed out....*

When the repair is complete, the Other removes the staff or rod or whatever it is and walks away, off to tend to another of the trapped. The thing that fell out of her is left behind, and after a while it begins to move, making moist sounds as sticky limbs slide against each other. Finally, it stands, and she can hear the wet sounds of its bare feet moving as it readjusts its weight, struggling to remain standing. It comes closer to her, puts its lips to her ear, and whispers its first words.

"Hello, Mother."

CHAPTER ONE

"Have you seen this woman?"

Jayce Lewis held out a flier with a color photo of Emory on it, one of a stack that he carried under his arm. Then, realizing how clichéd and impersonal the question sounded, he added, "She's my daughter, and she used to work here. She's…missing."

He hated using the word *missing*. As if she'd merely been misplaced. But it was better than *abducted*, and infinitely better than *dead*.

The man behind the CrazyQwik convenience store counter was in his early forties, Jayce guessed. About a decade younger than him. His hair was slate-gray and he wore it pulled back in a ponytail. He was clean-shaven, without a hint of stubble, despite the lateness of the hour. He was thin – unhealthily so – and his skin had a sickly cast. The man – Virgil according to his nametag – didn't take the flier from Jayce. Instead, he leaned over the counter to get a closer look at it. He gave off a strange scent, an acrid-sweet odor, like rotting flowers, and Jayce wondered if the guy was ill. He smelled like he was being eaten away from the inside. Jayce tried to keep the disgust he felt from showing on his face as he drew his head back and turned it slightly to the side to avoid the worst of the smell. It didn't help, though. The odor was too strong.

Virgil stared at Emory's photo for several moments, not blinking the entire time, as if he was focusing all his concentration on it, absorbing every detail and committing it to memory.

"The picture's a couple years old," Jayce said. It was, in fact,

Emory's senior high school picture, and it had been taken about two years ago. It was the most recent photo of her that he had. In it, she wore a white blouse and posed with one arm across a blue velvet platform, chin resting lightly on her other hand. Her brown hair was long and straight, and she wore minimal makeup that highlighted her features without being obvious about it. Her mouth was quirked up at one side in a half smile, and there was a mischievous glint in her eyes that said, *I know something you don't.* She was beautiful, and this picture made her look even more so. Jayce wished he had a more ordinary, plain photo of her, though. He had the feeling that Virgil was staring so intently at her picture because of how she looked, not because the man gave a rat's ass about helping him find her.

This was the first time Jayce had been in CrazyQwik. He'd never seen one before, so he assumed it was a local store and not part of a chain. The store stocked the usual types of products – snacks, drinks, cigarettes, magazines, and the like – but there were odd differences, too. There was a small section for what looked like taxidermy supplies labeled *Necromantia*, and a section called *Ferricles* that displayed twisted pieces of rust-covered scrap metal. What anyone would want with those, Jayce had no idea. The coolers in the rear of the store contained another oddity. Inside were clay jars, lids sealed with wax, none of them the exact same size and shape. There were markings carved onto their surfaces, symbols that made no sense to Jayce, and he figured they must indicate the jars' contents. Jayce wasn't the only customer in CrazyQwik that evening. A woman stood in front of the cooler, a contemplative look on her face, as if she was trying to decide which jar to select. She made no move to open the cooler door, though. Instead, she took a step back, as if to get a broader perspective on the problem.

Jayce guessed her to be in her mid-to-late thirties, although it was difficult to tell her age from the way she was dressed. She wore all black – a long-sleeved blouse, glasses, skirt, leggings, and knee-high boots with thick rubber soles. She wore large silver hoop earrings that had gossamer-thin filaments inside that shimmered in the light and made him think of dew-covered spider silk. It was a strange effect, but beautiful. The woman was short, five feet tall, maybe an inch or two shorter. Her long black hair was thick and full of body, and it looked slightly mussed, like she'd just gotten out of bed. She wasn't typically pretty, but she *was* striking. Her features were sharp, and she exuded a relaxed confidence that Jayce found attractive and more than a little intimidating.

Virgil finished examining Emory's picture, and he leaned back and looked at Jayce.

"Don't know her. Sorry."

"Like I said, it's an older picture of her. She worked here for a while, though." He didn't say how long because he didn't know. There was a lot he didn't know about Emory. Too much.

Virgil shrugged again.

That shrug was starting to piss Jayce off. But he kept his irritation from showing on his face or in his voice. Suppressing his emotions came easily to him. Too easily, according to his ex-wife.

"Who schedules the employees? Is there a manager I can talk to?"

"We don't have managers *per se*," Virgil said. "We don't really have schedules, either."

Jayce frowned. "How does *that* work?"

He gave another goddamned shrug. "It's hard to explain. Basically, you show up when you want to, work for as long as you want, and then leave."

Jayce wondered if the man was putting him on.

"How do you get paid?"

"We take money out of the register before we go. Only five percent, though. You can't take any more. If you do...." Another shrug.

Jayce *was* pissed now, but still fought to keep from showing it.

"Look, I don't mind you messing with me, as long as you tell me the truth about my daughter. So I'll ask one more time, and please – no joking. Do you know her?"

Before Virgil could respond, a woman's hand reached out and took the flier from Jayce. The woman in black held a clay jar in her left hand, and the flier in her right as she examined Emory's picture. There were words on the flier, too, of course. Details about Emory – age, height, weight, the date she went missing, where she was last seen, a contact number for Jayce, and a promise of a reward for information leading to her being found: $5,000. Not much, Jayce supposed, but it was all he had in savings.

"She's lovely." The woman gazed at Emory's face a moment before handing the flier back to Jayce. "I'm sorry."

He took it from her, unsure what to say. Now that they were face to face, he could see she had bright, almost piercing green eyes, and having them trained on him was exciting and intimidating in equal measure. Like Virgil, she had an odd scent, but unlike his, hers wasn't unpleasant. She had a faint woody odor, kind of like acorns. A strange choice for a perfume, he thought, but he liked it. It reminded him of being in the woods.

"Have you seen her?" he managed to get out. "She's been missing for two weeks. Eighteen days, actually. I guess that's almost three weeks, isn't it?" Time flew when your daughter vanished off the face of the Earth.

The woman didn't take the flier from him to give it a second look. She kept her green-eyed gaze fixed on him as she answered.

"No, I haven't."

Jayce nodded for lack of any other response. Then he returned his attention to Virgil.

"Can I leave a flier here for you to put up in the window?" He held the flier out, and after a moment's hesitation, Virgil took it.

"I'll tape it to the counter," he said. "Stuff doesn't last long in the window, a half hour tops, and it's gone. Just kind of…decays, you know?"

Jayce didn't know if the man was making another joke or if he was a few letters short of an alphabet. Maybe both, he decided. But he didn't want the guy to crumple the flier and toss it in the trash after he left, so he smiled and thanked him. He gave the woman a parting smile as well, then turned and headed for the door.

Behind him he heard a soft thump as the woman put her jar on the counter, and then heard voices as she and Virgil began speaking to one another. Were they talking about him? Why else would they be talking so softly? He told himself he was being paranoid, but he couldn't shake the feeling that they were discussing him – or perhaps Emory.

He tried to put his suspicions out of his mind and focus on the positive. If Virgil made good on his promise to display the flier, there was an excellent chance one or more of the CrazyQwik's customers would recognize Emory, and maybe – just maybe – someone might have some information about what had happened to her and where she was.

Jayce wasn't surprised the store – and its employee – was weird. The Cannery was a mix of fast-food joints, hole-in-the-wall restaurants, seedy bars, funky small businesses, and more than a few abandoned and boarded-up buildings. It wasn't exactly the safest place in Oakmont, and he wouldn't have ventured into it if it hadn't been for Emory.

He opened the door, setting off a two-note electronic tone – *bee-baw* – and stepped out into the night. It was the first week of March, and a light rain fell. It had snowed last week, and several inches remained on the ground. The roads and sidewalks had long since been cleared, though, and Jayce hoped winter was finally on its way out. It had been a hard one, with heavier-than-average snowfall and frigid temperatures, and he wouldn't be sorry to see it go. And if Emory were out on the streets somewhere, living homeless, at least she wouldn't have to deal with extreme cold. Then again, if she *was* on the streets of the Cannery, he supposed the weather would be among the least of her worries.

He wore a leather jacket with a removable lining to provide extra protection from the cold. He had gloves, but he'd left them in his pocket. He didn't have a hat, hated wearing the damn things. They always mussed his hair and filled it with static. He unzipped his jacket halfway and tucked the fliers inside to protect them from the rain. He held them close to his body and then zipped up the jacket. He'd started at CrazyQwik because Emory had worked there, but he had a lot of fliers, and he was determined to pass them all out before he went home. This evening, frustrated by the police's lack of interest in Emory's case – *Young girls take off all the time without telling their families, she'll get in touch when she's ready* – he'd decided to begin searching on his own. He'd gone home after work and started making a missing-person flier on his laptop. It took him a while to get to the point where he was satisfied with it, though. He was an insurance agent, not a graphic designer, but he thought the final result wasn't half bad. When it was finished, he printed fifty copies and then, after reconsidering, printed fifty more. CrazyQwik had been his first stop, and he was disappointed in how it had turned out. He knew it was foolish, but he'd hoped that he'd learn something important there. Maybe even discover that Emory wasn't really missing after all.

Emory? Yeah, she hasn't been in here for a while. She moved in with a new boyfriend. Bobby Something. He works at the Harley-Davidson store on the other side of town.

So now that CrazyQwik had turned out to be a bust, he wasn't certain where to try next. He knew so little of the life his daughter had made for herself since graduating high school, and he had no idea where to continue looking for her. Whatever he did next, he didn't want to keep standing out here in the rain, even as light as it was. He decided he'd try the businesses on either side of CrazyQwik, a tattoo shop called Stained and a secondhand store called Dregs. He decided on Dregs first. Emory couldn't have made much money working at CrazyQwik, and there was a good chance she shopped for clothes at Dregs. He turned right and headed for the store.

Traffic cruised by in both directions, not heavy but steady. The sidewalks weren't crowded, probably due to the rain, but then again, it was a Tuesday night. Things probably picked up around here on the weekends. The buildings were old in the Cannery and set close together, and the street was narrow. There were streetlamps, old-fashioned things that put out weak yellow light that did little to illuminate the neighborhood. Shadows were everywhere, clinging to buildings like a black coating, pooling on the sidewalks and in the gutters like dark water, filling the alleys like something solid.

He heard his mother's voice then, whispering a warning.

Be careful. The world's a dangerous place.

How many times had he heard her say that while he was growing up? Thousands, he supposed. But that didn't make her wrong.

As he passed in front of the alley between CrazyQwik and Dregs, he heard movement. Scuffling, skittering, a growl, a *chunk*, then a brief sharp whine. He knew better than to stop, knew he should keep going to Dregs, or maybe head straight to his car, go home, and come back tomorrow when it was light out. But he did stop, for reasons that weren't entirely clear to him, and he turned to face the darkness that filled the alley. He heard new sounds now – wet tearing noises followed by moans of satisfaction. He felt a warning prickle on the back of his neck, accompanied by a surge of cold panic in his chest. He needed to get out of here. *Now.*

"What the fuck are *you* looking at?"

A man's voice, followed by shuffling footsteps.

"You some kind of pervert?"

The second voice was female, and she sounded even angrier than her companion.

You could run.

His mother's voice, sounding far calmer than he felt.

He was fifty-one years old, and he spent most of his time sitting behind a desk. He was twenty pounds overweight – at least – and the most exercise he got was walking to and from his car. Even with the help of adrenaline, he doubted he'd make it an entire block without having to stop and gulp for air. Besides, if he ran, he might drop the fliers, and he couldn't bear the thought of them being scattered on the sidewalk to be rained on and stepped on. So he stood his ground as a pair of figures emerged from the alley. They were younger than he expected, in their teens, and both wore jackets, jeans, and sneakers. The girl was brunette, her hair buzzed short in a military-style cut. The boy's hair was black and it was cut in the same style. But their similar hairstyles didn't make much of an impression on Jayce. He was too busy staring at the dark smears around their mouths and the dark splotches on their clothes. But far more disturbing were the large hunting knives the teens carried. The blades were slick with the same dark substance that smeared their lips, and thick drops fell from the metal and hit the ground with audible *plaps*.

It's blood, he thought. He'd never seen blood in dim light before, and he was surprised by how black it looked.

The teens rushed toward him, and the boy reached forward, grabbed hold of Jayce's jacket collar with his free hand, and pulled him into the alley with surprising strength. He shoved Jayce against the alley wall and pressed the point of his knife to the fleshy underside of Jayce's chin. The back of Jayce's head smacked against brick when the kid shoved him, and bright pain flared behind his eyes.

"I asked what you were looking at," the boy said.

They were still close enough to the alley's mouth for the streetlamp's feeble light to penetrate, and Jayce saw that the boy's teeth came to sharp little points. The girl hung back, but she smiled, revealing equally sharp teeth. The newly shaved heads, the filed teeth…were these two in some kind of bizarre gang? If so, it was one Jayce had never heard of.

Jayce's head throbbed, and he felt dizzy and nauseated. He forced himself to stay calm, though – or at least as calm as possible – as he spoke.

"Have…. Have either of you seen my daughter?"

The boy frowned, then he turned to the girl and they exchanged confused looks.

"She's missing," Jayce continued. "I have fliers in my jacket. I'll show you one if you'll…."

The boy returned his attention to Jayce, looked at him for a moment, and then nodded. He took the knife away from Jayce's throat and stepped back, but he didn't lower his blade. Moving slowly, Jayce unzipped his jacket and removed the fliers. They'd gotten a bit crumpled when the boy had shoved him against the wall, but they were still usable. He held the entire stack out for the teens to look at. The girl came forward then and the two of them leaned their heads forward slightly and squinted, and he had the impression that they could make out Emory's picture fine despite the poor light in the alley. A strong odor like wet dog came from the teens, and since Jayce was already nauseated from the head blow, the stink brought him close to vomiting.

"She's pretty," the girl said.

The rain had picked up by this point, and it had washed most of the blood from her mouth, but not all. And quite a bit still clung to her knife.

"Don't be stupid, Reta," the boy snapped. "It's a trick. The poster's fake. He probably doesn't even *have* a daughter."

She turned to him, a skeptical expression on her face. "Why would he be walking around the Cannery with a fake poster?"

"Because he wants our meat." The boy shot Jayce a dark look. "Don't you?"

Jayce had no idea what the kid was talking about, but the teens' blood-smeared mouths and knives told him that whatever *meat* meant in this instance, it wasn't good.

"I don't," Jayce said. "Really. I just want to find my daughter."

The girl stepped forward and examined Emory's picture more closely.

"She *does* look kind of old."

The boy nodded. "Not exactly an Amber Alert candidate, right?"

This is what you get for coming down here at night, Mother said. *You should've stayed at home and let the police do the searching.*

Jayce wanted to explain to the teens that adults went missing too, but he was suddenly struck by the bizarre absurdity of the situation. He was standing with his back against an alley wall, head throbbing, gut twisted with nausea, while sharp-toothed, knife-wielding teenagers debated about whether or not his flier was legit.

"Look, I don't care if you believe me," Jayce said. "But I've got a lot more fliers to distribute, so—"

He started to step away from the wall, hoping that if he could make it back to the sidewalk the kids might leave him alone. But before he could move more than a couple inches, the boy rushed toward him and swept his knife in a horizontal arc. The tip of the blade sliced the back of Jayce's hand, and he dropped the stack of fliers he'd been holding. The papers tumbled to the alley floor, and at first he was more upset about that than he was by the wound on his hand. But then the pain registered, and he drew in a hissing breath and held up his hand to examine it. The boy had sliced a thin line just behind his knuckles and blood poured from the cut. It fell onto the fliers scattered on the ground at his feet, the thick drops splattering on the paper like crimson rain.

Jayce grabbed his hand to put pressure on the wound and cradled it to his chest. Blood smeared on his jacket, but he barely noticed.

Told you, Mother said, sounding smug.

"What the *fuck* is wrong with you?" Jayce shouted at the boy.

"Why don't you go back to cutting up whatever the hell you were working on and leave me alone?"

The girl gave the boy a doubtful look. "I think he really might be telling the truth, Zach."

The boy gave Jayce a venomous glare.

"Bullshit. He's a meat-thief, plain and simple. And you know what we do to those." He grinned, displaying his sharpened teeth.

"I don't want to waste time on him," the girl said in a near-whine. "I'm *hungry*."

Zach held up his knife and angled it back and forth slowly, as if he were imagining doing the same thing with the blade inside Jayce's body.

"Don't worry," he said. "It won't take long."

Jayce's yelling at the boy had been fueled by adrenaline and anger, but now all he felt was fear.

"Fine." The girl sighed theatrically. "It'll go faster if I help."

She stepped toward Jayce and raised her own knife as she came.

He might have been able to fight off one of them, but two?

I always figured you'd end up dead in an alley somewhere, Mother said. *If you'd listened to me....*

"I can't believe you've left your kill unattended for so long."

Jayce and the teens looked toward the mouth of the alley. A woman stood there, the one who Jayce had seen in the CrazyQwik. She held a white plastic bag which he assumed contained the clay jar she'd bought. Her tone was calm and her body relaxed, but her eyes were cold and serious.

"Fuck off, cunt," Zach said.

"Hey!" Reta smacked him hard on the shoulder. "Show some respect!"

"Fine." He looked at the woman again. "Fuck off, *Ms.* Cunt."

"That's better," Reta said, then giggled.

The woman's body language didn't change, but her gaze grew even colder. She reached into the plastic bag, removed the clay jar, and held it up so the teens could see it. Neither of them said anything for several seconds. They just looked at the jar, expressions unreadable. Finally, Zach spoke.

"So you've got a vessel. Big deal." A pause, and then in a less-confident voice, "What's in it?"

"The screams of a hundred dying men," the woman said. "Can you imagine the kind of damage they'd do if I released them in an enclosed space like this?"

Jayce had no idea what the hell she was talking about, but as long as it kept the sharp-toothed teens from gutting him, he didn't care.

Zach and Reta exchanged glances.

"A hundred's not so many," Reta said, sounding uncertain. "Besides, anything that happens to us happens to him too." She jerked her chin in Jayce's direction. "He's in the line of fire just as much as we are."

"What makes you think I give a shit about him?" the woman asked. "I don't like dog-eaters, that's all."

The teens bared their teeth at the woman, but they made no move toward her. The strange standoff continued for several long moments, Jayce cradling his bleeding hand and wondering if the situation would be resolved before he passed out from blood loss. Finally, the teens lowered their knives.

"C'mon," Zach said to Reta. "Let's go finish our dinner."

"About goddamned time," she muttered. She turned away, started walking deeper into the alley, and within seconds was swallowed by darkness.

Zach gave Jayce a parting look.

"I'll be watching for you, *thief*."

Then he too walked into the darkness and was gone. A moment later, the sounds of tearing flesh and loud chewing filled the air, and Jayce thought about what the woman had called them. *Dog-eaters*. He understood then that it wasn't merely an expression. His stomach lurched, and he almost threw up, but he concentrated on the pain in his hand and his nausea subsided. He turned to the mouth of the alley, intending to thank the woman for helping him, but she was gone. Of course she was.

He thought about retrieving the fliers he'd dropped, but they were wet from rain and blood, and he left them where they were. He could always print out more. Still cradling his wounded hand to his chest and putting pressure on the cut, he walked out of the alley and headed toward his car – a silver Altima – a trip to the emergency room in his immediate future.

★   ★   ★

It didn't take Reta and Zach long to finish the dog – a bull terrier that hadn't been on the street too long, so it still had plenty of meat on it. Their bellies full, they held their knives out and let the rain wash them clean, then they slid them into the sheaths on their belts. They turned their faces skyward and held out their hands so the rain could clean them as well. It wouldn't do much for their clothes, but that was okay. They liked wearing bloodstained clothing, liked the stiff feel of the fabric and especially liked the smell. They wore their clothes as long as they could, until they became so disgusting even they couldn't stand it anymore, and only then did they get new ones.

When they were clean – or at least clean enough – Zach took one of the terrier's ribs to gnaw on. Reta didn't like chewing on bones if there wasn't any meat on them, so she walked away from the carcass and headed toward the mouth of the alley. She saw the scattered, sodden fliers that the meat-thief had dropped, and she picked one up, handling the wet paper gently so it wouldn't tear. She knew Zach believed the fliers to be fake, a part of the meat-thief's ruse, but she wasn't so sure. Who's to say the man couldn't have been a meat-thief *and* the father of a missing daughter? She felt sorry for him. It must be awful to lose someone and not know what—

Zach screamed. Or rather, he started to scream, but his voice cut off abruptly.

Reta dropped the flier and whirled around. She drew her knife and started running back toward the terrier's carcass, heart pounding in her ears. All she could think about was Zach. They'd been close since they were born, and they'd stayed together even after the rest of their litter-mates had gone their separate ways. He was brother, lover, and hunting partner, and she would do anything to protect him.

But as she raced toward Zach, a figure emerged from the alley's darkness before her. It opened its mouth wide and an ebon cloud gusted forth to engulf her.

Her scream was even shorter than Zach's.

★   ★   ★

The alley was silent after that except for the patter of falling rain. The Harvest Man walked to the end of the alley, crouched down, and picked up the flier Reta had been looking at. He gazed upon it for a time, reading far more from it than the information printed on its surface. He held it to his nose and, even though it appeared clean, he could still detect the scent of Jayce's blood. He stood then, crumpled the flier into a wet ball, squeezed it tight in one hand, and inserted it into his mouth and began chewing.

He then turned, walked past two piles of black dust that were already being washed away by the rain, and headed back into the darkness from which he'd come.

CHAPTER TWO

Jayce sat in his doctor's waiting room, staring at a small flat-screen mounted in the corner of the wall. Health information appeared on the screen, mostly still photos and text, like a slicker version of a PowerPoint presentation. Most of the info started with *Did You Know?* and then went on to talk about such basic health concerns as proper nutrition, regular exercise, good sleep, hygiene, and so on. Normally, he would've brought a book to read or he might read the news on his phone, but he still had a mild headache from last night, and the simple info on the screen was as much as he could manage to take in right now.

It was early morning, but the waiting room was already full, mostly older people in their seventies and up. Retirees, Jayce figured, people who needed to see a doctor regularly and had the time to do so. There were some younger people, most notably a mother with a toddler-aged girl. The girl looked flushed and listless, and Jayce guessed she had a fever. The mother looked tired, probably from being up most of the night taking care of her daughter. He felt sorry for the girl, but seeing her brought a sad smile to his face. He'd sat up with Emory many nights. Mackenzie was a heavy sleeper who needed a full, uninterrupted eight hours, otherwise she could be a real bitch all day. Because of this, he'd tended to take night duty with Emory, but he hadn't minded it. He could forgo sleep when necessary without ill effect, and he liked spending time alone with Emory, just the two of them, as if there was no one else in the entire world. A damn shame it had only happened when she was sick, but that was a parent's duty – to provide aid and comfort when needed, without asking for anything in return. He wondered where Emory was at this moment. Was she in need of his help? Not knowing and not being able to do anything for her ate away at him like acid, and it baffled him that her mother didn't seem nearly as concerned about Emory's disappearance as he was.

She's twenty, Mackenzie had said when he'd first called her about Emory. *You know how kids are at that age. Impulsive. Erratic. She probably took up with some boy, and she's so caught up in her new romance it hasn't occurred for her to get in touch with either of us and let us know how she's doing. We'll hear from her when she comes up for air. Or when the relationship has run its course. Don't be such a worrywart.*

That's what she called him whenever he became — as she put it — *obsessive* about something, usually a threat of some sort, real or perceived. He hated the term, not only because Mackenzie had used it so often, but because she always said it with a sneer in her voice.

Worrywart.

He looked back at the screen to distract himself from thinking about his daughter and ex-wife. A message about erectile dysfunction was on, and a good-looking woman in her late thirties was talking, but there was no sound, so at least he didn't have to listen to her going on about limp dicks.

His fellow patients were a mix of runny noses and deep, phlegmy coughs and he imagined their germs drifting in the office air like snow.

You'll catch your death, Mother said.

He'd rarely seen a doctor growing up. His mother refused to take him. *Too damn many sick people there,* she'd say whenever he asked her why. Just one more danger in a world full of death and destruction as far as she'd been concerned. Her fears hadn't kept the adult Jayce from seeking medical attention when he needed it or from getting yearly checkups. As an insurance professional, he knew the importance of regular medical care. But he couldn't help feeling uneasy whenever he visited the doctor, and after what he'd been through last night, he felt more uncomfortable than usual. After the bizarre experience in the alley, he'd driven himself to the closest emergency room. He'd had to wait about an hour for someone to see him, and then he got a doctor so young he looked like he was still in high school. The doctor examined him, found no sign of concussion, then a nurse cleaned his hand wound and the doctor returned to stitch it closed. The doctor bandaged it and told Jayce to go see his regular doctor in the morning, especially if he still had a headache. He'd sent Jayce away with a prescription for Vicodin, but he hadn't filled it. He didn't like to take strong medicine unless it was absolutely necessary. He took a couple ibuprofen and acetaminophen when he got home to the small apartment he'd lived in since divorcing Mackenzie several years ago and tried to get some sleep. The medicine only did so much to blunt the pain in his head and hand, though, and what sleep he got was fitful. He finally gave up and got out of bed around 6:30 and called the office to leave a voicemail informing them he wouldn't be in today. He rarely took sick days, and he was reluctant to take one now, but given how little sleep he'd managed to get, he figured he wouldn't be much good at work anyway. He'd probably end up nodding off in front of his computer. He wasn't especially worried about his injuries, but he'd chosen to follow the ER doctor's advice anyway. Better safe than sorry, he figured. It was, after all, the insurance professional's motto.

Although the pain of his injuries had contributed to his spotty sleep, he attributed most of it to what had happened in the alley. Those kids had been so strange, with their sharp teeth, blood-smeared faces, and hunting knives. And that name the black-haired woman had called them – *dog-eaters*. That had to be some kind of gang name, right? They hadn't really been—

Meat-thief they'd called him. He remembered hearing a whine come from deeper in the alley, and they *did* have blood on their faces as well as on their knife blades.... He didn't want to believe it, but deep down inside, he knew dog-eaters was the right term for them. What the hell *were* they? The woman had acted as if they weren't anything out of the ordinary to her. And that jar of hers – the *vessel* – the one she'd claimed held the screams of a hundred dying men.... The dog-eaters had seemed to believe her claim. It was ridiculous, of course, but then why had the teens taken her seriously? Maybe it was some kind of weird prank, and the three of them had been working together. That explanation made the most sense. So why didn't it feel right?

Several of the other patients had been called back to examination rooms while he'd been thinking, and he figured his turn was coming soon. He decided to try his best to put last night out of his mind. Whatever had been really going on, he supposed he'd never know the truth behind it. Life was like that sometimes. Strange shit occurred without any apparent rhyme or reason, and once it was over with, that was it. Nothing to do but shrug and move on. That was exactly what he intended to do, and he might have succeeded. But then *she* walked into the waiting room: the black-haired woman.

She was dressed so differently from last night that at first he wasn't convinced it really was her. She wore a navy blue suit jacket and matching slacks, a white blouse, and glossy black shoes. Her hair was up in a ponytail, her makeup was minimal but effective, and she wore a pair of small pearl earrings. She looked every inch a professional woman, and not like someone who saved hapless middle-aged men from sharp-toothed killer teenagers. She carried a thick black case in her left hand. When she reached the reception counter – after passing him without any sign of recognition – she knelt slightly, put the case on the floor, and straightened again. He had no doubt it was her, though. He recognized the unmistakable scent of acorns coming off her. Jayce listened closely as the office manager greeted her.

"Hey, Nicola. Here to see Dr. Vikram today?"

So…she was a pharmaceutical rep. Not a profession he would've guessed for her based on last night's encounter.

The office manager – whose name Jayce could never remember – was a heavy-set woman in her forties with red hair that was so bright he suspected she dyed it. She smiled at Nicola and seemed genuinely pleased to see her. She brought a clipboard from beneath the counter, on it pieces of paper with a series of pre-printed lines. She slid the clipboard across the counter to Nicola and handed the woman a pen. Nicola signed the sheet and then handed the clipboard and pen back to the office manager.

Nicola smiled. "If the doctor's not too busy this morning, I've got some samples of a new decongestant I'd like to give her. It dries you up so fast, they should've named it Sahara."

The office manager laughed.

"Things have been hopping around here all morning, but I'm sure she can find a couple minutes to see you. Go on back."

Nicola thanked her, took hold of her case – which Jayce assumed contained her samples, brochures, and the like – and headed to the door that separated the waiting area from the examination rooms. She opened it, stepped through, and then she was gone. Not once had she looked at him.

He considered going up to the front counter and somehow trying to get a look at the sheet she'd signed, so he could learn her full name. But he didn't know how to convince the office manager to let him. He'd need some kind of excuse, and he couldn't think of one. The truth wouldn't do, that was for certain.

"Excuse me, but the woman you just let go back to see the doctor. Nicola? She saved me from a pair of knife-wielding dog-eaters last night, but she didn't tell me her last name. I'd really like to thank her, so if you could just let me take a peek at her signature…."

One of the physicians' assistants opened the door to the examination area and stood in the doorway. She was younger and thinner than the office manager, with short black hair.

"Jayce?" she called.

He started to stand, but then he stopped himself. If he went back to an examination room now, Nicola would most likely be gone by the time Dr. Vikram had finally finished with him. Since he didn't know Nicola's last name, he would have no way of finding her, and he wanted to talk with her about last night. *Needed* to, desperately.

"Jayce?" the physician's assistant called again.

This time he stood, but instead of walking toward the examination area, he headed for the front door and stepped through into the parking lot.

★ ★ ★

For the next fifteen minutes, Jayce sat in his Altima, keeping watch on the entrance to the doctor's office. Several people exited during that time, but not Nicola. He was beginning to think she'd left by an employee entrance of some kind and he'd missed her, but then she finally emerged. It was a bit chilly this morning, in the mid-forties, but the cold didn't seem to bother her. She walked to a Honda CR-V, put her case on the passenger seat, then climbed into the driver's seat, turned on the engine, and began backing out of her space.

Jayce turned on his car, feeling a small thrill of excitement as he did. He knew it was foolish, but he couldn't help it. He'd never tailed anyone before, and he felt like he was a character in a spy movie. He thought about the dog-eaters again, their teeth and their knives.

Wrong kind of movie, he thought.

Dr. Vikram's practice was located in an office park, set apart from the main neighborhood. The access road curved around in a large U, and there were a number of neighboring businesses. A dentist, a Realtor, a vet, a financial planner, and a lawyer. Nicola turned right as she left the parking lot, and Jayce backed out of his space and hurried to follow, hoping he didn't look like he was hurrying. There was no posted speed limit on the access road, but people normally drove around 30 mph, given how narrow the road was and how sharply it curved. Nicola drove faster, though. Probably because she had other stops to make, Jayce thought. He hung back a bit, not wanting to ride her bumper. He was tempted to take out his phone and try to get a picture of her license plate, just in case they became separated in traffic, but he realized it was a stupid idea. Not only was there a chance that she might glance at her rearview mirror and catch him taking the photo, but once he had it, what could he do with it? He wasn't a cop, and he didn't know any. If he couldn't get access to a vehicle registration database, the plate number would be useless to him.

Nicola turned right onto Montillo Street. There was usually a steady stream of traffic on this road, and today was no exception. Jayce couldn't afford to wait to pull out after her if he wanted to prevent any vehicles from coming between them. So he hit the gas and whipped his steering wheel to the right. He made it onto the road just before a red pickup would've cut him off. The driver blasted his horn in irritation, but Jayce ignored him and concentrated on following Nicola.

She stopped at two other doctor's offices, and she spent 10 minutes at one and 20 minutes at the other. Both times Jayce tried to park as far away from her as possible, but at the second doctor's the only space available was right next to her. Seeing no other alternative, he parked next to her vehicle and waited. She hadn't recognized him at Dr. Vikram's office, so he figured there was a decent chance that she wouldn't notice him when she returned to her car. Still, he didn't want to take chances, so he considered ways that he might be able to hide when she came out. He couldn't just duck down in his seat. That would look stupid and it would draw her attention. He decided that his best bet was to lean across his seat when she returned to her car, his face averted, and pretend to root around in his glove box for something. He opened the glove box so he'd be ready when the time came, and he was startled when someone tapped on the driver's side window. His first thought was that Nicola had come out sooner than he'd expected and had seen him, and he desperately tried to think of an excuse for why he was following her as he turned to the window. But it wasn't her, and Jayce was so surprised that for a moment all he could do was stare.

The man was tall and stocky. He had plenty of weight on him, but he was solid-looking rather than fat. He had a thick shock of brownish-blond hair and sported a 1970s porn star mustache. His neck was so thick it looked like his head had sprouted directly from his shoulders. His eyes were blue but they seemed too small and set too far apart. His ears were folded back against the sides of his head, and his thick lips resembled a pair of earthworms lying one on top of the other. The man's eyes were fixed on Jayce, their blue cold and intense. He raised sausage-thick fingers and tapped on the window again, harder this time.

"Get out of the car," the man said, voice low, tone dangerous. When Jayce didn't respond, the man made a fist and slammed it against the window, the impact causing a small crack to appear in the glass. The man's face reddened with fury.

"*Now.*"

The last thing Jayce wanted to do was confront this lunatic, especially after what he'd been through last night, but if he turned on his engine, put his car in reverse, and got the hell out of here, he'd lose his chance to keep following Nicola. More than that, he'd lose his chance to learn more about what had happened in the alley, and maybe – just maybe – gain some insight into what had happened to Emory.

He thumbed the switch to unlock the car. When the man heard the locks disengage, he stepped away from the door to give Jayce room to get out. Jayce opened his car door, climbed out, and then closed it behind him. He instantly regretted closing the door. Shouldn't he have left it open, in case he needed to get away from this guy fast? Too late now.

The man had stepped far enough back from Jayce's Altima to give himself sufficient maneuvering room. Smart. Now that the man wasn't bending down to tap on his window, Jayce could see that he wore a T-shirt, jeans, and heavy brown work boots. No jacket, even though it was still chilly out. His T-shirt was light brown and on the chest were the words *I Will Buttfuck Your Soul.* Behind him, parked so that it blocked Jayce's car and Nicola's Honda, was a red RAM 1500 pickup, engine still running, personalized plates that read OHIO PIG. Jayce recognized it as the truck he'd cut off leaving Dr. Vikram's office.

Shit, Jayce thought.

Before he could say anything, the man spoke.

"You got a hard-on for doctors or something? This is the third doctor's office you've visited. And why the fuck don't you get out of your car? Are you some kind of freak?"

You're one to talk, Jayce thought. Aloud, he said, "Why didn't you talk to me before this?"

The man looked puzzled. "What?"

"You've been following me since I cut you off on Montillo, right? So if you saw me stop at the last two doctor's offices, why did you wait until now to confront me?"

What are you doing? Mother said. *Don't antagonize him. He's obviously crazy as fuck!*

Jayce couldn't argue with this last part. He was scared, there was no denying it, but he couldn't allow some road-raging asshole to get in the way of his finding Emory.

You've already been to the ER once in the last twelve hours, Mother said. *Are you so eager to go back?*

He ignored her. He knew her 'voice' was really just a projection of his own fears and that he was only talking to himself.

"Well?" he demanded.

"I was checking you out," the man said. "Getting the lay of the land, so to speak. I don't go into a situation without getting intel first, you know what I'm saying?"

"Actually, I have no idea. But let's cut to the chase. I'm sorry I pulled out in front of you like that. I thought I had more room, but I obviously miscalculated. Please accept my most sincere apologies." Then he stepped forward and offered his bandaged hand to the man to shake.

The man looked at Jayce's hand as if it were a snake that might be poisonous.

Jayce knew from his years selling insurance that the best way to put people off balance was to be direct. This man was angry, so instead of allowing his anger to continue building, Jayce would defuse it by admitting he made a mistake and asking for the man's forgiveness. He liked to think of tactics like this as social kung-fu. He just hoped it would work with 'Ohio Pig'.

The man continued staring at Jayce's proffered hand for several seconds, then he looked up and met Jayce's gaze.

"You're fucked up, man, and I mean monumentally. I can smell it coming off you. You are mixed up in some seriously twisted shit, aren't you? Well, I ain't touching your damn hand. I don't want to catch any of your freak cooties. But I don't give up easy. I'll get what's coming to me, you can be goddamned sure of that."

The man backed away, keeping close watch on Jayce the entire time. Then he climbed into his truck, put the engine in gear, tromped on the gas, and roared out of the parking lot.

"That was weird."

Jayce spun around to see Nicola standing between their two vehicles, case in hand, looking at him. She smiled.

"Want to have lunch?"

CHAPTER THREE

"Why not?"

Jayce is thirteen. It's Saturday morning, but he's not watching cartoons. He likes to think he's too old for them, but the truth is he would love to watch them. He likes superhero ones the best, but there's only one TV in the house, and his mother – who doesn't work on Saturdays and Sundays – rules it. He's free to watch it with her, but he has to watch whatever she picks, and he can't complain about it. It's why he spends a lot of time in his room on the weekends.

"Because I said so."

Valerie Lewis is in her mid-thirties, but she looks older. There are worry lines at the corners of her eyes and mouth, and her brown hair holds more than a few gray strands. The fingers on her right hand are yellow from nicotine, but the house doesn't smell like smoke. She always goes outside whenever she wants a cigarette. She sits on the front porch or strolls through the backyard in good weather. In rain or deep cold, she smokes in the garage. She's thin, and the baggy clothes she likes to wear – at least two sizes too large for her – make her seem almost cadaverous. This thinness adds to her older appearance, and more than once a stranger, a sales clerk at the mall or one of Jayce's teachers during conference time, has assumed she's his grandmother.

She's been like this for as long as Jayce can remember. Once, when he was five, he'd gotten curious and, in the thoughtless, unselfconscious way of children, had asked her why she was so skinny. She told him it was because his father had taken the best from her before he left them both. Jayce wasn't sure what his mom meant by this, and he never asked her again.

Since it's Saturday, Valerie wears baggy gray sweatpants and an oversized Bengals T-shirt. Looking at her, Jayce thinks if she pulled in her head, arms, and legs, she could disappear into the cloth, like a turtle withdrawing into its shell.

"But I'll be back before dark."

Valerie has a thing – almost an obsession, really – about him being outside after dark. The only time she permits it is if she's with him, and even then, she doesn't allow it very long.

There are things in the dark, Jayce. We may not be able to see them, but they can damn sure see us.

She's watching a rerun of *Hogan's Heroes*, and she doesn't take her eyes off the TV screen as she answers.

"No."

"Bryan and his mom can give me a ride. She can bring me home too."

Their living room is sparsely furnished. An uncomfortable love seat that neither of them uses and the overstuffed chair his mother – and only her – sits in. Regardless of the time of year, Valerie is always cold, and so she sits covered in a blanket. In the wintertime she sits under two or three. The only pictures on the wall are framed copies of his school photos throughout the years. Jayce hates having to constantly look at these younger versions of himself. He looks stupid and goofy in each picture, and they prevent him from believing that no version of himself ever existed except the one that woke up this morning.

There are no photos of his mother or of the two of them together. She used to keep old pictures in a box under her bed, and he found them one day several years ago while she was taking a bath. The photos were loose in the box and most were unlabeled. Many of them were black and white and were of people he didn't know, men, women, and children, all of them strangers to him. Except his mother. There were pictures of Valerie as a child, a teenager, a young woman. There were no pictures of Jayce or his father. The pictures of his mother fascinated him. She looked so different in them. She smiled in a lot of the photos, and she wasn't so skinny back then. She looked healthy, and seeing her like that was startling to Jayce and more than a little sad.

He put the photos away and left her room before she finished her bath, but she must've somehow known what he did, because the next time he snuck into her room to look at the photos, the box was gone. He'd searched the house for it, but he never found it again.

"I don't trust Bryan's mother. She drinks."

As far as Jayce knows, Valerie hasn't exchanged more than a dozen words with Bryan's mom, and then only over the phone and only to tell her that Jayce wasn't allowed to go to sleepovers or birthday parties.

"No, she doesn't!" He has no more idea about the woman's alcohol consumption than his mother does, but he has to say something. Yesterday at school Bryan was talking about a new movie that had come out called *Star Wars*. He'd already seen it twice and was going to see it for a third time on Saturday. When Jayce sheepishly admitted that he hadn't seen the movie, Bryan insisted he come with him. *Ask your mom,* he said, as if it were that simple. Jayce almost didn't bother, had put it off until this morning. But now that he *has* asked and gotten the expected no, he finds himself getting angry. He's thirteen, damn it. He's not a little boy. He should be allowed to see a stupid movie if he wants to. He should be allowed to do *something*.

When Valerie doesn't respond, he adds, "She'll stay with us the whole time. We won't be alone." This is a lie. The plan is for her to drop Bryan and Jayce off at the mall and pick them up after the movie's over. But there's no way Jayce will tell this to his mother. She would freak out at the idea of him running around the mall without adult supervision.

His mother takes her attention from the TV, reluctantly, he thinks, and looks at him. Her expression is stern, and there's anger in her gaze. But there's something else there too, something he can't name. Something hidden. Secret.

"What have I told you?"

He knows she's not referring to their current conversation. This is a question she's asked him many times before, and he knows how he's supposed to answer. He sighs and gives the required response.

"The world is a dangerous place."

Some of the anger drains from her gaze, and her expression softens the tiniest bit.

"And because it is, we have to be careful. You're the most precious thing in the world to me. I couldn't stand it if something bad happened to you."

You couldn't stand it if something good happened to me, either, he thinks.

Her expression softens even further and she smiles.

"Now come give your mother a kiss."

He's suddenly struck by how frail she is. Skin and bones mostly, and more of the latter than the former. She's a living skeleton, and although he's only thirteen, he realizes he probably outweighs her. If he decided to walk out the door right now, there's nothing she could do to stop him physically. If she tried to grab hold of his arm, he could easily shrug off her grip. And if she persisted, he could shove her away, even hit her if he wanted. As thin and weak as she is, what could she do about it? Nothing. But despite his realization that the power dynamic between them has shifted in a profound and not altogether understandable way, he walks to her, bends down, and gently kisses her cheek. Her skin is cold and parchment-dry against his lips, and he has to suppress a shudder of revulsion.

When he draws back, she says, "Go on and play now," and then she returns her attention to the TV. Colonel Klink yells, "Hogan!"

He turns away, walks to his room and closes the door. They live in a one-story house, and he puts on his sneakers, grabs some money from the *Jaws* bank on his dresser, opens his sole window, pushes out the screen, and climbs through. He props the screen against the outside wall, and pulls his window down almost all the way, leaving it cracked just enough so he can get back in again later. His ten-speed leans against the wall close to his room. He leaves it here for occasions like this, when he has to get out of the house or else he'll go crazy. Valerie can spend hours in front of the TV, barely moving a muscle, and when she settles in for a weekend of marathon TV watching, Jayce knows he can escape and return without her knowing he's been gone. Much like the POWs in Stalag 13, coming and going as they please in order to carry out their plans to sabotage the Third Reich. He imagines Colonel Klink yelling his name.

Jayce!

He walks his bike halfway down the block before hopping onto it and pedaling. He rolls down the sidewalk, the early June day warm, sun shining, wind blowing in his face. He's free, for a little while, at least, and he loves it.

★ ★ ★

He rides to Bryan's house, but by the time he gets there no one answers the door, and he realizes Bryan and his mom have already left. He's disappointed and angry at his mom. Too angry to just give up and return home. The mall isn't *that* far away, and he decides to ride there. Even if he doesn't get there in time to see the movie, just going to the mall will feel like a triumph.

He has to ride on the road most of the way because there aren't any sidewalks here. Cars rush past him, some of the drivers honking their horns at him in irritation. One man yells through his open passenger window. *"Get off the road, you dumbass!"* Jayce just laughs.

His mother would be horrified at what he's doing. The speed limit is only thirty-five mph, but most of the vehicles are traveling faster, and they pass within a few feet of him. All it would take is for one to come a little too close and him to drift a little to the left, and he'd be hit. He wonders what it would feel like. He imagines a jarring thump, a dizzying whirl of images as he's spun around, the sound of crumpling metal, the impact of hitting asphalt and sliding. And then the pain would register, and depending on how badly he was hurt, he might cry out, might even scream. Would there be blood, too? Probably.

Maybe even a lot of it. He wonders how Valerie would react once she found out what had happened to him. The thought is so compelling that for a moment he's tempted to turn his handlebars to the left and veer into traffic. But he doesn't, and he eventually arrives at the mall in one piece.

He doesn't have a bike chain, so he parks his ten-speed behind some shrubs next to one of the mall entrances. The shrubs aren't tall enough to hide his bike completely, so there's still a chance that someone might steal it, but he'll just have to take that risk.

Once inside the mall, he hurries to the movie theater and sure enough, he's fifteen minutes late for *Star Wars*. He considers going in anyway, but he doesn't want to miss any of it. He decides to wander around for a while and come back in time for the next showing. Seeing the movie alone won't be as much fun as seeing it with Bryan, but it'll still be good.

For the next half hour he walks through the mall, not going into any of the stores, just looking at the people passing by and thinking to himself that this is what ordinary people do. They go places, see and do things, be around each other. They *live* life, and he wonders why his mother can't do the same. Sadness and anger well up inside him, the combination so strong and overwhelming that he feels as if he might start crying. The thought of bursting into tears in the middle of the mall, of everyone looking at him and wondering what's wrong, of some adult or other coming forward to ask if he needs help, is intolerable.

He walks – not runs – to the nearest restroom. It's empty, thank God, but he goes into a stall anyway, in case someone comes in. The toilet lid is up and he can see the bowl is filled with urine and a large mass of sodden toilet paper. It's gross and he considers flushing it, but with that much toilet paper in it, he's afraid it will overflow. So he puts the lid down, sits on top of it, and lets the tears come. He cries quietly, not wanting to make any noise, and he grabs handfuls of toilet tissue to wipe the tears and blow his nose. He feels so defeated. He might have physically escaped his house, but he hasn't escaped his mother. Wherever he goes, he carries her with him, and he's afraid it will always be so. Now he wishes he *had* turned his bike into traffic earlier. Death is the only real escape possible to him, unless Valerie finds a way to follow him into the darkness. He wouldn't put it past her.

After a time his sorrow fades, as does his anger, leaving him feeling empty and spent. Screw the movie. He's not in the mood for it now. He might as well go home and sneak back into his room. He hopes Valerie hasn't noticed his absence. The last thing he wants right now is to have to deal with her yelling at him for daring to leave the safety of their home. He stands and reaches for the stall door, but before he can open it, he hears the outer door's hinges squeak as someone enters the restroom.

The door thumps shut, and he listens for footsteps but hears none. Did whoever it was change his mind about coming in? Maybe he decided he didn't have to go that bad, or maybe he realized he had somewhere he needed to be right away and couldn't afford to take the time to hit the restroom. Jayce is about to open the stall door when he senses he's not alone. A tingle on the back of his neck, a tightening of his stomach muscles, a sharpening of all his senses…. All of these things scream at him that someone else is in the restroom. More, that this someone else is now on the other side of the stall door. He still hasn't heard whoever it is make so much as a whisper of a noise, but when he looks down at the floor he sees a pair of bare feet standing there, framed between the floor and the bottom edge of the stall door, and he has to clap his hand over his mouth to keep from crying out.

The feet are mottled gray, the bottoms calloused and dry, skin cracking around the edges. The toenails are overlong, black and sharp, almost claws. The man wears jeans, the cuffs frayed and ragged. A smell hits Jayce then, so strong it overpowers the stink of urine coming from the toilet bowl. It's the smell of autumn leaves on a crisp moonlit night. But beneath that is another smell, one of freshly overturned soil and the musty stink of old rot. A sense of wrongness strikes Jayce then, a feeling that he's in the presence of something that cannot be real but somehow is. His anger, sadness, and frustration over the state of his life are wiped away, obliterated into nothingness by a deep-seated atavistic terror of the thing standing on the other side of the stall door. If he wasn't trapped in the stall, he would run as fast and as far as he could to escape. But he *is* trapped, and there's nowhere to go and nothing he can do except sit there and hope that whatever the thing outside is, it will lose interest in him and go away. He wants that to happen so badly that, even though he was not brought up to believe in a deity, he prays to whatever god or gods might exist for deliverance.

Jayce hears a soft sound, then. It reminds him of a winter wind blowing against his bedroom window at night. Cold, desolate, and lonely. It takes him a moment to realize that what he's hearing are words, but they're being spoken so softly and in such a strange cadence that he cannot decipher their meaning. For all he knows, they might be nonsensical muttering, but he detects a pattern to the sounds, as if the same words are being repeated over and over. *It's a message,* he thinks. He doesn't know why he believes this. He just does.

The stall door is locked from the inside, but it's not much of a lock, a small metal bar that slides into place. No protection at all, really. An adult would be able to break it and force the door open with minimal effort. And even if the flimsy lock managed to hold, whoever – *whatever* – is outside could climb under or over the stall door. The safety the lock offers is only illusory, Jayce realizes, and for the first time in his young life, he understands that flimsy locks, thin doors, and breakable windows are all that stand between people and the awful things of the world, and that these so-called protections are nothing of the sort. They're all illusions. Lies. Ultimately no more effective at keeping the dark things at bay than the air which surrounds us. He thinks he might go mad then, and maybe he does, a little.

Then the lock slides back of its own volition with a soft *snick* that to his ears sounds loud as a shotgun blast. His pulse, already racing, picks up speed, and he wonders if it's possible for a thirteen-year-old to have a heart attack, and if so, if he's having one now.

There's a creak as the door opens a few inches. He feels an impulse to rush forward and attempt to hold the door shut, but he's frozen, unable to move or breathe, unable to do anything more than watch as the door continues to open and listen to the trip-hammer beat of his heart pounding in his ears. Then, with a sudden swift motion, the stall door is pushed all the way open, and he sees…he sees….

*   *   *

He's standing at his front door, body slick with sweat, breathing hard. He glances to the side, sees his ten-speed lying in the grass, rear tire spinning slowly. He has no memory of how he got here. He assumes he rode home, but he doesn't know for certain. He remembers being trapped in the bathroom stall, remembers the horrible whispering thing standing on the other side of the door, remembers it opening…and then nothing.

The front door is unlocked, and he rushes inside, calling for his mother in a voice so high-pitched that it's almost a shriek. Valerie is still sitting in front of the TV – *I Dream of Jeannie* is on now – and she rises from her chair as he races into the living room. Before she can ask him what's wrong, he throws himself against her and wraps his arms around her. She's so thin and frail that she almost seems to disappear in his arms.

"You were right," he sobs. "You were right."

He presses his face to her shoulder and weeps, and after a moment she reaches up and pats him gently on the back.

CHAPTER FOUR

Jayce sat across a table from the black-haired woman, who'd introduced herself as Nicola Castell. The restaurant she'd suggested for lunch wasn't particularly impressive. It was small, with simple tables and chairs and no real décor to speak of. The color scheme was bland oranges and yellows, the floor tiles were scuffed and cracked, and the ceiling was dotted with water stains. Some kind of traditional Asian music – high-pitched twangy strings that were plucked instead of strummed – played over crackling speakers. The air was overly warm and felt greasy, as if whatever cooking oils were used in the kitchen had completely suffused the place.

"I know it doesn't look like much," Nicola said. "But they serve the best Thai food in town."

The restaurant was called About Thaime – a terrible pun as far as Jayce was concerned – and despite its unimpressive appearance, it had a full crowd for lunch. A number of the patrons were Asian, and he took that as a good sign. There were no servers. You ordered your food at the counter, and when it was ready, your name was called and you went to the counter to pick it up. There was a self-serve soda machine for drinks, although most of the diners settled for water. Jayce and Nicola didn't have long to wait once they'd ordered, and when their names were called, they got their food – pad Thai with chicken for her, Thai curry for him – filled foam cups with water, picked a table, sat down, and started eating. Jayce took a bite of his food and was surprised at how good it was. It had a lot more heat than he usually preferred, but the spiciness only added to the dish's flavor.

Nicola smiled. "Told you."

They ate in silence for several minutes, and despite the strangeness of the situation – here he was, having lunch with a woman who'd saved him from being killed by a pair of dog-eaters – he was actually enjoying himself.

After a bit, Nicola said, "Tell me about your daughter."

The question took Jayce aback at first. He didn't know this woman, and although she'd helped him last night, he had no reason to trust her. But she had known about the dog-eaters and more importantly, how to handle them. She knew a side of Oakmont that he'd never suspected existed – a side he wasn't sure he wanted to know more about. But maybe, just maybe, she might know something that would help lead him to Emory. And so he began talking.

"She disappeared a couple weeks ago. We don't know exactly when, since no one reported her missing. She lived alone, and as far as we know, she wasn't dating anyone."

"We?" Nicola asked.

"Her mother and I. We divorced several years ago, while Emory was still in high school. Emory and Mackenzie talk on the phone several times a week. I try to stay in touch with her too, but we're not as close as I'd like. We don't have much in common, and we have a difficult time finding things to talk about."

He felt a certain amount of shame admitting this, but there was no sign of judgment on Nicola's part. Her expression was neutral, and he had the impression that she was simply listening. Encouraged, he went on.

"I hadn't heard from Emory for almost a month, and she hadn't returned any of my calls or responded to the texts I sent. I checked with her mother to see if everything was all right, and Mackenzie told me that she had spoken to Emory recently. I asked her *how* recently, and she said two weeks, maybe three. It was unlike Emory to remain out of touch that long, but Mackenzie wasn't concerned. She said it was a natural process, that children become more focused on their own lives as they get older and don't need as much contact with their parents."

"But you didn't agree with her?"

"At first I did, or at least I tried to. I'm…more inclined to look at the negative aspects of life than my ex-wife, and because of this, I rely on other people for reality checks. What Mackenzie said seemed reasonable, but despite that, I decided to go to Emory's apartment, for no other reason than to assure myself that all was well. I'd helped her move in when she decided to move out of her dorm last year, and even though I hadn't been there since, I had no trouble finding the place again. She didn't answer her door when I knocked, so I went to the rental office. According to the apartment manager, not only had he not he seen Emory recently, she owed two months' rent. I wrote the man a check, and then left. I called Mackenzie to let her know about what I'd learned, but she told me I was being paranoid and Emory would get in touch with us when she was ready. By that point, I feared something bad had happened to Emory, so I went to the police."

"And they didn't take you seriously," Nicola said.

Jayce nodded. "Young people take off all the time, they said. They skip out on rent, shack up with some guy, girl, or group somewhere. She's probably partying too hard and we'll hear from her when she sobers up enough to remember her name."

"So you decided to make some fliers and go looking for her on your own."

"That's right. I had to do *something*. The first forty-eight hours after someone goes missing are supposed to be the most important, aren't they? After that, the odds of finding someone −" he didn't want to say *alive*, not out loud "− are supposed to go way down. It's been a lot longer than forty-eight hours since Emory disappeared. I hope the police are right, I really do. I hope that this will turn out to be another case of Dad letting his imagination run away with him, but just in case…."

Nicola had continued eating while Jayce talked, and she'd almost finished her pad Thai, whereas he'd barely touched his curry. She put her plastic fork on her foam plate and pushed it aside. Jayce didn't bother taking another bite of his food. He wasn't really hungry.

"If I were in your position," Nicola said, "I'd do the same thing, I think. I don't have children, and I've never been married – praise Oblivion – but I wouldn't feel right standing around and doing nothing when someone I loved might be in danger."

Jayce felt a rush of gratitude toward her for understanding. Odd that a complete stranger would have more sympathy for what he was doing than Emory's mother, but when it came to her emotional make-up, Mackenzie wasn't exactly normal, was she?

"Have you had any luck so far?"

"No. I spoke to her apartment manager again early last night, but he had no idea where she might have gone. Or if she'd gone at all. I asked him to let me into her apartment so I could take a look around and see if I could find something that might give me a clue where to look for her, but he refused. I might resemble Emory and I might really be her father, but did I have any proof? The question shocked me. I realized that I didn't have any concrete evidence that I was Emory's father. What proof does any parent have of their relationship to their child, beyond a birth certificate? There's no such thing as a parent ID card. I gave up trying to convince the man and headed for CrazyQwik. I don't really know my way around the Cannery, and I walked around a while before I found it. I might've gone past it a half dozen times before I finally saw it." He shrugged. "I guess I was too upset and wasn't thinking straight."

"Maybe it didn't want you to see it until it was ready." She went on before Jayce could ask what she meant. "What's the name of the apartment complex where Emory lives?"

"Springhill Apartments."

She didn't react to the name, so Jayce had no idea if she was familiar with the place.

"What about the manager? Was there anything about him that struck you as out of the ordinary?"

Jayce frowned. "I'm not sure what you mean."

She waved the question aside. "Tell me about Emory. What's she like?"

He started to answer, but then he paused. No one had ever asked him to talk about the kind of person his daughter was. It should've been simple enough. After all, he *was* her father. He kept thinking of what she looked like, but he knew that wasn't what Nicola wanted to hear. Besides, she'd seen the picture of Emory on the flier last night. Nicola was asking for something much deeper than a mere catalogue of his daughter's physical features. But he had no idea where to begin.

"She's stubborn," he said, then smiled. "That sounds negative, doesn't it? Maybe I should say strong-willed. She was like that when she was a baby. If she wasn't tired, she refused to go to bed. If she wasn't hungry, she wouldn't eat. She didn't make a big fuss or anything. Didn't cry, didn't pout. But you couldn't get her to do anything she didn't want to do. It had to be her idea, and no one else's."

"I don't want to upset you, but she sounds like the kind of person who, if she wanted to take a break from her usual routine for a couple weeks – or even longer – might not tell anyone. Especially not the people she was taking a break from."

He didn't appreciate the last bit Nicola said, but as much as he wanted to, he couldn't argue with it.

"I thought of that," he admitted. "But I can't escape the feeling that something bad has happened to her. I suppose you can call it father's intuition." He broke off then, his attention caught by a new customer entering the restaurant.

The man was in his thirties, wore a gray suit with a dark red tie, and he carried a metal briefcase. All of that was ordinary enough, but what struck Jayce as odd was what he wore on his hands: a pair of bright green rubber gloves that went from his fingers to his elbows. They looked like industrial gloves of some kind, the sort of thing people who worked with dangerous chemicals might wear to protect themselves. The man didn't walk up to the counter to order, though. Instead, he ignored the woman at the register, grabbed a handful of spicy Thai sauce packets from a serving container next to her, and then walked to an empty table. He put the sauce packets on the table, pulled out a chair, put his briefcase on it, and then pulled out another chair for himself. He sat and began removing napkins from the table dispenser with his gloved fingers. As he removed each one, he placed it carefully on the table and neatly laid the next one atop it. He continued this process until he'd emptied the dispenser and all the napkins lay in an orderly pile before him. He then took the sauce packets and opened them one at a time. Jayce couldn't figure out how the man managed to tear the packets while wearing those gloves. How could he get a grip on the plastic with his fingers covered by thick rubber? But he had no difficulty. As each packet was opened, he squeezed its contents onto the pile of napkins. He placed each empty packet carefully on the table next to the napkins, and when he was finished, the napkins were a red-soaked mess. No one else in the restaurant paid any attention to the man. As near as Jayce could tell, they were completely unaware of his presence.

The man gazed upon the mess he'd created with undisguised hunger, bordering on lust. Then he picked up the napkins and began eating them. He started slowly at first, but he gained speed with each mouthful until by the end he was jamming napkins into his mouth as fast as he could, sauce smearing his face and splattering onto his suit.

Still no one seemed to notice.

When the man finished, his gloves were coated with sauce.

Jayce thought he might remove them then, that perhaps he'd worn them to keep his hands clean during his disgusting meal. Although why he'd worry about getting his hands messy when he didn't seem to care about his face and clothes, Jayce had no idea. But he kept his gloves on, and he made no attempt to clean the sauce from them. Nor did he wipe the sauce from his face. How could he? He'd eaten all his napkins.

The man stood and picked up his briefcase. Jayce had stared at him the entire time he ate, but the man had paid no attention to him. But now he looked toward Jayce, and the two men locked gazes. There was nothing especially intimidating about the man's eyes. No hint of anger, no sign of madness, no trace of emotion whatsoever. Finally, he gave Jayce a nod and headed for the exit. As he left the restaurant, he left a smear of sauce on the door handle.

"Thank you. Come again!" the woman behind the counter called after him.

Jayce turned to Nicola, but before he could ask her if she'd seen the same thing he had, she spoke.

"I've seen him around. Don't know his name. He always has that case with him. I wonder what's in it."

Jayce frowned. "You saw what he ate, right?"

"Of course I did. Believe me, it's not the worst thing I've seen someone eat. But what interests me is that *you* saw it. You've got the Eye."

"I have no idea what you're talking about."

"You see things that most people don't." She nodded toward the table splattered with Thai sauce and littered with empty packets. "Like our friend with the green gloves."

"I've never seen anything like him before. Same for those kids in the alley last night."

She frowned. "Really? I mean, it was obvious you didn't know how to handle dog-eaters, but you're saying you're not used to seeing...." She paused, as if trying to find the right way to put it.

"Weird things?" she finished.

He was going to say he wasn't, but then he thought of seeing the gray-hued feet outside the restroom stall when he was thirteen.

"Not usually."

She looked at him a moment before shrugging. "Maybe you're a late bloomer. Or maybe there's another reason. It doesn't matter. What's important is that it might just help you find your daughter."

She reached into her purse, removed a business card from a plastic holder, found a pen, and wrote something on the back of the card. She then put her pen away and handed the card to Jayce. He read what she'd written.

11:00 pm. 1407 Mercantile Drive.

"Meet me there tonight," she said, "and we'll see what we can do about finding Emory."

Without waiting for his reply, she stood, smiled at him, and then walked out of the restaurant. He turned and watched through the front window as she got into her car, pulled out of the parking lot, and headed down the road, presumably on her way to the next doctor's office on her list for the day.

He turned away from the window, looked down at the back of Nicola's card once more, and then looked at the sauce splatter the man with the green gloves had left on the surface of his table. He had no idea what was going on, but if there was any chance that Nicola could help him, then he'd meet her tonight. But he couldn't help wondering what the hell he was getting himself into.

★   ★   ★

Because Jayce's back was to the window, he didn't notice a red pickup truck with license plates that read OHIO PIG drive slowly past the restaurant. Nor did he see the man behind the wheel glare at his back before driving away.

★   ★   ★

Since Jayce had called off work, he went directly home after leaving About Thaime. Mackenzie got the house in the divorce, and he'd moved into a one-bedroom apartment not far from the office where he worked. When he'd been looking for a new place to live, he'd been half-tempted to move into Springhill Apartments so he could be close to Emory, but he'd wisely decided against it. He didn't want to cramp Emory's style, and he didn't want her to think her father was overly needy – even if at that time in his life he was. Now he wished he *had* moved there. Maybe he would've been able to forge a closer relationship with his daughter. If he had, maybe he'd know more about her life and he'd have a better idea of where to look for her. Or maybe she wouldn't have gone missing in the first place.

Once inside his apartment, he went to the kitchen to take some pain meds. His head wasn't hurting too bad, but his hand was throbbing like a sonofabitch. He took four ibuprofen with water, and then went into his bedroom, where his laptop and printer rested atop an old card table positioned in one corner. He booted up his computer, turned on the printer, and printed more Emory fliers, more to have something to do than for any other reason. While they were printing, he logged onto the Internet and looked up the address Nicola had given him, but he didn't find any references to it. He entered the address into a direction-finding website, but he again came up empty. He supposed he shouldn't be surprised. It was just one more bit of weirdness to add to what was becoming a rather lengthy list.

He considered taking a nap, but he wasn't tired, and naps tended to make him feel groggy when he woke up. He couldn't bring himself to plunk his ass down in front of the TV and zone out while he waited for nighttime, though. His mind was buzzing with everything that had happened since last night, and his divorced, middle-aged bachelor pad felt smaller, shabbier, and more confining than usual.

As he waited for the fliers to finish printing, he thought about what Nicola had said at the restaurant. *You've got the Eye.* If he did, he sure as hell could do without it. He liked living in a world where he knew nothing about teenagers who devoured stray dogs and men who ate napkins while wearing green rubber gloves. A memory tickled at the back of his mind then, but he couldn't recall any specific details about it. Couldn't – or didn't want to? He forced himself to concentrate, and slowly some details returned to him. It had happened when Emory was a child, when he and Mackenzie took her someplace special. The zoo or maybe the circus. Animals were involved, he was sure about that. His color printer was old and had seen plenty of use in its time, and it took a while for it to print each flier. The printer still had a ways to go, and on impulse, he took his phone from his pocket and called Mackenzie.

The phone rang on the other end a number of times, and he thought the call was going to go through to voicemail, but then Mackenzie answered.

"Hello, Jayce. What do you want?"

For a long time when he'd called after the divorce, she'd sounded exasperated. But these days, she just sounded bored.

"Just checking to see if you've heard from Emory."

"We've been over this before. If I hear from her, I'll let you know. Immediately."

Her tone was that of a frustrated teacher repeating something for a particularly inattentive – and not particularly bright – student.

"That's not really an answer," he said.

She sighed. "I don't have time for this right now. I was in the middle of something when you called."

Mackenzie's new husband, a high-end real estate agent, made plenty of money, and she didn't need to work these days. What did she have to do that was so important? Count all their money and stack it in neat, even piles?

He hurried on before she could say goodbye and disconnect. "Do you remember the time we took Emory to the—" Which was it? He took a guess. "Zoo?"

Mackenzie didn't answer right away, and he wondered if she'd disconnected without him realizing it. But then she answered.

"We took her to the zoo a number of times."

"I'm talking about the time when the strange thing happened." He fought to dredge up more details. "When Emory *saw* something."

"I really don't have time for this, Jayce. I'm sure Emory will get in contact with one or both of us soon."

She disconnected before he could say anything else, and without saying goodbye.

He tucked his phone back into his pants pocket. He'd been married to Mackenzie for fifteen years, and he could tell when she was uncomfortable discussing a subject. Her words became clipped, she spoke more rapidly, and she bailed on the conversation as soon as she could. He'd definitely touched a nerve, but he hadn't—

His headache had lingered in the background while he spoke with Mackenzie, but now it came roaring back to life, far worse than before. He gritted his teeth and squeezed his eyes shut. He grabbed hold of the sides of his head as if he feared it might explode and was desperately trying to keep it from doing so. His skull felt like one of those boxes magicians put their assistants in and then inserted one sword after another. Each blade of pain was more agonizing than the last, and he fell to his knees, rolled onto the floor, and curled up in a ball of utter misery. What the fuck was wrong with him? Had the doctor who'd examined him at the ER screwed up and not realized how seriously he'd been hurt last night, when the back of his head collided with the alley wall? Maybe his brain had been injured to the point where it was bleeding, and the blood had built up inside and now, trapped by his skull, it had nowhere to go. Maybe instead of exploding, his head would implode, the pressure squeezing his brain into tapioca. But then the pain – all of it – vanished. The sudden relief caught him off guard, so much so that he drew in a surprised gasp.

And then he remembered.

*   *   *

"Look, Daddy! There's a jaff!"

Emory, five years old, points to an enclosure where a pair of giraffes stand motionless, and Jayce wonders if the heat's too much for them. It's July, and the sunlight beats down with almost physical force. There's weight with the heat, making each step, each movement an effort. Not for Emory, though. She seems immune to the heat, full of energy and excited by each new animal she encounters. He's envious of her. All he wants to do is leave, get in the car, crank the AC as high as it will go, and head home and jump in an ice-cold shower.

"It's *giraffe*, dear."

Mackenzie draws out the word – *juh-raaaafff* – to make sure Emory hears the difference from the way she pronounced it. Mackenzie is thirty-three, but she looks ten years younger. She's slender, muscles toned from regular exercise, and she moves with easy, confident grace. She wears her straight brown hair in a ponytail to keep it off her neck, and although she's slathered herself in sunscreen – and made sure Jayce and Emory did too – her skin has red blotches here and there. Mackenzie and the sun do *not* get along. Her white Put-in-Bay T-shirt, shorts, and flip-flops are supposed to help her deal with the heat, but she still looks as miserable as Jayce feels. Despite how obviously uncomfortable she is – or maybe, in a strange way, because of it – he finds her heartachingly beautiful at this moment. He thinks he's the luckiest man alive, and he breaks out in a wide grin. Mackenzie notices, frowns slightly, and cocks her head to the side, as if asking what he's smiling about. But then Emory starts running toward the giraffe enclosure and the both of them hurry to catch up to her.

Jayce, like Mackenzie, is wearing a T-shirt and shorts. His shirt says *Do You Know What Time It Is?* It's the slogan for the insurance company he works for. He likes the slogan because it's provocative and a little enigmatic. When he wears the shirt, sometimes people ask him what the slogan means, which gives him the opportunity to talk to them about their insurance needs and give them one of his cards. He's not an overly aggressive salesperson, but he believes in taking advantage when an opportunity presents itself.

Emory stands at the edge of the 'jaff' enclosure. There's a metal fence with a thick, rounded railing on top. It's taller than Emory, and when Jayce and Mackenzie get there, she turns to Jayce and holds up her arms. Jayce smiles and picks her up so she can have a better view. Her skin is dry but she's hot as a miniature oven, and it doesn't take long for the added heat to make him feel nauseous. He doesn't put her down, though. He's a daddy, and daddies tough it out.

A moat of sorts surrounds the enclosure. Empty of water, but it's effective at keeping distance between the animals and the people who come to stare at them. The ground within is simple packed earth, but there are fake rock formations that Jayce supposes are designed to make the enclosure appear more wild, but they just look stupid to him. The giraffes gaze at them, standing motionless, not so much as twitching an ear. They could be museum replicas of giraffes, formed of plastic, metal, and wire beneath their artificial spotted hides.

"Why don't they do something?" Emory asks. She sounds equal parts frustrated and irritated.

"They come from Africa," Jayce says. "They're used to the heat, and they know that standing still will help them conserve their strength and keep them from getting overheated." He knows next to nothing about the animals, but this sounds like a reasonable explanation, and it seems to satisfy Emory. She shifts restlessly in his arms, and he knows she's still frustrated, though.

The zoo is not crowded today. Most people aren't dumb enough to venture out into this heat. They're sitting comfortably inside their air-conditioned houses, sipping glasses of ice water, and congratulating themselves on how smart they are. Right now, Jayce hates every one of them.

Another family approaches the enclosure – a man, woman, and a boy a couple years older than Emory. Jayce doesn't pay them much attention at first, but then Emory tugs on his T-shirt.

"Daddy...." She sounds frightened, and when she points to the family – who stand at the railing a dozen feet away – he turns to look at them.

At first he doesn't notice anything remarkable about them, certainly nothing to frighten a little girl. But then he realizes their features aren't symmetrical. Their eyes don't line up, their noses are bent and twisted, the nostrils different sizes, one ear is higher than the other, and their mouths droop at one corner. The longer he looks, the more odd details he notices, and he wonders how he could've ever mistaken them for normal. Their flesh sags on their bones, as if their skin has been designed for people that are grotesquely obese but has somehow ended up on people who are stick-thin.

Jayce has a disturbing thought, then.

It's the heat. They're melting.

He turns to Mackenzie. She isn't looking at the Incredible Melting Family, though. She's looking at the giraffes without any particular interest. From her weary expression, he guesses she's too busy trying not to think about how goddamned hot it is to pay attention to anything else.

Jayce's first thought is he's crazy, but Emory sees the family too. Does that mean they're *both* crazy? Maybe it's a hallucination brought on by the heat. But if that's the case, how can two people share the same hallucination? He decides to ask Emory what she sees when she looks at the family. Maybe they aren't seeing the exact same thing. But before he can speak, a sudden flash of memory overtakes him. For a moment he's thirteen again, sitting on a toilet in a bathroom stall, and looking at a pair of gray-tinged feet that belong to whatever stands on the other side of the door. The memory is so powerful that his legs buckle and his vision momentarily goes gray. He might fall to his knees, maybe even faint, but he has hold of his daughter, and he won't allow himself to drop her. The weakness passes, his vision clears, and he grips Emory tighter to make sure he won't lose his hold on her.

How could he have ever forgotten the man – or *thing* – he saw in the restroom at the mall? How can anyone forget something like that? But he has, and he wonders if he's forgotten any other bizarre experiences like that one. If he has, how would he ever know? But right then he doesn't care how many other dark memories might be locked deep in the recesses of his mind. All he wants to do is get Emory the hell away from the Melting Family. Bad enough that he has some nasty memories lurking in his head – ones so bad that he's evidently done all he can to forget them – but he wants to spare Emory from beginning a collection of her own.

He speaks then, his voice shaky.

"How about we go see the tigers, sweetie? They'll be a lot more interesting than...."

He breaks off as a half dozen shapes emerge from behind the fake rocks. No, he realizes, from *inside* them. Each is a yard long, cylindrical and thick-bodied. They are snail-belly white and undulate like caterpillars, but they have no legs that Jayce can see. They have no eyes, either. The only features they possess are insect-like mandibles that protrude from their heads, black, slimy, and cruel-looking. *More a weapon than a mouth,* he thinks. He doesn't have to ask Emory if she sees them too. She stares at the creatures, eyes wide, and despite the oppressive heat, he feels her shiver in his arms. He also doesn't have to ask if Mackenzie sees them. He knows she doesn't. The Melting Family does, though. The child squeals in glee, his voice gurgling as if his throat is clogged with phlegm. He claps his hands together, the saggy, loose flesh around them making a moist smacking sound. Jayce can't be certain, given the way the family's skin droops, but he has the impression that all three of them are grinning, or at least attempting to.

The boy points. "Look, Daddy!" he says in his phlegmy voice. "Cankerworms!"

Neither giraffe seems to notice the slug-things at first. The animals continue standing, motionless and unconcerned. The six creatures converge on the giraffe closest to them, picking up speed as they draw closer. The first creature to reach the giraffe begins undulating up the animal's leg, and it is quickly followed by two others. The giraffe lets out a cry of alarm that sounds uncomfortably close to a human scream as the slug-things move swiftly up the legs and onto the central part of its body. The rest of the creatures mount the giraffe, and soon all six of them are clustered on the animal's sides, belly, and back, covering it in a throbbing white mass. The giraffe rears onto its hind legs and whips its head from side to side, as if trying to dislodge the creatures, but without success. The second giraffe shows no sign of alarm at what's happening to its companion, but it does move off, putting some distance between them, as if it is only partially aware of the attack on the other animal.

Jayce expects the slug-things to begin biting into their victim's hide, but what they do is far worse. Just as they emerged from the rock, passing through it as if it were no more substantial than mist, they enter the giraffe's body without breaking the skin. The giraffe's torso swells as the slug-things – cankerworms, the saggy-fleshed boy called them – fill it, and the animal screams in agony.

Emory presses her face against his chest, eyes squeezed shut, tears running from them, soaking his already sweat-sodden shirt.

"Make it stop, Daddy, make it stop!"

All he can do is hold her tighter. Mackenzie continues looking at the enclosure, a listless expression on her face.

How can she not see this? Jayce thinks. Fuck *seeing.* Why can't she *hear* the giraffe scream?

He expects the giraffe's torso to explode like a boil so overfilled with pus that the skin can no longer contain it. But instead, the giraffe's legs buckle and it falls onto its side. Its screams give way to weak bleating sounds, and then the animal's neck, legs, and tail begin to shrink as they are pulled toward the swollen mass that's the center of its body. The torso swells more as the legs and neck are pulled into it. The tail is the first to disappear into the mass, and the legs go next. The neck is longer, so it's absorbed last. By this point the giraffe's bleating has dwindled to quiet whimpers, which are silenced as the head is pulled into the bulging central mass. *It's like it's drowning inside itself,* Jayce thinks. All that remains of the giraffe is a swollen blob, white with brown spots. The colors begin to edge toward white as the mass shrinks, and then it's gone, and only the cluster of cankerworms remains. They hold together for several more seconds before slowly detaching themselves from the group. Their bodies are thicker than before, evidence that they've fed and fed well. One by one, they begin undulating back toward the rock they emerged from, passing into it with the same ease with which they came. Within moments, the cankerworms are gone. Nothing is left of the giraffe they attacked. No scraps of flesh or pieces of hide. No fragments of bone or splashes of blood. It's as if the animal never existed.

The remaining giraffe walks slowly over to the spot where its companion was...devoured? Absorbed? Unmade? It lowers its head to the spot as if trying to pick up its companion's scent. After a moment, it raises its head and walks off. Its movements are slow, ponderous, and Jayce wonders if it's grieving the loss of its friend.

The Incredible Melting Family applaud as if they've just witnessed a spectacular performance. They move off then, their sagging flaps of skin quivering. Jayce watches them go and wonders what animals they'll visit next and what horrible things they might witness there. Emory is still crying, and Mackenzie comes over and puts her hand on top of their daughter's head.

"What's wrong, sweetie? Are you sad the giraffe's alone? Don't worry. Maybe one day the zookeepers will bring in a friend to live with it."

★　　★　　★

Jayce sat on the edge of his bed, shaking from the intensity of the memory he'd experienced, one so vivid it had almost been like reliving it. How the hell could he have ever forgotten something like that? Forgetting what you had for breakfast on Thursday last week, that was normal. But forgetting seeing a giraffe being absorbed by monstrous white worms that can crawl through solid objects? It seemed impossible. But he *had* forgotten it, just as he'd forgotten seeing the bare gray feet on the other side of the restroom stall. As awful as these memories were, maybe it wasn't so surprising that he'd suppressed them. Given a choice, who would want to live with such nightmarish images scuttling around in their mind?

One thing reliving this memory had taught him – Nicola was right. He *did* have 'the Eye'. And he'd learned something else. Emory had it as well.

He had one other thought, and this one was the worst of them all. What other memories might be hidden deep within his mind? It was a question he didn't want to know the answer to, but he feared he was going to find out anyway, like it or not.

CHAPTER FIVE

Jayce pulled into the parking lot of Springhill Apartments at a quarter to five. He drove to the rental office and parked, but he didn't get out of his car right away. He sat, hands still gripping the steering wheel, and stared at the OPEN sign in the office's front window.

The name *Springhill* conjured images of countryside. Trees with lush green leaves, rolling hills covered with grass and dotted with flowers. The name also implied quiet and tranquility, a place of peace and calm repose. The reality, however, was far different. The Springhill Apartments were a cramped cluster of shabby buildings located on the edge of the Cannery, only a few miles from the CrazyQwik where Emory had worked. Or at least, where she'd *claimed* to work. She'd once told Jayce that while Springhill didn't look like much, the rent − while not cheap − was doable, and it was close enough for her to walk to work, which saved on gas. He hadn't been comfortable with the idea of her walking alone in the Cannery, especially at night, but she was stubborn, just like her mom, and he hadn't been able to convince her how dangerous it was, and now she was gone.

You're her father, Mother said. *You should've tried harder to convince her, should've made her listen to you.*

He couldn't argue with that, so rather than continuing to sit in his car and wallow in guilt, he got out and started toward the rental office. He wasn't certain why he'd come back here. The manager he'd spoken to about Emory hadn't been any help before. But he had to do something. He'd been going crazy sitting at home, and he hadn't been able to take it anymore. He had six hours before he was supposed to meet Nicola, and he might as well do something useful with them.

The short walkway that led to the office was cracked in numerous places, and it looked so old Jayce wouldn't have been surprised if it had crumbled to dust beneath the weight of his footsteps. The rental office was a small building, almost a hut really, with a number of shingles missing from the roof, grime-streaked windows, and brick that looked soft and porous, like sandstone. Jayce imagined a strong rain would wash it away. It wasn't just the physical characteristics of Springhill that created an impression of age, decay, and dissolution. The air was flat, stale, and lifeless, and when he breathed it, it felt as if it gave his lungs no nourishment. Jayce supposed there were more depressing places to live in town, but he had a hard time believing it.

You should never have let her stay here. This is the kind of place where women get raped in every hole they have, filleted like fish, and tossed in a dumpster like last week's trash.

He ignored his mother's voice, and when he reached the door, he took hold of the knob – the metal discolored with age – and turned it. At least he tried to, but the door was locked. He looked to the window in time to see someone inside turn the OPEN sign around to the CLOSED side. There were no posted hours of operation on the window or door, but it wasn't five yet. Why were they closing early?

They saw you coming, Mother said, *and they don't want to talk with you. They know something about Emory, and they want to keep it from you.*

Jayce tried to see who'd turned the sign, but the window was so dirty, all he could make out was a silhouette on the other side of the glass.

He knocked on the door, waited, then knocked again. No one answered. He knocked again, this time pounding the door with his fist.

"Hey!" he shouted. "I just want to talk to you for a couple minutes! It's important!"

No answer.

Sudden anger welled within him, strong and overpowering, and he envisioned himself stepping back, placing a well-aimed kick next to the doorknob, and hearing wood splinter as the door gave beneath the impact. He'd never been a violent person before, and the intensity of the anger – coupled with the feeling of exhilaration that accompanied it – shocked him. He almost did it, though, actually took a step backward, fixed his gaze on the point where his foot would make contact with the wood, tensed his muscles in preparation....

But his anger drained away as suddenly as it had come, and he turned and walked back to his car.

A real father would do whatever it took to find his daughter.

He got in the car, turned on the engine, and backed out of the space.

"How the fuck am I supposed to know what a father would do?" he said. "I never had one."

Valerie didn't respond to that, and he felt more than a little satisfaction at having shut her up. Imaginary or not, her nagging wore him down, and he was glad to be rid of it, if only for now. He wasn't planning on leaving, though. A remnant of the anger that had erupted inside him remained, and he used it to fuel his determination to do something, anything, that might lead him to his daughter. If the goddamned apartment manager wouldn't talk to him, he'd go see what he could find out for himself.

He didn't understand the manager's seeming reluctance to talk with him. The man had been a bit standoffish the last time they'd spoken, but he'd been cooperative enough. What had changed? Maybe nothing. Maybe it was simply that the man wanted to close a bit early today. Maybe he had something to do, errands to run, or even a hot date. Maybe he wasn't feeling well or was just tired after a long day. Maybe. But Jayce couldn't escape the feeling that something else was going on, something far less benign.

He drove to the building where Emory's apartment was, parked, and got out of his car. His head had started hurting again, and his injured hand throbbed, but he barely registered the pain. His vision swam in and out of focus too, but he ignored it. And a moment later, it stabilized.

Maybe you should go back to the doctor, Mother said.

"Maybe you should just shut the fuck up."

He stopped to regard Emory's building. It was two stories tall and contained four separate units. It was in the same shape as the rental office: cracked walkways, grimy windows, shutters slightly askew, friable brick, missing roof tiles. The building itself was lopsided, listing several degrees to the left. The overall impression was that of a structure perpetually on the verge of collapse, and he'd never been comfortable with Emory living here. His sad little apartment was nothing to brag about, but at least it wasn't a shithole like this place. A few weeks after Emory had moved in, he'd considered trying to urge her to switch to his complex, but he'd abandoned the idea. They'd barely been on speaking terms then, and he hadn't wanted her to think that he was trying to exert some kind of parental authority over her to which she felt he wasn't entitled. But now he wished he had insisted she move, had offered to help pay her rent at a new place if she couldn't afford it. If he had done these things, she might have accepted. And if she had, she might not have gone missing.

He did his best to thrust such thoughts aside. He hadn't come here to obsess over what he should've done. He'd come here to see what he could do *now*.

He didn't bother going to the building's entrance. The door to Emory's apartment would be locked, and he didn't have a key. If that bastard manager had answered his knock, maybe he *would* have a key, but the fucker hadn't, and that meant Jayce was going to have to get creative if he wanted to get into his daughter's apartment.

He started walking toward the back of the building.

★   ★   ★

Jayce didn't look back as he headed for the rear of the building. If he had, he would've seen a red pickup pull up and park next to his car, he would've seen the plate OHIO PIG, and he would've seen the driver get out of his truck and follow him.

★   ★   ★

A narrow sidewalk ran behind the building, the concrete in even worse shape than the front. It had buckled in numerous places, and large chunks were missing, exposing the ground beneath. The soil was still wet from last night's rain, and Jayce was careful to avoid stepping in it. If he intended to break into Emory's apartment – and he did – he didn't want to leave muddy footprints all over the carpet. A line of scraggly, near-leafless trees stretched behind the building, a piss-poor attempt at creating a privacy boundary between it and the next.

The ground units had fenced-in patios, while the upper units had wooden decks with a set of stairs leading down. The patios had slabs of concrete – weathered, cracked, and broken – along with a small strip of ground between them and the fence. Jayce assumed there was supposed to be grass on the ground, like a tiny lawn, but the earth was bare and wet. Fat earthworms writhed in the soil, reminding him too much of cankerworms. He didn't want to think about that zoo trip now, maybe not ever again, so he looked away from the worms and continued on. The fences were falling apart, slats missing, the wood so old it was peeling away in threads. The decks of the upper units were in seriously poor condition, and their flooring sagged. Jayce couldn't imagine that those boards could support the weight of anything larger than a sparrow.

The building seemed even more rundown and ramshackle than he remembered. Was this another case of his 'Eye' seeing what had been there all along, or had it really gotten that much worse since his last visit?

Emory's patio had no furniture, not even a lone plastic chair that she could sit on when the weather was nice. She'd planted no flowers in the small patch of ground, nor were any decorations visible through the small kitchen window. There were no personal touches of any kind outside, not a single thing to show that Emory – or anyone else, for that matter – lived here. The patio's anonymity made Jayce suddenly doubt himself, and for a moment, he feared he'd come to the wrong building. How could he tell for sure that this unit was hers? He *thought* it was, but given the lack of distinguishing details.... Then he noticed a large gouge in the planks that made up the small gate built into the fence. It was large and deep, slanted from right to left, and cut across several boards. He'd noted it when he'd visited on Emory's birthday, and she'd taken him onto the patio so they could talk while she smoked. Jayce didn't approve of her smoking, wasn't even sure when she'd picked up the habit. He didn't smoke, and neither did Mackenzie. Even though he hadn't said anything, she'd sensed how he felt and they'd ended up arguing, and she'd gone back inside her apartment, slamming the patio door so hard he'd been surprised the glass hadn't shattered. Feeling it would be wiser if he didn't go back inside, he'd opened the patio gate and left using the rear walkway. He'd noticed the gouge in the wood during his departure, and he'd wondered what could've made it. Had someone used a knife? Had some sort of animal done it? Ohio had coyotes. There hadn't been any in the state when Jayce had been growing up, but they'd gradually moved into the area during the last couple decades. The damned things were perpetually hungry, and they seemed to have little fear of humans, scrounging outside their houses – or apartments – in search of any scraps of food that might satisfy, however temporarily, the yawning pit at the core of their being. The gouge looked too wide and deep to be coyote work, but whatever had made it, it told him that he was in the right place.

An image passed through his mind then – a gray-skinned hand, fingers terminating in sharp black talons, an index finger extended, the nail being drawn across the fence, making a single deep groove, curled wood shavings falling to the ground.... The image passed as quickly as it had come, but it left him uneasy.

He opened the patio gate, the wood feeling moist and soft beneath his fingers, the creaking of its hinges sounding loud as a gunshot to his ears. So far, he hadn't seen any of the building's occupants, but that didn't mean it was empty. Plus, people would be getting home from work soon, and he didn't want to be caught prowling around the building. He left the gate open to avoid making any more noise, and then he walked to the patio door. He tried to open it and wasn't surprised to find it locked. Breaking the glass wasn't an option. Not only would it make far more noise than a squeaky gate, it would be the kind of noise that prompted people to call the police.

And you'd probably end up slicing your hand to ribbons and bleeding to death before you could get help, Mother said.

"True enough."

He stepped up to the patio door and tried to look inside, but not only was the glass dirty, the vertical blinds were pulled closed. Emory had once told him that the latch on her patio door didn't lock tight, and if you pulled on it hard enough, the lock would disengage and the door would slide open. He'd told her to get an old broom handle and cut off a length of it that she could insert in the door's track to prevent anyone from opening it. She'd told him she would, but in a way that indicated she'd said so only to make him feel better. He'd have made a rod for her, but he'd known she'd only resent him for it, so he hadn't. He gripped the door handle and pulled, putting his weight into it. The door resisted at first, but then it gave way with a soft *snick* and slid open. The door's motion caused the blinds to swing and make soft clacking sounds as they bumped into each other. Jayce pushed the slats aside and stepped through.

The air in the apartment was stale and musty, as if the place had been closed for a long time. There were no lights on, so the room was dim, but he could see well enough. Emory's furnishings were minimal – chair, couch, small wall-mounted TV, a table with two mismatched chairs – everything except the television purchased at secondhand stores. Same for the artwork, a framed print of geese on a winter lake and another of wild horses galloping across an open plain. Emory liked to keep her space neat, always had ever since she was a child, and there were no signs of untidiness. No shoes in the middle of the floor, no clothes draped over the back of the chair or couch. She'd inherited this quality from him. She certainly hadn't gotten it from her mother, who believed that cleaning was something you paid other people to do for you.

He knew Emory wasn't here. He could feel the apartment's emptiness. But he still called out for her, just in case.

"Emory? Are you here? It's Dad. I've just come to check and make sure you're all right."

Silence.

Despite knowing he'd receive no answer, he couldn't help feeling disappointed. He'd much rather have his daughter come storming out of her bedroom yelling at him for breaking into her apartment like a crazy man than be confronted by the quiet reality of her absence.

"Where are you, sweetie?" he said softly. There was no reply, of course, not even from the part of him that spoke in his mother's voice.

He began making his way through the apartment, searching, but for what, he didn't know. Something, anything, that might give him some indication of what had happened to Emory. There was nothing in the living room, so he moved on to the kitchen. The counters were clean, save for a small stack of mail. He looked through it but found nothing of interest, just bills and junk mail. The sink was empty, but the dishwasher was full of clean dishes. If she'd planned on going away for some time, would she have left the dishwasher full like this? Many people – maybe most – would have, but Emory bordered on being OCD when it came to neatness. He had a hard time imagining her leaving her apartment for any length of time without putting the dishes away. He checked the cupboards next, more to be thorough than because he expected to find anything important there. There were a lot of easy-to-make boxed meals, various kinds of rice, canned soups.... The shelves were far from full, and he wondered if she ate out a lot. The thought saddened him. When she'd been a child, he'd known her eating preferences and habits as well as he did his own. But looking into her partially stocked cupboards made him realize once more just how little he really knew about the woman Emory had become.

He shut the final cupboard door and turned to the refrigerator. Would he find it even emptier than the cupboards? If Emory hadn't been back here for a while – which seemed to be the case – there was bound to be spoiled food inside. Sour milk, rotting meat, unidentifiable substances green with mold.... What good would it do to look at that?

It would give you some idea how long she's been gone, he told himself, although there might have been a bit of his mother's voice in there as well. If the milk was fresh, that would mean she had been here recently. If it was well on its way to becoming cheese, it would tell a different story. So he opened the fridge.

It was far from empty, but it didn't contain plastic jugs of milk, liters of soda, bottles of ketchup or mustard, half-full bottles of wine, or plastic storage containers with leftovers inside. Instead, the shelves were lined with clay jars, the kind sold at CrazyQwik. Nicola had purchased one last night, but he hadn't thought to ask her about it – or what was *really* in it – during lunch. Seeing these jars.... He tried to remember what the dog-eater Zach had called them last night. Was it...vessels? That sounded right. Seeing these vessels in Emory's refrigerator struck him two different ways. It was a validation that, despite what that fucker working the counter last night – Virgil – had said, Emory did work at CrazyQwik. Or at the very least, she shopped at the place. But on the other hand, the sight of all those vessels – there must have been close to thirty of them – was more than a little disturbing. There wasn't anything else in the refrigerator, just the jars. They varied somewhat in size and shape, and they had symbols on the front that Jayce didn't recognize but which hurt his eyes to look at.

He hesitated, and then he reached in, chose a jar at random, and lifted it out to examine. He left the refrigerator door open and cool air slowly surrounded him as he gazed at the vessel. The markings consisted of a series of curving and interlocking lines that refused to make sense, no matter how hard he stared at them. The jar felt cold in his hand, far colder than could be accounted for by being in the refrigerator. So cold, in fact, that it was more than a little uncomfortable to hold. He brought the jar close to his face and inhaled through his nostrils. The smell of hardened clay was strongest, but there were other scents as well, subtler ones. He couldn't put a name to them, but they summoned images in his mind. One was of a snow-covered landscape at night, illuminated by the sickly glow of a swollen pus-yellow moon. Hundreds, thousands of skeletal arms jutted upward from the snow, as if reaching toward the moon. Another image was of a large slime-coated sea creature with a mottled grayish-white hide, tusked and spiked, thousands of tiny crab-like creatures clinging to its body, working industriously to strip the flesh from its bones as it swam through a night-dark sea. There were other, even stranger images, but these were the only ones he could make even partial sense of. He moved the vessel away from his face, and the images ceased. He was trembling so violently in the aftermath of these visions that he almost dropped the jar, but fear of what might emerge from it should it plunge to the floor and shatter helped him maintain his grip. If it had given him visions that strong when it was closed, what the hell would happen to him if its contents were released?

What the hell was in there? Some kind of drug? If so, it had to be goddamned powerful to make him hallucinate like that. But if it was a drug, how could CrazyQwik get away with selling it out in the open, stored in one of their coolers, no less? Hand still trembling, he put the jar back in the refrigerator. Whatever the jars were, based on the different markings on their surfaces, no two were the same. He thought about examining another, but instead he closed the refrigerator door. One was more than enough.

He reluctantly checked the freezer and was relieved to find it contained only a few low-calorie microwaveable meals. He left the kitchen then, walked through the living room, and down a short hallway. The apartment's layout was almost identical to his, and this thought depressed him, although he wasn't sure why. Maybe because he was in his fifties and living no better than his twenty-year-old daughter. Or maybe it was because she wasn't living any better than her failure of a father. The apartment's sole bathroom was located in the hall, and he stopped to check it out. There was makeup on the sink counter – mascara, eyeliner, lipstick – along with some haircare products. He found body wash, shampoo, and conditioner in the shower. A quick search of the sink cabinet drawers revealed nothing of interest. After what he'd found in the refrigerator, he was reluctant to open the medicine chest, but he did. He found several unlabeled prescription bottles. There was no way to tell what the pills inside them were, and he put the bottles back, closed the medicine chest, and left.

There was a linen closet next to the bathroom, but all he found there were towels, washcloths, and an extra set of sheets. He was starting to feel like an idiot. What the hell had he expected to find by searching Emory's apartment? A diary that contained all of her deepest, darkest secrets? A calendar or datebook with appointments written down, detailing her daily schedule? Or better yet, a note saying where she'd gone, why she'd gone, and when she'd be back?

A few more steps and he was at her bedroom door. It was closed, and he stood there for a moment, debating whether he should enter, if he could bring himself to violate Emory's privacy to this extent.

You've already broken into her apartment, he thought. *You might as well go all the way.*

He opened the door and stepped inside.

He'd never been inside her bedroom before, and being here made him feel more like an intruder than at any point since he'd forced open the patio door. Even when Emory had been little, he hadn't gone into her bedroom often, mostly at nighttime to read her a story, tuck her into bed, and give her a goodnight kiss on her forehead. She'd stopped wanting stories – and kisses – by the time she reached middle school, and he and Mackenzie had divorced not long after that. Emory had kept him at arm's length ever since, so the sudden intimacy of being in her most private of places made him uncomfortable. It reminded him of how much she was a stranger to him, and vice versa. The bedroom was a far more intimate place to him than the bathroom. He viewed bathrooms as utilitarian places for eliminating waste, for cleansing and grooming one's body. But this was where she slept, where she dressed, where she brought lovers to or, if she was alone, where she pleasured herself.

Her bedroom was as sparsely furnished as the rest of her place. A single bed, a lone nightstand, a small dresser. No artwork on the walls here, no photos, either. The bed wasn't made, the sheet and comforter pulled back as if Emory had just gotten up. As neat as she was, he was surprised she'd left the bed unmade. Maybe she'd been late for work that day. Maybe she'd been late for something else. Whatever the reason, it seemed she'd left in a hurry.

The air inside her bedroom held a strange tang that reminded him of a pet shop. Sawdust bedding, ammonia, and the musty-acrid odor of mingled animal scents. But underlying this was the rank smell of sex – sour semen and vaginal musk. His stomach roiled as a sudden wave of nausea hit him. He wasn't one of those fathers who freaked out at the thought of his daughter as a sexual being. He wanted her to have a happy, healthy life, and sex was a natural part of that. But this smell – this *stink* – was like a room in a whorehouse, or maybe a hotel room where a porno had been filming all day. It was a smell of raw animal lust, mindless and meaningless.

He tried to think of the smell dispassionately. It meant that Emory had been here recently, maybe as recently as the last few hours. Except that didn't feel right. The smell was strong, yes, but it felt old, as if whatever had taken place in here had happened a while ago and the stained sheets hadn't been removed from the bed and washed. But that didn't explain why the stink was so goddamned strong. He couldn't imagine only two people being responsible for this smell. Had Emory brought a small army of men into her bedroom and they'd all stood round the bed, jerking off and squirting semen all over her? As soon as the image came to him, he regretted it, and for the first time since he'd started searching for his daughter, he wondered if he should stop. By continuing to look for her, he might discover things that he'd be happier not knowing. He thought of the dog-eaters and the man with the green gloves at the Thai restaurant. He'd already encountered some goddamned disturbing things while looking for Emory, and he had a bad feeling it was only going to get worse from this point forward. And the things he'd encountered had started to stir up memories that he'd buried – the man with the gray skin, the cankerworms devouring the giraffe.... If he kept going, what else might get dredged up from his subconscious? Were there even worse memories hidden there? He feared there were, and if he was forced to remember them, could he handle it?

For his own sake, he should leave the bedroom, shut the door, and get the hell out of Emory's apartment. He shouldn't be here anyway. He was violating her privacy, not to mention breaking the law. Mackenzie was probably right. Emory was most likely fine and he was just letting his imagination run away with him, as it often did when it came to the possibility of something bad happening, thanks to his mother, who'd instilled in him a deep paranoia and distrust of the world and everything in it. He should go home, try to rest, get a decent night's sleep, head on in to work tomorrow, and wait patiently for Emory to get in touch with him or Mackenzie. And as for Nicola.... He didn't really know her, did he? And just because she'd helped him out in the alley last night didn't mean her motives for being willing to continue helping him were entirely altruistic. She knew about the dog-eaters and hadn't seen anything especially odd about the man in the green rubber gloves. Whatever sort of bizarre world those weird people inhabited, Nicola was a part of it somehow, and for that reason, if no other, she couldn't be trusted. This was his last chance to walk away. If he continued now, there would be no turning back, for better or – more likely – worse.

He almost did it. But he thought of the little girl at the zoo, the one clinging to him and pressing her face against his chest so she wouldn't have to look at something that was bad – *really* bad. He had been there for her on that day, and he wouldn't turn his back on her now.

He stepped into the bedroom.

He started with her dresser and found it held only neatly folded clothes. The closet was the same – blouses, slacks, and dresses hanging up, shoes arranged in a row on the floor. Nothing else. He moved to the nightstand next, fearing he'd discover items of a more *personal* nature there. But when he slid the drawer open, all he found were bottles of hand lotion, headache pills, decongestants, and a book bound in black leather. At first he thought it was a Bible, which he found odd as neither he nor Mackenzie was religious. They'd never discouraged Emory from learning about religion, but she'd never displayed any particular interest. People changed, though, and if she had taken up a religion, it might explain her apparent disappearance. Maybe she was so caught up in the newness of it all — the people, the services, the Bible study — that she'd been neglecting her secular life. And since he and Mackenzie didn't subscribe to any religion, maybe she was reluctant to tell them about her new passion in life. Jayce wasn't certain how he'd respond to Emory if she'd found God — especially if, like a lot of new converts, she was overzealous or worse, fanatical. But he'd find a way to accept whatever she was into, as long as it meant she was safe. He pulled the book out of the drawer and examined it. The title was embossed on the cover in gold foil letters, as he'd anticipated, but it wasn't written in English. He thought it might be Latin.

Liber Ab Oblivione.

A bookmark stuck out from the pages about a third of the way in, and Jayce opened the book to that point. The text was written in English, but that didn't help him understand it any better. There were terms mentioned that he wasn't familiar with. *The Gyre. Purgatum. Shadow. The Nightway. The Vast.* The bookmark had something printed on it, an ad for the store where Emory had presumably bought it. *Tainted Pages. New and Used Books. Esoterica a Specialty.*

He put the book back in the nightstand drawer but he folded the bookmark and put it in his wallet. He almost turned to leave then, but he realized there was one last place to search. He got down on his hands and knees and peered under the bed. At most, he thought he might find a couple plastic storage containers for extra clothes, but the only object beneath the bed was a cardboard shoebox. It was the kind of thing that people kept photos or other memorabilia in. Or maybe receipts. Receipts would give him an insight into where Emory usually went, where she spent her money. They'd give him other places to look for her. More, they'd help him better understand the person his daughter had become. He was beginning to believe that if he was going to have any hope of finding her, it wouldn't be because of one specific clue, but because he'd finally, after all these years, gotten to know who she was. It was a sad realization, one accompanied by deep guilt and self-loathing, but he did his best to ignore those feelings. They weren't going to help him find his daughter.

He sat cross-legged on the floor next to Emory's bed, shoebox on his lap. He removed the lid, put it on the floor, and looked inside. No receipts, no memorabilia. Inside was a bright pink rubber object, and at first he thought it was a sex toy of some kind. The discovery made him feel even more like an intruder – a *violator* – in his daughter's private space. His first impulse was to put the lid back on the box, slide it under the bed, and get the hell out of there. But the longer he examined the object, the more he realized it didn't look like any sex toy he was familiar with – not that he was an expert, by any means. It wasn't shaped like a phallus and it didn't have any visible controls, like a vibrator would have. No buttons, no dial to twist. It was a coiled length of what looked like solid tubing about an inch thick. He tried to guess how long it would be if he removed it from the box and straightened it. Four feet, he guessed, maybe longer. He felt an urge to touch it, if only to get a better idea of what it was, but he resisted. Maybe this wasn't a sex toy, but if it was, if it was something Emory had used to pleasure herself, he did *not* want to handle it. The very idea disgusted him. In a sense, it would be incestuous, maybe not technically but emotionally, and that was a line he wasn't willing to cross, not for any reason. He reached for the lid, but before he could take hold of it, the object in the box shifted.

He stared down at it, not trusting what he'd felt, putting it down to a combination of imagination and guilt over spying on his daughter.

Oh, it moved all right, Mother said. *And you'd better do something before it—*

One end of the pink tubing lifted out of the box and, moving so fast it was little more than a blur, it wrapped itself around Jayce's wrist. The rubbery surface felt vaguely slimy, and the sensation of its touch disturbed him almost as much as the fact that it had moved. He yanked his wrist back in reflex, but instead of freeing himself, he only pulled the rest of the tubing out of the box. The entire length was moving now, writhing in the air, long body whipping back and forth like a pissed-off snake.

He let out a cry of disgust and jumped to his feet. He grabbed hold of the tubing's other end and tried to pull it off him. But that end coiled around his other wrist, and the thing had him cuffed. He tried pulling both hands free by jerking his arms violently outward, but whatever the hell this thing was, it was too strong. A thin tendril emerged from the middle section of tubing and stretched toward his neck, while another emerged and moved toward his crotch. Both tendrils thickened as they extended until they were the same size as the main mass. One of the tendrils wrapped around his neck, while the other forced its way into his pants, slithered through his pubic hair and wrapped around his penis. Panic set in and he began thrashing back and forth, attempting to free his hands so he could grab hold of the other tendrils and pull them off him. But his exertions proved no more effective than before, and all he managed to do was lose his balance.

He flopped onto the bed, still struggling to pull free of the coils encircling his wrists. The tendril around his neck tightened slowly, compressing his airway bit by bit. The tendril in his pants began squeezing his cock, firmly but not so hard that it hurt. The tendril began to grow warmer, and the slime on the outer surface became thicker. The cock-tendril worked his shaft with all the skill and precision of a high-class whore, and despite the situation he grew erect in its rubbery embrace. While the cock-tendril went to town on his stiff member, the neck-tendril continued its slow, inexorable tightening. He mentally detached himself from what was being done to him beneath the waist. As bad as that was, it was nothing compared to having his oxygen supply cut off. He tried tensing his neck muscles, turning his head, shaking it back and forth, but none of his exertions loosened the neck-tendril. All he'd accomplished was to waste oxygen with his movements. He tried crying out for help, not caring if he were discovered having broken into his daughter's apartment, but he could no longer draw in enough air to shout, could only manage a weak breathy wheeze that only vaguely resembled the word *help*.

His head began to pound with migraine intensity, and his vision began to blur, a soft gray haze nibbling at the corners of his eyes. Distantly, he was aware of his cock throbbing, the skin stretched so tight it felt as if it might tear any second. His testicles felt as if they were on fire as his body built toward an orgasm he didn't want. He wondered if he'd come before he lost consciousness or if his body would betray him after he passed out. He remembered reading somewhere that when men were hanged, their cocks fired off a last desperate blast of semen, on the off chance that somehow there might be a receptive egg nearby. Evolution's last-ditch evacuation plan. *Dead man cumming!* he thought, feeling lightheaded now. He would've laughed if he could've drawn enough air into his lungs to do so.

As darkness began to slip over him and his orgasm drew imminent, he thought of Emory. Hoped that wherever she was, she was safe and happy. He also hoped that someone else would find his body so she wouldn't have to. He didn't want her last memory of him to be that of a purple-faced corpse with cum-stained pants sprawled across her bed.

He heard movement then, a scuffing thump on the carpet, and then, through his dimming vision, he saw a swift blur of motion. It was followed by a tug on his neck, and then a sharp piercing cry. Another blur of motion, another tug, this one on his cock. He'd already been on the verge of ejaculating, and this last sensation sent him over the edge. His dick spasmed and an electric jolt lanced through his prostate. It was the most powerful orgasm he'd ever experienced, and for several seconds he was unable to control himself as endorphins flooded his system and his body bucked as if he were having a seizure. When it was over, he lay back, gasping, his underwear soaked with warm sticky cum. The fact that he could breathe was something of a miracle, and he realized that the coil around his neck had been loosened. He tried to move his arms, but he couldn't. His wrists were still bound by those coils as strongly as ever.

His vision began to clear, and he looked up to see Ohio Pig standing next to the bed, looking down at him. The man grinned.

"Was it as good for you as it was for me?"

CHAPTER SIX

The man held a large hunting knife – not much different from the kind the dog-eaters had carried – the blade slick with blood. At first Jayce thought it was his blood, but then he saw the stumps where the neck and cock tendrils had been attached to the pink creature, blood running from both ragged openings. The severed neck-tendril lay on his chest, the cock-tendril on his crotch, both twitching weakly, well on their way to dying. As far as Jayce was concerned, they couldn't get there fast enough.

He looked up at Ohio Pig, intending to ask the man to cut his hands free. But before he could speak, the man sat on the bed next to him and placed the edge of the knife to Jayce's neck.

The Pig shook his head. "You people are sick, you know that? I can't believe you snuck into someone's apartment just so you could get off in their bedroom. And with a Pink Devil yet. Don't you know how dangerous those things are?"

"I'm...starting to get an idea," Jayce said, throat hurting and voice raspy. He'd forgotten about his headache during his orgasm, but it was back now, not quite as agonizing as before, but still damned painful. He should've been terrified that this man had a big-ass knife to his neck, blood from the Pink Devil oozing off the metal and onto his flesh. But after what he'd just been through, he didn't feel any emotion as he asked, "Why are you holding a knife to my throat? You're not still mad about me cutting you off in traffic, are you? I said I was sorry."

The man looked at Jayce as if he'd made the stupidest statement imaginable.

"It's *because* I'm holding the knife that I get to ask the questions instead of you. Got it?"

Jayce nodded. His semen cooled against his wilted cock and blood continued dripping from the Pink Devil's wounds. The color of its rubbery substance was fading, the pink edging toward white, and the tendrils wrapped around his wrist didn't feel so tight anymore. He pulled experimentally, making sure to keep the movement minimal. The coils hadn't loosened enough for him to pull free yet, but they would. He just needed to be patient.

Ohio Pig smiled again, revealing crooked, yellowed teeth. One of his front teeth was missing, and this caused a slight, almost undetectable whistle when he spoke.

"That's better. I'm going to ask you some questions, and you're going to answer them with a simple yes or no. If I want you to say any more than that, I'll tell you. Got it?"

"Yes."

The Pig lowered his head closer to Jayce and looked him deep in the eyes, as if trying to gauge his sincerity. Whatever he saw in Jayce's gaze must have satisfied him, and he asked his first question.

"Are you one of *them*?"

Jayce didn't know how to respond to that, and after several seconds passed, the Pig added, "You know what I mean. Are you a Shadower?"

Jayce had no idea what that was, but from the way the Pig's upper lip curled when he said the word, Jayce figured his safest bet was to answer no, and he did.

"Then what the fuck were you doing having lunch with that woman?"

Jayce hesitated, and the man said, "Forget yes or no. Just answer."

"My daughter's missing. I went to the convenience store where she worked to see if I could learn anything that might help me find her. Outside, a couple" – he felt silly saying the word – "dog-eaters attacked me. Nicola chased them off. She thinks she might be able to help me find my daughter."

He'd left out some of the details, but he figured he'd covered the most important parts.

"Dog-eaters, huh? I *hate* those fuckers. They're like goddamned cockroaches. Kill one and a dozen more take its place."

Kill? Mother said. *You hear that?*

He sure as shit had.

He tested his bonds again. Looser, but still not loose enough.

"Whose place is this? Your daughter's?"

"Yes."

"You find anything in here that gave you a clue as to what might've happened to her?"

Jayce thought of the bookmark folded in his wallet. "No."

The Pig's mouth worked itself into a grimace of distaste. "Do you feel like a perv sneaking around in your daughter's bedroom? Looking in her drawers, her closet…fucking around with her Pink Devil. 'Cause if I was in your place, I would feel like a real lowlife. A true sleazeball, you know? What's your daughter's name? Don't lie to me. I'll know if you do."

The man might be bluffing, probably was, but after everything Jayce had seen since setting foot inside the CrazyQwik last night, he decided not to take any chances.

"Emory Lewis."

"Describe her."

Jayce was reluctant to do so, but the Pig pressed the knife blade more firmly against his throat to emphasize who was in charge, and Jayce complied, describing Emory in the most general terms. The Pig didn't ask for further details.

"Is *she* a Shadower?"

"No." *At least, not as far as I know,* he thought.

The Pig gave Jayce a skeptical look, then pressed the knife even harder against his neck, the blade dimpling the skin. Jayce held his breath, afraid to move. He could feel the Pink Devil's coils slackening further, and in another few seconds he would be able to pull himself free at last. But once he could use his hands again, how was he going to get Ohio Pig away from him without getting his throat slashed?

The man smiled, once more showing his mouthful of yellowed teeth.

"All right. I believe you."

He pulled the knife away from Jayce's neck and with a single swift motion sliced through the nearly bone-white length of the formerly Pink Devil. There was little blood left in the thing, so only a few drops oozed from where the Pig's knife cut it. Once the blade had done its work, the last of the life went out of the tendrils wrapped around Jayce's wrists. They were no longer shiny and rubbery but dry and brittle. The Pig wiped his knife on Emory's sheets, then slid it into his right boot. He then glanced down at the wet spot on Jayce's crotch and wrinkled his nose.

"Christ, man, you should go home and get yourself a fresh pair of undies."

He stood and moved away from the bed. Jayce sat up and pulled the remains of the Pink Devil from his wrists and let the pieces fall onto the bed to join the rest of the creature. Blood stained the sheets and his clothes, and if anyone had been here to see him, that person would've thought the Pig had stabbed Jayce repeatedly. He stood and turned his back to the other man as he reached into his pants and picked the dead pieces of the Pink Devil off his dick. They were sticky with drying cum, but he didn't care. He couldn't stand having the goddamned things touching his skin any longer – especially down *there*.

The sheets were already a mess, so he tossed the last bits of the Devil onto the bed with the rest. When he figured he'd gotten most of the Pink Devil out of his underwear, he turned to face the Pig.

"If you think I'm going to shake your hand – either of them – after that, you're insane," the man said.

Now that he was no longer in immediate danger of getting his throat cut, the emotional impact of what had happened – being raped by some kind of living sex toy, then being interrogated at knifepoint by a lunatic – was starting to hit him. A dozen different emotions collided within him – chief among them shame, revulsion, and denial. But the strongest of them was anger.

"Why the *fuck* would I shake *your* hand?" he demanded. "You held a goddamned knife to my throat!"

Ohio Pig didn't seem offended by Jayce's outburst.

"I freed you from the Pink Devil." He paused, then added, "Eventually. But the biggest reason you should want to shake my hand is because I'm going to help you."

Jayce couldn't believe what he was hearing. First the sonofabitch threatened him, and now he claimed he wanted to *help* him somehow?

Don't trust him, Mother said. *You can't trust anyone but family, and sometimes not even them.*

"Help me how?"

"What happened? Did the Pink Devil squeeze out all your brains when it milked your cock? I'm going to help you find your daughter. My guess is she's fallen in with some Shadowers, got herself in too deep, and needs some help finding her way home. I'll track her down, even if she doesn't want to be found. That just makes the hunt sweeter, know what I mean?" He grinned, but his eyes were cold and hard as black pebbles coated with ice. "You got a cell number where I can get in touch with you?"

Ohio Pig – the same guy who'd threatened him outside the doctor's office this morning and had held him at knifepoint only moments ago – was now offering his services, whatever they might be, as an ally in the search for Emory. It seemed like far too abrupt a turnaround for the man, and Jayce didn't trust it.

"Why do you care what happened to my daughter?"

"I don't. But I hate Shadowers, and I never miss a chance to fuck them up." He looked Jayce up and down, as if only now noticing how stained his clothes were. "Man, go home, burn those clothes, and take a goddamn shower." He paused, as if reconsidering. "On second thought, take two."

★   ★   ★

Jayce gave Ohio Pig one of his work cards with both his office and cell number on it. The man left after that, and Jayce spent a few minutes cleaning up Emory's bedroom. He got a plastic trash bag from beneath the kitchen sink and put the remains of the Pink Devil in it. The creature's carcass was now dry and light as dehydrated coral, but he still didn't like touching the pieces of it. He tied the bag closed, then removed the comforter and sheet from the bed. He was relieved to see that the mattress itself was unstained. The bedding – and, for that matter, he himself – had caught the Pink Devil's blood. He wadded the bedclothes into a ball and held them against his chest to hide the bloodstains on his shirt. He carried the trash bag holding the Pink Devil's desiccated corpse in his left hand and walked through the apartment and out the patio door. He engaged the lock, closed the door behind him, and walked across the patio to the gate he'd left open. He didn't close it, still wanting to avoid making the hinges creak and alerting someone to his presence. As he headed down the rear sidewalk, he felt numb, detached from reality – which, considering what he'd experienced inside his daughter's apartment, only made sense. He'd left normal reality behind when he'd stepped into the CrazyQwik last night, and he was beginning to wonder if he'd ever find his way back to it.

As difficult as it was to believe that a thing like the Pink Devil could exist, he had an even more difficult time imagining Emory using it. It wasn't the idea of her getting off with it that bothered him. Well, not *too* much. It was how violent and dangerous the Pink Devil was. Had Emory been unaware of the risk of using the device, or had she been turned on by it? Had she enjoyed the thrill of knowing that the machine-creature might well kill her even as it pleasured her? An image came unbidden to his mind: Emory, naked, riding the Pink Devil which had formed a multipronged member and thrust it deep inside her, other extrusions stretched upward and wrapped around her throat, choking her forcefully as she came. He had vowed to accept the woman his daughter had become, but could he accept – let alone understand – a woman who enjoyed such dark pleasures? And could that woman accept him in return?

A sudden rustling of leaves broke him out of his thoughts and he glanced to his left. The row of scraggly trees that formed an ineffective boundary between Emory's building and the next were no longer quite so scraggly. Not only that, but there seemed to be more trees than before. The trunks and limbs were thicker, although their bark appeared unhealthy, dry and cracked, mottled with greenish-gray mold. The branches held more leaves than before, but instead of being green, they were autumnal browns, yellows, and reds. And although there was still plenty of light left, the trees were draped in shadow so dark and thick it was difficult to say where one ended and the other began. A slight breeze passed through the trees, stirring the branches and breaking off several leaves, which drifted to the ground. One landed next to the sidewalk where Jayce stood, and he knelt down, put Emory's bedclothes and the trash bag on the concrete, and picked up the leaf. It was brown and felt real enough. He held it to his nose and inhaled. It smelled like an autumn leaf should – earthy and with a hint of sweet decay. The smell reminded him of something, but he couldn't—

—and then it came to him. He'd smelled the same odor when he'd been thirteen and the man...no, the *thing* with the gray feet had appeared. The realization brought fear, but with it came a great weariness. He'd been through so much since coming to Springhill Apartments, and he didn't think he could take any more right more.

Please, he thought. *Not now.*

The leaves grew still, and despite the apartment complex being located in the Cannery, Jayce heard no sounds of traffic. It was as if the entire world had paused to consider his silent plea.

A swift breeze came up out of nowhere, plucked the leaf from his hand and bore it away. The breeze rushed past his ears, and he thought he heard a single whispered word.

Soon.

When he looked to the trees again, he saw they had returned to the way they'd been before. Thin, spindly branched things with almost no leaves. The shadow that had cloaked them was gone as well, and Jayce wasn't sorry in the slightest to see it go. He released a long, shuddering sigh, bent down to retrieve the soiled bedding and the trash bag containing the Pink Devil's remains, and continued walking to his car.

★　　★　　★

Ten o'clock that night, Jayce drove through the streets of the Cannery.

He didn't know how the district had gotten its name. There'd never been an actual canning company in Oakmont as far as he knew. He figured it was some kind of nickname, the origin of which had been long forgotten. It was one of the most run-down sections of the city, with abandoned and boarded-up businesses and empty warehouses. There were people on the streets, most of them keeping to the shadows. Only the prostitutes – male, female, shemale, and whatever variation or combination you desired – ventured into the streetlights' bright wash, the better to display their wares. The streets had more potholes than asphalt, and the billboards displayed only ragged scraps of old advertisements so weathered and faded that it was impossible to guess what they'd once been trying to sell. Traffic here was light, a mix of old rust buckets that looked as if they'd fall apart any second and newer vehicles, only a few years old at most. Suburbanites came to the Cannery to purchase the dark delights they couldn't get in their own neighborhoods, and because there was minimal police presence there. Maybe the cops kept a low profile. Maybe they were paid good money to stay away. Maybe they just didn't give a damn. Or maybe they were simply too smart to go there.

Jayce hadn't been to the Cannery much before last night. Even when he was a kid, it had a reputation as a bad place, like a wound that refuses to heal, festering year after year. His mother had constantly warned him against going to the Cannery, underscoring her words with lurid phrases like *Not unless you want to end up with your privates cut off and shoved down your throat* or *Not unless you want to be hogtied and ass-raped with a nail-studded baseball bat.*

Now that he was older than she'd been when she'd spoken those words, he found them not only batshit-crazy but almost comical. Where the hell had she come up with that stuff? More to the point, what made her think it was appropriate to tell a kid that kind of shit? But then again, he'd stayed away from the Cannery most of his life, so he supposed her warnings had worked. Until last night, that is.

He had a difficult time finding the address Nicola had written down on the back of her card. He drove up and down the streets in the area, unable to find Mercantile Drive, let alone the specific address. He might've thought that Nicola had written down a fake address, except the GPS on his phone claimed the street existed. But when he tried to follow his GPS app's directions, he ended up at a different place each time. The first was a vacant lot that held a small homeless camp – patched-up tents, sleeping bags spread out on the ground, fires burning in a couple metal drums, bundled-up people standing around, looking at him with suspicion in their heavy-lidded gazes. He'd pulled up to the curb, lowered his window, and asked the nearest person – who was swaddled in so many layers of cloth that his or her gender was impossible to identify – if this was Mercantile Drive. The person had turned to him, the eyes the only part of his/her face visible between winter hat and wool scarf. Eyes that were large and white as cue balls.

Jayce hit the gas and got out of there. He didn't look in his rearview mirror, but he could feel those eyes watching him depart.

The next attempt brought him to a small park with rusty playground equipment and a basketball court. There were no people in the park, but the playground equipment – swings, slide, merry-go-round, and the basketball hoops and backboards – was covered with the black shapes of what Jayce at first took to be birds. But then he noticed they had tails, long curving things like a monkey's. Their eyes reflected the light from his headlights as he approached, making it seem as if they glowed with an internal fire. The creatures, whatever they were, continued to look at him as he drove past, not stirring from their perches, just watching him, seemingly unafraid and only mildly interested.

His third attempt proved to be the charm. The GPS led him to Mercantile Drive and a two-story brick building with 1407 painted in large white numbers above the entrance. An African-American man stood in front, smoking a cigarette and looking bored. There was no place to park in front of the building, so Jayce continued until he saw a lopsided sign with red letters that said PARKING: $5.00. He pulled into the lot, expecting there to be someone at the entrance to take his money, but there was no one. The lot was full and cramped, and he drove slowly as he searched for a space. He had no trouble seeing. The lot was lit by buzzing fluorescent lights that glowed so brightly he wouldn't have been surprised if they overloaded and shattered.

As he drove, he was struck by the odd variety of vehicles. Roughly half were normal cars, vans, and SUVs – some so new they looked fresh off the lot, others so old they looked held together by duct tape and wishful thinking. But the other half were...different. They weren't any make or model that Jayce recognized, and some were patchwork things, put together from mismatched pieces of vehicles, colors and styles clashing. The lines and angles were wrong on some of the vehicles, making them look like an M.C. Escher illusion, and it hurt his eyes to look at them too long. Some of the chassis appeared to have been made from something other than metal. One looked like it was covered with a fine layer of fur, while another was covered in a glossy black material that reminded him of a beetle's shell. Parked in one spot was a vehicle that resembled a railway handcar, the kind of thing powered by two people pumping the handles up and down. It appeared to be made of brightly colored ceramic, however, and the wheels – grooved to fit onto rails – looked like they'd been fashioned from gold.

He found a space between a silver Lexus sedan and an old-fashioned race car – low to the ground, body made of sturdy metal, wheels jutting out from the sides, ridiculously small windshield, the number 28 painted on the side. As he'd driven through the lot he'd kept an eye out for Ohio Pig's pickup, but he'd seen no sign of the lunatic's vehicle. He was relieved. He'd already had enough encounters with that bastard in one day to last him the rest of his life.

He undid his seatbelt, turned off the ignition, removed the keys, and slipped them into his pants pocket. But instead of getting out of his car, he remained seated. It wasn't 11:00 yet, and he still had some time before he was to meet Nicola.

Fuck Nicola! Mother snapped. *You are in an extremely bad place, and you need to get the hell out before it's too late.*

"It's already too late," he said. He had the Eye, and he'd seen – and remembered – too much in the last twenty-four hours.

You forgot bad things before, and you'll forget them again. It won't take long, a few days at most. Then your life will be back to normal. All you need to do is start your car, back out of this space, drive away, and never look back.

If it was true, if he really could forget, it was tempting. His mother had always impressed upon him one thing, repeating it so often over the years as he was growing up that he'd come to think of it as Valerie's First Law: the world is a dangerous place. Since becoming an adult he'd done his best not to let her paranoid philosophy ruin his life. But before setting foot in the CrazyQwik last night, he'd only thought he'd understood how dangerous the world was. But since starting his search for Emory, he'd realized that he didn't know shit about the world and the things that crawled through its darker places. He was in *way* over his head, and if he didn't want to drown, he should head home, stop at a liquor store on the way, buy a big bottle of Jack, lock the door once he was inside his apartment, and drink until he passed out. With any luck, when he woke the next day, all of this would seem like nothing more than a nightmare. But doing that would mean abandoning Emory. Could he give up on finding his daughter to save his own skin – and perhaps more importantly, his sanity? Could he fail her one more time?

This is a matter for the police, Mother said.

"Fuck the police. I'm her father."

He got out of the car and started walking.

*   *   *

The night air was chilly, but not so much that his leather jacket couldn't fend off the worst of the cold. He walked toward the building with 1407 painted above a pair of wooden doors with vertical brass handles. He hadn't noticed it before, but now he could see that all the windows were painted black. As he approached, he saw a group of four people coming from the opposite direction. The man Jayce assumed was working the door didn't bother to glance at them. From the way the quartet walked close to one another, Jayce assumed they were together, but they appeared to have nothing in common. Two male, two female. One of the males looked to be in his nineties – a wrinkled bag of flesh draped over a stooped skeleton. The other male was in his late teens to early twenties, at least based on his boyish face. He was so grotesquely obese that his features seemed in danger of sinking into his puffy face and being lost forever. The first woman was a petite, middle-aged blonde wearing running clothes, complete with a paper number 28 affixed to her back, as if she'd just finished a marathon. She smiled broadly and exuded an aura of positivity and high energy. The last of the four was a young girl, around seven, Jayce guessed. She wore a hospital gown, had sunken cheeks, and hollows for eyes. She didn't have any hair, the top of her head smooth and so shiny he wondered if she polished it.

The quartet entered the building without the doorman – if indeed that's what he was – so much as glancing in their direction. Jayce decided he was probably just hanging around on the street, passing the time while he waited for someone. But as Jayce walked toward the entrance, the man turned to him and held up his hand for him to stop.

There was nothing specific to suggest the man was watching the entrance. The building had no sign to indicate it was a nightclub, hotel, or apartment building, and the man had no uniform. He wore a brown bomber jacket, jeans, and cowboy boots.

"Hold up there, brother."

Jayce stopped three feet away from the man. His first instinct was to tell him to fuck off, but then he noticed the man's eyes, or rather, lack thereof. His eye sockets were empty, the skin around them smooth as a baby's. Jayce couldn't tell if the man had been born like this or if he'd lost his eyes somewhere along the way.

If the latter, he'd had an excellent surgeon. There was absolutely no scarring.

He held the cigarette to his lips, and after he inhaled, smoke curled forth from his eye sockets, making it look as if his brain was smoldering. Jayce couldn't help staring at the tendrils of smoke coiling upward from the man's head. The effect was startling, yes, but also hypnotic in its own way.

Now that Jayce was close to the man, he could see that the rest of his skin was in far worse condition than that in his eye sockets. He had blotchy patches on his face and hands. Flecks of dead skin covered the patches, and as the man moved they sloughed off and floated in the air around him for several seconds before drifting down to the sidewalk. Jayce wasn't certain, but he thought he heard soft high-pitched sounds, as if the skin flakes screamed on the way down.

The man scowled then.

"What are you looking at?" he demanded.

"Uh…nothing. Sorry."

The man *hrumpfed* but otherwise said nothing. He took another drag on his cigarette and fresh smoke drifted from his eye sockets.

"I'm supposed to meet someone here." Jayce took his wallet out of his back pocket, removed Nicola's card, and started to hand it to the man, but then he stopped, feeling like an idiot.

The man reached out and took the card before Jayce could put it away. He held it up to his nose, sniffed it, and then gently touched the tip of his tongue to one corner. After a moment, the man nodded and handed Nicola's card back to Jayce. Bits of skin clung to the card, and Jayce hesitated before taking it.

Don't touch that! Mother said. *Whatever he has might be contagious!*

Jayce ignored her and returned the card to his wallet, after giving it a quick shake first. Now the man held the cigarette in his mouth, and smoke continued to curl from his eye sockets. The smoke smelled like the stink wafting from an overflowing sewer, and the odor turned Jayce's stomach. After what had happened at Emory's apartment, he hadn't any appetite, so he'd skipped dinner. Now he was glad, because if he'd had anything in his stomach, it would've come rushing up now.

"So?" Jayce asked, taking a couple steps back to get away from the stench of the man's smoke. "Can I go in?"

The man frowned as if he were deeply considering the matter. While he did so, another man came walking down the sidewalk toward the building. It was the green-gloved man that Jayce had seen at the Thai restaurant that afternoon, the one he'd come to think of as the Napkin Eater. The man still carried his metal case, and he walked at a brisk pace, like he had important places to go and even more important people to see. The doorman didn't glance in the man's direction, but his nostrils widened as he drew in a deep breath of air, giving Jayce the impression that the man was checking the Napkin Eater's scent. The Napkin Eater saw Jayce looking at him, and he smiled, raised one of his rubber-gloved hands in a wave of acknowledgement, and then entered the building.

A moment later, the doorman said, "Sorry. I can't let you in."

"Why not?" Jayce snapped, starting to get angry.

The man's face wrinkled in mild disgust, causing a number of skin flakes to break away and float in the air around his head.

"You smell funny."

Jayce stared at the man in disbelief.

"Are you kidding me? How can you smell anything other than that cigarette of yours? It stinks like it's packed with shit instead of tobacco."

"That's because it is," the man said matter-of-factly. "Feces collected from the bowels of dying accident victims, to be specific. I'll admit it's an acquired taste, but the buzz is amazing." He removed the cigarette from his mouth and held it out to Jayce.

"Want to try a drag?"

Jayce's gorge rose and he felt hot bile at the back of his throat. "No thanks."

The man shrugged and returned the cigarette to his mouth. Smoke started coiling from his eye sockets once more.

"You've got a scent about you that I can't identify," the doorman said, "but there's something wrong about it. *Seriously* wrong. Dead leaves, rot, sour-yellow moonlight.... If I didn't know better, I'd say it—" He broke off, paused, and spoke a name then, saying it so softly that Jayce wasn't sure he heard it right. It sounded like he'd said *the Harvest Man.*

Before Jayce could ask the doorman what he meant, he heard the sound of heels clacking on the sidewalk behind him. He turned and saw Nicola approaching. She looked like she was dressed for a night on the town. She wore a little black dress – emphasis on the *little* – pearl earrings, gold chain necklace, and a gold bracelet on her left wrist. She had on full makeup – red lipstick, eyeliner, and light green eyeshadow, and she carried a small black purse cradled against her side. She looked great, and for a moment all Jayce could do was stare at her. Despite the fact she wasn't wearing a coat, she didn't appear to be bothered by the night's chill.

"You're early," she said.

He smiled back. He felt as if he should compliment her on how she looked, but that seemed absurd. They weren't meeting for a date.

She looked past him to the man Jayce had begun to think of as Shit-Smoker.

"How's it going, Trevor?"

By this point the man's cigarette had burned almost all the way down. He took a last drag, dropped the butt to the sidewalk, and crushed it with a boot. The cigarette might have been extinguished, but its stomach-churning stench lingered like a toxic cloud.

"Same as usual. This guy says he's a friend of yours. Is that true?"

She stepped closer to Jayce and slipped her hand under his arm.

"Oh, yes. We go *way* back."

She looked at Jayce and gave him a wink. Jayce smiled again but otherwise didn't reply. She faced Trevor once more.

"Is there a problem?" she asked.

"He wants to go in, but he smells wrong."

"I'll vouch for him. That should be good enough, shouldn't it?"

Trevor looked doubtful. He pulled another cigarette and a packet of matches from his shirt pocket, lit the cigarette, tossed the dead match away, and put the rest back in his pocket.

He shook his head, cigarette clamped tight in his mouth, but he said, "Okay, you can go inside. Just don't start any trouble, okay?"

Jayce started to protest, but Nicola tightened her hand on his arm. He got the message and kept his mouth shut. And then she and Jayce stepped through a cloud of screaming skin flakes and foul-smelling smoke and entered the building.

CHAPTER SEVEN

They entered an empty lobby that looked as if it hadn't been used since the Sixties. The tiled floor had a bland design – black swirls and streaks of gray – and the furniture was blocky and covered with stiff-looking orange fabric. There was a reception desk inside made from heavy dark wood, with a leather-covered office chair behind it. The surface of the desk was clear of equipment – no phone and certainly no computer. There was a large fake plant in a brown plastic pot sitting on the floor next to the desk, with flat fronds colored an unconvincing artificial green. A clock hung on the lime-green wall behind the desk, a minimalist thing with the numbers represented by gold-colored metal line segments and the thin hour and minute hands made of the same material. There was no second hand. The time was 11:05.

The thing that struck Jayce as most strange about the lobby wasn't its anachronistic look but the fact that everything appeared brand new, and there wasn't a speck of dust anywhere.

"What is this place?" he asked. "Some kind of office building?"

"Once," Nicola said. "The top two floors aren't used much anymore." She paused, then added, "Not by anything you'd want to meet, that is. We're going downstairs. That's where all the action is."

She led him across the lobby, her heels clacking on the tiles, toward a lone elevator, the door painted a lackluster taupe.

"Why does this place have a blind doorman?" he asked.

"Why do you think?" Nicola countered.

He thought of how Trevor had inhaled through his nostrils

when Jayce had approached him. *You've got a scent about you that I can't identify, but there's something wrong about it. Seriously wrong.*

The answer came to him then. "Because he can smell trouble."

Nicola grinned. "Exactly!"

Is that what Trevor had scented on him? Trouble? If so, it hadn't been enough for him to forbid Jayce entry, not with Nicola as his escort. He thought about telling Nicola what Trevor had said and asking her who or what the Harvest Man was, but it didn't feel like the right time. Besides, he was here because Nicola had offered to help him find Emory, and he should be focusing on his daughter, not on what some weird guy who exhaled through his eye sockets had said.

They reached the elevator and Nicola pressed the down button. In response, a loud metallic grinding sound came from behind the door, and Jayce could feel the tiles vibrate beneath his feet. He imagined ancient machinery straining in the walls, rotors spinning, fraying cables rising and lowering. It took a while, but the elevator juddered to a halt on the first floor, a *ding* sounding to announce its arrival, and the door slid slowly open to reveal the car was empty. Nicola stepped in, pulling Jayce with her. She pushed a button labeled *Lower Level*, the door closed, and the elevator started to descend with ratcheting, grinding, and clanking sounds.

"Whoever keeps the place clean doesn't know dick about maintaining elevator equipment," Jayce said. He glanced at Nicola. She looked good in her black dress. *Real* good.

"I feel underdressed standing next to you," he said.

"Don't worry. There isn't a dress code."

As the elevator continued its tortuous descent, Jayce detected a high-pitched sound. He felt more than heard it, and it set his teeth on edge.

"Do you hear that? It's like some kind of electronic whine."

She nodded. "It takes some getting used to."

The elevator came to a halt, and the door opened with another *ding*.

"We're here," Nicola said. She took Jayce's arm once more and led him out of the elevator.

The building's lower level was a large open space with stone columns placed at regular intervals for support. The floor was concrete, marred with dark stains that Jayce didn't want to think about too much. The ceiling lights gave off a dim red glow that barely illuminated the place, making everything shadowy and sinister. There was a bar on one side and a raised stage against the opposite wall. There was an open space in front of the stage, for dancing presumably, and while there were people on it, they stood talking in pairs or small groups. There were tables and chairs, most of them occupied, but despite the number of people present, it wasn't noisy. The people spoke in hushed tones, their voices joining to create a sound not unlike a strong, steady wind. But floating above this was another sound, the high-pitched tone Jayce had detected earlier. It was more intense in here, so piercing that it felt like someone had implanted a metal wire in his brain and was running a current through it. It was impossible to determine where the sound originated; it seemed to be coming from all around them. But some instinct pulled his gaze toward the stage where a naked woman sat cross-legged, wisps of white hair clinging to her otherwise bald head. To say she was old would've been a gross understatement. She was little more than a thin layer of bark-like skin stretched tight over a skeleton. She looked like a scarecrow made of old cloth and sticks, Jayce thought, and given everything he'd experienced in the last day, he wouldn't have been surprised if she were. Her eyes were closed, her mouth wide open, revealing gums through which only a few gray nubs of teeth protruded.

"I think she's supposed to be some kind of entertainment," Nicola said. "She's always here, sitting just like that, and she never takes a break."

"So she's making that sound?"

Nicola nodded. "The first few times I came here, I ended up with a terrible headache by the time I left. Come on. Let's get some drinks."

She took his arm once again and steered him over to the bar. They threaded between tables as they made their way, and Jayce looked at the people they passed. Most of them appeared normal enough at first glance, but there was a handful of people whose physical appearance was so dramatically distorted that Jayce wasn't sure they qualified as human. These folk sat by themselves at tables where the shadows were thickest. Jayce couldn't make out much more than their general outlines, but their limbs were mismatched – different lengths and thicknesses – shoulders uneven, heads too big or too small. He felt a deep sense of wrongness coming from them, one that only partially had to do with their physical appearance. It was a psychic impression, as if their presence alone was a violation of reality.

The woman behind the bar was a redhead in her thirties. At least, Jayce guessed she was a redhead because of the freckles on her face. The crimson lights made it difficult to determine her actual hair color. She appeared normal enough at first, but as she mixed a drink, he noticed that she had two extra fingers on each hand, and that all her fingers moved in a flopping, rubbery way, like tentacles. There were several chairs at the bar, each of them taken. The men and women who sat there were like the bartender, appearing generally normal until you took a closer look at them. One man had a left eye larger than his right one, about the size of a softball, and Jayce had to fight to keep from staring at it. Next to him sat a woman whose ears were shaped like a horse's and covered with light fur. Most of the people in the club dressed normally enough, but some wore suits or dresses that looked like they belonged in a different decade, if not in a different century.

There was a glassed-in refrigerated cabinet mounted on the wall behind the bar, but instead of displaying bottles of various types of alcohol, they held vessels, several dozen in all, some large, some small, all with the same strange symbols engraved into their surfaces. Jayce checked out the people sitting at the bar, curious to see if any of them held a vessel instead of a glass, but none did. The bartender finished making a drink, served it to one of the customers seated at the bar, then turned to Nicola.

"Hey, Nicola. What'll it be?" she asked.

"I'll have a white wine, Nyla. As for my friend...."

"A beer's fine."

Jayce felt the weight of numerous gazes on him as he and Nicola waited for their drinks. He sensed curiosity, suspicion, and hostility, along with a growing sense of menace. It was as if the club's denizens were sizing him up, trying to determine whether he was predator or prey. From the dark looks and hungry smiles directed his way, it looked like the general consensus had come down on the side of prey. Nyla brought them their drinks, Nicola paid for them, and then led Jayce to an empty table. He tried not to meet anyone's gaze as they walked. He looked straight ahead and tried to appear casual and relaxed, as if he belonged here. But he walked stiffly and his skin was coated with nervous sweat, and he doubted he could've looked more like a stranger if he tried. He thought of the dog-eaters, and he wondered if there were any of them – or things even worse – in here. If so, was he in danger of being attacked? He thought of the stains on the floor, and he wished he'd brought some kind of weapon with him, if only for the illusion of comfort it would've provided.

They sat, and each took a sip of their drink. As Nicola put her glass down on the table, she said, "This place is called Crimson Splendor. It's a...I suppose *gathering spot* is the best way to describe it. It's kind of like a private club for people like me, and – I suspect – like your daughter."

There wasn't much *splendor* here that he could see.

"People like you?" he asked.

"Shadowers. People who can see – and interact with – the darker aspects of existence. You know how a snake grows a new layer of skin and then sheds the old one? Well, reality is the same way. Each nanosecond is sloughed off as a new one takes its place, and all of these dead bits of reality eventually start to pile up, creating a...." She paused, searching for the right words. "Not a parallel reality, exactly. More like a dark reflection. It's usually called Shadow, which is as good a name as any, I suppose. It lies alongside ordinary reality, but most people aren't aware of it. Sometimes they sense it, though. They have a feeling that someone's watching them, but when they turn around, no one's there. They experience a chill on the back of their neck for some unknown reason. They catch a glimpse of a figure out of the corner of their eye, a figure which vanishes when they try to look at it straight on. Shadow is tricky. It often resembles the real world so closely that it can be difficult to tell the difference between the two. But there are people who can see Shadow for what it is and move within it."

"People with the Eye," Jayce said.

"Yes. No one seems to know for sure why some people have the Eye and some don't. Some say you have to be born with it. Some say you develop it if something from Shadow reaches out and touches you – assuming you survive the encounter, that is."

Jayce thought of the thing that stood on the other side of the restroom stall. His memory was a blank from the moment he saw the creature's gray feet to the moment he found himself back home. What had happened to him in between? Whatever it was, had it been responsible for causing him to develop the Eye? And had he, in turn, passed it on to Emory?

"A lot of people in Shadow – maybe most of them – are like you and me, people who can not only see Shadow, but who find themselves drawn to interacting with it. So much so that some of them become permanent residents."

"Are those the ones who look...." He glanced at the tables closest to them and then lowered his voice. "Different?"

"Yes. Exposure to Shadow changes you. Sometimes faster,

sometimes slower, sometimes in big ways, sometimes in small ones. But it *always* changes you, one way or another."

"You still seem…."

"Normal?" she smiled. "Some changes are less obvious than others. And I'm really just a dabbler when it comes to Shadow. It's like I'm swimming in a vast dark ocean, so I make sure to stay close to shore where the water's not too deep."

He thought about asking how Shadow had changed her, but he decided he didn't know her well enough to ask that. Besides, maybe he'd be better off not knowing.

"Shadow is everywhere, but it concentrates more in some places than others," she said. "Areas like the Cannery – run-down and mostly deserted – are prime places for Shadow to thrive. Entropy's stronger there, and where there's entropy, there's Shadow. Anyway, I brought you here because I figured there was a greater chance you'd believe me about Shadow once you'd experienced Crimson Splendor in all its bizarre glory. You could always tell yourself that what happened last night, while weird, had some kind of logical explanation, but this" – she gestured to take in the people around them – "is a bit harder to rationalize. That's my hope, anyway."

Jayce had to admit that her strategy had been a sound one. He supposed it was possible that all this was some sort of elaborate practical joke, but why would anyone go to such effort and expense? And the deformities he'd seen – if that was even the right word for them – looked absolutely real. He didn't believe that makeup and special effects could create an illusion this convincing.

"Do you think that's what happened to Emory? That she has the Eye and has been…exploring Shadow and got lost in it somehow?"

"It wouldn't be the first time something bad happened to someone who got too curious about Shadow, believe me."

She sounded bitter, and Jayce guessed there was a story behind her words.

"Shadow is dangerous," she continued. "And not just because

of the people who are changed by it. There are beings native to Shadow, creatures that feed on the decaying cast-offs of reality, like carrion-eaters disposing of a dead animal in the woods."

Jayce felt a fist of ice punch him in the gut. "Are you saying you think Emory is dead?"

"I'm saying there are all kinds of things that can happen to people in Shadow if they aren't careful – and even if they are – and all of them are bad."

"You make it sound like there's no point in looking for her. If you think it's so damn hopeless, why did you offer to help me?"

Nicola smiled and reached across the table and took his hand. The contact startled him, and he almost jerked his hand away. It was the first time since he divorced Mackenzie that a woman had touched him. Had it really been that long?

"I didn't say it was hopeless. But if you're going to start poking around in Shadow looking for her, you need to know what you're getting into – and you need to be prepared for the possibility that your search may not turn out the way you want."

"So she might be dead." He thought of what he'd found in her apartment – the vessels in her refrigerator, and most of all, the Pink Devil that had raped him. "Or she might be changed."

"Yes," Nicola said.

They sat in silence for several moments after that. Nicola drank her wine, while Jayce sat, leaving his beer untouched as he processed everything she had told him. Then, when he was ready, he began speaking again.

"After we had lunch, I couldn't make myself sit around and wait to meet you here, so I visited Emory's apartment." He then proceeded to tell her everything that had happened between their meeting at the restaurant and the moment she'd approached him outside Crimson Splendor. He even told her about his encounter with the Pink Devil, although he edited that account considerably.

When he was finished, Nicola said, "Ohio Pig? That man is a

lunatic. Some people who can see into Shadow are revolted by it – even more so by their attraction to it. This self-loathing prompts them to lash out at other denizens of Shadow, and in the Pig's case, it spurs him to violence. You're lucky he didn't hurt you. You're not so lucky that he's taken it on himself to search for your daughter. His kind of help you don't need. He's so damn erratic, though, that there's a good chance he'll end up getting distracted by something else and will forget about her."

She sounded doubtful about this last part, and Jayce wished he hadn't answered Ohio Pig's questions. Yeah, the man had been holding a knife to his throat, but what if he turned out to be a danger to Emory and he'd put him on her trail?

"I'm sorry you got a surprise tentacle-job from the Pink Devil," Nicola said. "Those things can get out of control fast if you don't know what you're doing – and sometimes even if you do."

Jayce burned with shame as he thought about what the creature or machine or whatever the hell it was had done to him, and how his body had responded, even though he hadn't wanted it to.

"I know where she bought it," Nicola continued, "so that's one place we can check out. Same for the bookstore where she picked up *Liber Ab Oblivione,* or in English, *The Book of Oblivion.* It's kind of a starter's guide to Shadow. It's mostly harmless, not like *The Book of Masks* or *The Book of Depravity.*"

"I found a bunch of clay jars in her refrigerator, like the one you bought at CrazyQwik last night. What are they?"

"They're called vessels. They're made of clay mixed with bits of Shadow itself. They can hold all sorts of things. Things you didn't know could exist as well as things that shouldn't exist."

Jayce thought about the many vessels in Emory's refrigerator, and he wondered what dark dangers – and wonders – they contained.

"Last night you told the dog-eaters that your vessel held the screams of a hundred men. Was that true?"

Nicola just smiled, and Jayce decided to change the subject.

"What about the strange voice I heard after leaving Emory's apartment?"

He remembered hearing the single word whispered in a soft, dark voice – *Soon* – and frost collected on his spine.

"I honestly have no idea what it might have been. Once you start interacting with Shadow, you can draw the attention of all kinds of nasty things. If you ignore them, most of the time they'll leave you alone."

Most of the time. Jayce didn't like the sound of that.

He was beginning to despair that he'd never find Emory. The normal world was dangerous enough, but Shadow was a nightmare world filled with lunatics and monsters. The odds that something bad had happened to Emory were excellent, and from what he'd seen so far, death wasn't the worst thing that could happen to someone in Shadow. Not by a long shot.

"Everyone comes to Crimson Splendor," Nicola said, "and even if your daughter's like me – someone who's careful not to step too far into Shadow – she'd at least come here once in a while. She might even be a regular. This place is relatively safe, at least compared to some. So I figured it would make a good starting point to begin looking for her."

"So what do we do? Walk around and ask people about her? I have fliers in my car, but I didn't bring them in with me. Should I go get them?"

Nicola shook her head.

"I said this place was *relatively* safe, but it's not a good idea to randomly approach people here – not unless you want to get your face ripped off. I called a friend of mine earlier. She knows a hell of a lot more about what goes on in the Shadow-side of town than I do. I'm hoping she might know your daughter, or at least have seen her around. She might be able to give us a lead."

"Is your friend here now?" He looked around, as if hoping to see a woman walking toward their table, but there was no one.

"Not yet. She usually doesn't make an appearance until around

THE MOUTH OF THE DARK • 101

midnight. She should be here soon." She paused before going on. "Are you sure you want to do this? I'm not talking about finding Emory. Of course you want to do that. But are you sure you want to keep looking in Shadow? It's not safe – well, you know that by now – but like I said earlier, Shadow *changes* you if you spend too much time in it, and it changes you in ways you can't anticipate. Are you willing to risk that?"

He didn't have to think about his answer.

"Yes."

It was what any concerned parent would say, he knew that. He also knew that he'd only had the briefest of introductions to Shadow, and that as bad as it seemed so far, it could – and likely would – get far worse. He suspected that not only would he be risking his life, but his sanity, and maybe even his very soul. But none of this changed his answer. Emory was his daughter, and he'd do whatever it took to find her.

You're a fool, Mother said.

Maybe so, but it still didn't change his answer.

"Outside, Trevor said he smelled something on me. Dead leaves and moonlight, something like that. He also spoke a name: the Harvest Man. Do you know who or what that is?"

Up to this point in their limited acquaintance, Nicola had struck Jayce as cool, calm, and utterly confident. But now she froze, wineglass halfway to her mouth, eyes wide. She recovered quickly and brought the glass the rest of the way to her mouth, but her hand shook as she did so. She took a long drink, draining the rest of the glass, and set it down on the table. Her hand trembled less as she did this, but it still trembled.

"He's Shadow's version of the boogeyman. The story goes that the more people interact with Shadow, the more we inject life into it, slowing its rate of decay. If that rate slows too much, the Harvest Man appears to speed it back up again, to bring balance back to Shadow."

"How does he do that?"

Nicola ignored his question. "It's just a story. Even Shadow has its legends."

She gave him a smile then, but he didn't find it to be a particularly comforting one.

"You said you're helping me because you know what it's like to become lost in Shadow."

"Yes."

She was quiet for a time after that, and Jayce thought she wouldn't say more on the matter, but then she began talking.

"I've had glimpses of Shadow all my life. I'd see strange people and things that I couldn't explain, none of which my family and friends ever saw."

Jayce thought once more of the cankerworms devouring the giraffe. Nicola went on.

"One day when I was in junior high, a friend and I decided to walk to a gas station to get some slushies. We lived on the edge of the Cannery, but our neighborhood was safe. At least, that's what our parents thought. As we walked, a black van pulled up alongside us and the side door slid open. I can't tell you who or what was inside. I saw only darkness so thick it was like something solid. Then hands emerged from the darkness. They grabbed hold of me and Gretchen and yanked us inside. The door slammed shut, the van picked up speed, and Gretchen and I tried to scream but the darkness itself seemed to cover our mouths and muffle our voices."

She paused and tried to take a sip of her wine, only to find that her glass was empty. She put it down, more than a little regretfully, Jayce thought, and continued.

"I can't tell you where we were taken. I didn't know the Cannery back then. Some abandoned building. I remember going down stairs, Gretchen beside me, a dark figure behind us, cold hands on our shoulders. I don't remember anything after that until I found myself sitting on my parents' front porch. That was two weeks after I disappeared. Gretchen never came back."

Jayce still had half his beer left, and he handed it to Nicola. She took the bottle without comment and downed the rest of its contents.

"I was examined at the hospital," she said, "and as near as the doctors could determine, nothing was wrong with me. I hadn't been injured or sexually abused. The police questioned me, but I couldn't tell them much. They kept looking for Gretchen, but I knew they'd never find her. And they didn't. Afterward, I could see into Shadow more clearly than ever before, and I began tentatively exploring it, hoping to find Gretchen. I spent a good part of my adolescence in Shadow, learning everything I could about it while trying to be careful not to let it swallow me up the way it had her. I came to understand Shadow, even enjoy it, but I know better than to let my guard down, even for a second."

Jayce found it interesting that Nicola had experienced a period of missing time too, although hers had been far longer than his. And both their experiences had happened when they were roughly the same age. He almost told her about the man with the gray-skinned feet, but he decided against it. He wasn't sure why. Maybe because he didn't want to turn the conversation away from her and onto him. Maybe because even after almost forty years, he wasn't ready to talk about what had happened that day. Maybe he never would be.

Nicola really did know what it was like to become lost in Shadow, he thought, and the fact she had somehow escaped her captor − or for some unknown reason been set free − gave him hope that he'd find Emory and bring her home. Nicola's story was proof Shadow could be survived…at least sometimes.

"When did you first become aware that you could, you know. *See?*"

Nicola thought for a moment before answering. "I don't remember a time I couldn't. I've got three brothers and a sister, and none of them can See. Neither can my parents. At least, I don't think any of them can. I suppose any of them might be able to but have never felt comfortable talking about it." She smiled. "It's not the sort of thing you bring up over family dinners."

Or maybe they're like you, Jayce, Mother said. *They don't have the guts to remember the things they See.*

"I do remember the first time I realized most other people couldn't see the same thing I did. I was in preschool. The teacher's name was Mandy. I can't remember her last name. It was storytime, and the kids all sat on the floor while Mandy sat in a wooden chair and read a picture book to us, pausing after each page to make sure we all had a chance to look at the picture before turning to the next page. I remember the book she was reading that day. *Blueberries for Sal.* Do you know it?"

He nodded. "I used to read it to Emory. It was one of her favorites."

"While Mandy read, I noticed something out of the corner of my eye. When I turned to look, I saw a boy sitting a few feet away from me: Steve Slater. He had thin blond hair, and his skin was so pale it was almost chalk-white. He was quiet and kept to himself for the most part, unless Mandy had us do a group activity of some sort. He'd participate then, dutifully if not enthusiastically, and then he'd return to minding his own business. I'm not sure I even heard him speak, come to think of it. As Mandy read, Steve's gaze wasn't focused on the pictures in the book, but rather on a point in the air directly in front of his face. I didn't know what he was looking at. There was nothing there. Except, when I looked closely at the spot Steve stared at, I thought I could detect a faint shimmer, as if that small space wasn't quite as confident in its existence as the area surrounding it. And then a small round object appeared in front of Steve. A blue object. It hung in the air, motionless, and I grinned in delight. As I said, I'd been used to seeing strange things all my life, but up to this point I'd never witnessed anything appear out of thin air like that. I thought it was a wonderful trick.

"After a moment, Steve reached out with his too-white fingers and plucked the blueberry out of the air and popped it into his mouth. He bit down and there was a crunching noise followed by a muffled scream. It startled me, and I jumped. 'Are you all right, Nicola?' Mandy asked. She'd stopped reading and was looking at me with concern. The other kids were looking at me, some with confusion, some with small smiles and a gleam in their eyes, as if hoping I was going to get into trouble. 'Are the bears too scary for you?' Mandy asked."

Jayce remembered the story well. A mother takes her young daughter out to pick blueberries on a hillside. On the opposite side of the hill, a mother bear is showing her cub how to eat blueberries. The girl and the cub are both so absorbed with eating the luscious blueberries that they don't realize they accidently switch places, and the girl ends up following the mama bear and the cub ends up following the human mother. Eventually the two children – one human, one ursine – are reunited with their proper mothers and everything is right again.

"Of course the bears didn't scare me," Nicola said. "They weren't drawn scary and they didn't do anything scary in the story. But no one had turned to look at Steve as he bit down on the blueberry – or whatever it was – and it screamed as it died. They were all looking at *me*. I realized then that they weren't looking at him because they hadn't heard the scream. 'Nicola?' Mandy said. 'Do you need me to stop reading?' Another small blue sphere appeared in front of Steve and he took this one from the air just like the first and put it into his mouth. Another crunch and another scream, only this time as he chewed, a thin line of red trickled from one corner of his mouth. I knew it wasn't blueberry juice. It was blood. Again, no one but me noticed.

"I shook my head. 'No, Mandy,' I said. 'I'm okay now.' Mandy looked at me for one moment more, as if she didn't quite believe me, but then she smiled and returned to reading. Some of the kids giggled and whispered, giving me sidelong glances, but most returned their attention to Mandy and the story. Steve was looking at me now, and more lines of blood ran from his mouth. He grinned, displaying blood-slick teeth, and then he pursed his lips and put his index finger to them in a shushing motion, as if to say, *Don't tell. It'll be our secret.*

"He looked away from me and went on to eat four more of those magically appearing things. Each one screamed as it died, and by the time the story was finished, his chin was covered with blood, and it had dripped down and dotted the front of his T-shirt with dark splotches."

Nicola paused for several moments, thinking.

"I have no idea what happened to Steve. One day he stopped coming to school. Mandy never remarked on it, and neither did any of the other kids. It was as if he'd never existed. I sometimes wonder if something appeared in front of him that was too big and fast for him to eat, and it got him before he could get it."

She fell silent again for a time after that, lost in the memory, Jayce assumed. But she eventually gave him a sad smile.

"It's a lonely thing, having the Eye. Knowing that reality is far stranger – and darker – than most people will ever be able to perceive. It's why places like Crimson Splendor exist. It gives those of us who've been touched by Shadow, whether in big ways or small, a place to go where we can be around others like us. When you're in a place where everyone's strange—"

"No one is," Jayce finished.

She nodded. "I suppose that's why I was compelled to help you. You were alone, looking for a daughter who was like me. My family are all still alive, all still more or less healthy. But if I went missing, none of them would come looking for me. They wouldn't have the slightest clue where to start. But when you went to CrazyQwik, I could see that you saw how strange it was, and it didn't deter you. You were going to keep on looking for your daughter no matter how much crazy-ass shit you encountered. I wish I had someone who loved me that much." She gestured at the people near them. "We all do."

Jayce smiled at her. "I'll go get us some more drinks."

He rose and picked up her empty glass and his empty bottle, and when Nicola started to stand, he told her he wanted to go alone. He needed to learn to take care of himself in Shadow, and he thought a solo trip to the bar would be a good start.

Nicola sat back down. "Okay, but be careful."

He promised he would and then headed for the bar.

The high-pitched singing – if it could be called singing – coming from the woman on stage was making his head hurt. Maybe a second drink would help, especially considering he'd only had half of his first one. Thinking of his headache made him think of his skull colliding with the alley wall last night, and he wondered if the two dog-eaters who'd attacked him – Reta and Zach – were here. The last thing he needed was for them to see him and try to pick up where they'd left off last night. They were minors, sure, but he doubted that mattered here. Whatever factors Trevor used to determine who got into Crimson Splendor, Jayce doubted age was one of them. He looked around to see if he could spot them, but the damn crimson lighting made it difficult to make out anyone clearly who wasn't in his immediate vicinity. The two teens could be here and he wouldn't know it. Hopefully, the same would prove true for him, and if they were here they wouldn't spot him – or catch his scent.

He made it to the bar without anything more serious happening than having a few people give him hairy eyeballs as he passed their tables. He put the empties down on the bar and managed to order two more of the same without staring at Nyla's fourteen boneless fingers. As she handed him the drinks, her fingers brushed his, and they felt soft and squishy, like a surgical glove filled with thick syrup. He shuddered, paid with cash, told her to keep the change, and started back to the table. As he drew closer, he saw that Nicola was no longer alone.

The woman was Asian and older than Nicola, older than him

too, although how much older it was difficult to say. The crimson light made it difficult to judge her age, but Jayce thought he'd have a hard time guessing it even if she stood in broad daylight. She could've been in her sixties, seventies, or even eighties. She had a long oval face with high cheekbones and a sharp nose. Her lips were thin, and as near as he could tell in this light, she wore no makeup. Her hair was long and spilled down her back to her waist. He assumed it was white, gray, or silver, but the crimson lights made it look red, another factor that contributed to making her age ambiguous. She wore a black tuxedo with a bowtie, and while she wore no earrings, her long, slender fingers were covered with rings, three on each digit, two behind the knuckles, one in front.

When Jayce reached the table, he set Nicola's wine in front of her and put his beer down at the place where he'd been sitting. The woman in the tuxedo – who he presumed was the friend Nicola had been waiting for – looked up at him and smiled.

"I'm Jayce Lewis," he said, returning the smile. "Can I get you a drink?"

"Nice to meet you, Jayce. I'm Ivory. And while I appreciate your offer, there's no need."

Jayce wasn't certain what she meant, but then Nyla appeared and set a vessel in front of the woman. Nyla stood by while Ivory removed the lid and raised the jar to her face. She inhaled the vessel's scent, closed her eyes for a moment, and then smiled.

"Thank you, Nyla," she said, eyes still closed. "It's a wonderful choice."

Nyla grinned – looking more than a little relieved, Jayce thought – nodded once, and then headed back to the bar.

"What did she bring you?" Nicola asked. Jayce sat as the woman opened her eyes and answered.

"The last breaths of lovers who died during sex. Quite rare and sinfully expensive." She smiled at Jayce. "But what's the point of owning the place if you can't indulge yourself once in a while?" She raised the vessel to her face once more, and this time she inhaled deeply.

Jayce caught Nicola's attention and arched an eyebrow. It seemed she was better connected socially than he'd realized.

Ivory let out a contented sigh, put the vessel back on the table, and replaced the lid. Jayce wondered if she'd inhaled all the breaths stored within the jar or she was saving some for later. Ivory then turned her attention to him.

"Nicola tells me you have a problem that I might be able to help you with, Mr. Lewis. Your daughter is missing?"

"Yes." Jayce took his phone from his pants pocket, found a recent picture of Emory, and showed it to the woman. "This is her."

Ivory took the phone. She looked at Emory's picture for a moment, and then nodded.

"Oh, yes. I've seen her around. I wouldn't say she's a regular, but she comes here often enough that—" She broke off and cocked her head slightly to the side. She brought the phone closer to her face and peered at Emory's picture intently for several seconds. The light from the screen washed away some of the red from Ivory's face, and Jayce could see where she'd gotten her name from. Her skin was white as porcelain.

Without looking away from the screen again, she said, "What's your last name again?"

"Lewis," Jayce replied, unsure where this was going. At first he'd been thrilled when the woman remembered Emory, but now it seemed like something was wrong, and although he'd only become – consciously – aware of Shadow a little over twenty-four hours ago, he'd learned enough to know that things could go very wrong here indeed.

Ivory looked at Jayce now, but she made no move to return his phone.

"There was another woman who used to come in here some years back. She looked a great deal like your daughter and had the same last name as you do. I was younger then, of course. I'd just started my second century, and you know what they say. After the first hundred years, some of the finer details start to escape you. I'm trying to remember the woman's first name, but...." She shook her head, annoyed.

Jayce felt a cold pit open in his stomach.

"When you say *some years back*, how long are we talking about?"

"Several decades, at least," Ivory said. "Maybe even as much as a half century."

The pit at the center of his being yawned wider.

"Was her name Valerie?" He spoke softly, but Ivory had no trouble hearing him over the club's noise.

She smiled. "Yes, I think it was." She looked at Emory's picture once more. "Your daughter does favor her." She finally handed the phone back to Jayce. "Is Valerie a relative of yours?"

"She's my mother."

He waited for his mother's voice to say something, to confirm or deny what he'd just learned, but she was silent. Of course she was. Her voice wasn't really hers, but his. Now he understood why she'd been so paranoid and overprotective all those years, why she'd always kept insisting that the world was a dangerous place. If she, like her granddaughter, had gotten involved with the denizens of Shadow, had for a time been one of them, then she knew just how dangerous the world could truly be.

Ivory spoke again, but Jayce was so stunned by this revelation that what she said didn't register. It took an effort of will for him to focus on her voice.

"...places where your daughter might go. I could make some inquiries, but first I must know your reasons for searching for her."

At first he didn't understand what she was saying, but then he scowled.

"What reason do I need? I'm her *father*." The words came out more harshly than he'd intended.

Nicola reached out and put her hand over his.

"It's a valid question," she said. "Some people are drawn to Shadow to escape something bad in their lives. So bad that Shadow and its dangers are a better alternative. And a lot of times, that something is a person."

Jayce understood what the two women were getting at. He looked at Ivory.

"You're asking if I'm an abusive bastard trying to track down the daughter who ran away from me."

"You wouldn't be the first," Ivory said evenly.

Jayce wanted to protest, to shout that he wasn't a goddamned child-abuser. But everyone would claim that, wouldn't they? *Especially* an abuser. Besides, while he'd never raised a hand to his child, he didn't feel he was going to win Father of the Year anytime soon.

"I don't want to take her away from Shadow, not if it's the way she truly wants to live. I just want to know that she's safe, and I want her to know that I care what happens to her."

Ivory looked at him for several moments without blinking. Jayce wondered if she could somehow read his mind, and if so, what memories she might find in there that he kept locked away. But whether she read his thoughts or, more likely, simply came to a judgment about his character based on their conversation so far, she nodded.

"Very well. I'll start asking around and see what I can find out. Do you have a number I can reach you at?"

Jayce pulled his wallet from his back pocket and removed one of his work cards. He put his wallet away, and he handed the card to Ivory.

"My cell number's on there, right below my office number."

Ivory held the card close to her face and inspected it. As she did so, Jayce noticed movement out of the corner of his eye. He saw a figure — a large one — approaching their table with a brisk, purposeful stride. He turned to see Ohio Pig coming their way, a giant grin on his face. In his left hand he carried a canvas bag, the kind that environmentally conscious people used when buying groceries. The side of the bag bulged and it hung low, as if it contained something heavy. Then he realized the bottom of the bag was stained black. At least, it looked black in the club's crimson light. The Pig had a number of similar black stains on his clothes, some as large as half dollars.

The Pig stopped when he reached their table. He didn't acknowledge either Nicola or Ivory. He kept his wild-eyed gaze fixed on Jayce. He raised the bag, reached into it with his other hand, removed a large object, and tossed it onto the table. It hit with a heavy thud and bounced once, leaving a dark smeary blotch on the tabletop before coming to a stop. It was a severed head, and it faced Jayce, eyes open and staring, lips parted to reveal a glimpse of straight, even teeth. It had long brown hair and its neck was a ragged stump with a nub of bone jutting out.

"Told you I'd find her," Ohio Pig said, sounding very satisfied with himself.

The head, of course, was Emory's.

CHAPTER EIGHT

Jayce didn't move at first, didn't breathe. It felt as if his heart seized in his chest, and pain deeper and more intense than any he had ever imagined possible cut through the core of his being like a blade of white-hot steel. Nicola and Ivory both stared at Emory's head, Nicola in shocked surprise, Ivory with reserved interest. People at the surrounding tables looked over to see what was happening, and more than a few of them laughed.

Jayce's body began moving on its own, without any conscious control on his part. It stood, walked over to the grinning Pig, reached up, grabbed the back of the man's head, and then with a strength he didn't realize he possessed, Jayce slammed the Pig's face into the tabletop, crushing the man's nose and dislodging several teeth. Blood gushed outward from both sides of the Pig's nose, and he gave a strangled, gurgling cry of pained surprise. The impact of the Pig striking the table caused Emory's head to bounce and roll off the edge and onto the floor. Seeing his daughter's head fall from the table like a dropped scrap of food shattered his emotional paralysis and filled him with rage. He grabbed hold of the Pig's hair and yanked him upward, fully intending to slam his face onto the table once more and to keep slamming it until there was nothing left of the man's head but bloody paste and bone fragments. But before he could begin, the Pig swung his right arm out in a wide arc and struck Jayce on the side with his fist.

The blow knocked the air out of Jayce, and he released his grip on the Pig's hair and took a stagger-step backward. Before he could recover, the Pig straightened, turned, and came at him. The man's eyes bulged with fury and his face was a mask of blood. He roared as he rammed into Jayce and wrapped his arms around his midsection. The momentum of the Pig's rush drove both men into a nearby table, and it collapsed beneath their combined weight, wood splintering, mugs and glasses shattering. Three men and a woman had been sitting at the table. Two of them were knocked over when Jayce and the Pig destroyed their table, but the other two sprang to their feet and started shouting. Jayce was only partially aware of all this. The two men lay on the floor, the Pig holding Jayce in a tight embrace, squeezing his ribs and preventing him from breathing. He struggled to break free, squirming and rolling, cutting himself on broken glass, but barely feeling it. His exertions didn't help. The Pig held on to him with the tenacity of a starving pit bull.

Despite his violent attack on the Pig, Jayce had never been in a physical fight before. The closest he'd ever come was minor skirmishes at school when he was a kid, consisting primarily of name-calling and shoving. He'd never thrown a punch or received one. He still felt rage and shock at what Ohio Pig had done to Emory, and those emotions – coupled with animal instinct – told him what to do next. He opened his mouth wide, fastened his teeth on the Pig's cheek, and bit down hard. The man's skin was already slick with blood from his broken nose, but fresh warmth gushed into Jayce's mouth as his teeth penetrated the Pig's soft flesh. The man howled, more in anger than pain, Jayce thought, but instead of releasing him, the Pig only tightened his grip.

The man was damn strong, and Jayce felt his ribs grind together. He struggled to draw in a breath, but the most he could manage to pull in was a hissing gasp through his teeth. His mouth was still fastened onto the Pig's cheek, and with no other way left for him to fight, he bit down harder, sawing his jaw back and forth to cut through the meat. The Pig moaned in pain but kept up the pressure on Jayce's ribs. Jayce continued biting and sawing at the man's cheek until his teeth came together and a slick hunk of flesh lay wet and slippery on his tongue.

A pair of figures approached then, and at first Jayce thought Nicola and Ivory had decided to come to his aid. But then he realized that the figures were larger and more broad-shouldered than either woman. As the pair drew close, Jayce saw that they looked enough alike to be twins. Their heads were clean-shaven, and their eyebrows had been drawn on with heavy black liner. They had brutish faces – small, close-set eyes and wide, flat noses – but their lips were full and lush, and they possessed delicate shell-like ears. Their arms, however, were thick and well-muscled, chests wide, waists trim, legs like tree limbs. They were dressed the same: tight-fitting dark T-shirts, jeans, and black leather boots.

The twins stopped when they reached Jayce and the Ohio Pig. Moving in almost perfect unison, they each bent down, grabbed hold of one of the men's shoulders, and employing grips like iron, they pulled Jayce and the Pig apart from each other. The Pig struggled to free himself, but the twin had hold of him from the back, and the Pig couldn't move. The man glared at Jayce who, after being lifted to his feet by a twin, was allowed to stand without any sort of restraint.

The twins wore sidearms on their belts, along with sheathed knives, stun guns, and other objects Jayce couldn't identify. Things of bone, rock, and feathers lashed together with barbed wire. They also carried small hairy hands tucked into their belts. Were those actual monkey paws, Jayce wondered, like in the story?

"Why the fuck did you attack me?" With the Pig's broken nose and missing teeth, his words came out as mushy noise that was difficult to make sense of.

Jayce still had the bloody gobbet of the Pig's cheek in his mouth, and he spat it at the man. It struck his chest with a wet smacking sound, slid off, and fell to the floor with a *plap*.

"Because you cut my daughter's head off, you goddamned lunatic!"

Jayce screamed these words, and the twin behind him put a large hand on his shoulder to keep him from renewing his attack on the Pig.

Now that the fight had been broken up, Ivory and Nicola came over. Ivory nodded toward the twins.

"Thank you both." She then looked at Jayce. "The Therons are the best security I've ever had. They anticipate problems before they happen, and they were likely already halfway to our table before this man" – she glanced at the Pig in distaste – "pulled his little prank."

Jayce couldn't believe what he was hearing.

"*Prank?* The motherfucker killed my *daughter!*" He practically howled this last word.

He felt wetness on his cheeks, and he thought Ohio Pig had injured him without knowing and he was bleeding. But then he realized the wetness wasn't blood. He was crying.

Nicola came to his side.

"Are you all right, Jayce? Did he hurt you?"

His ribs ached, and he thought a couple might be cracked, but he didn't think any were broken, and he'd torn a couple of the stitches on his hand where one of the dog-eaters had cut him, and the wound was bleeding a bit. But none of that mattered right now. Emory was dead, decapitated by the madman being held by one of Ivory's security brutes only a few feet away from him. How could both Ivory and Nicola be so unaffected by what had happened to his daughter? Nicola had told him that exposure to Shadow changed people, and the longer and more intense the exposure was, the greater the change. Neither woman seemed changed outwardly, but inwardly? Given the lack of empathy they'd displayed since seeing Emory's head dropped onto the table in front of them like so much trash, maybe they were both as crazy in their own way as Ohio Pig.

His intense rage had burned itself out, leaving behind only soul-crushing sorrow. His little girl, his *Emmy*, was gone. She'd died a horrible, unimaginable death, and he hadn't been able to do jack shit to stop it. He'd failed her again, and this time it had cost Emory her life.

His mother's voice, silent for so long, spoke up now.

You should've kept your dick in your pants. The way she ended up, she would've been better off if she'd never been born.

He wanted to deny Valerie's words, but he couldn't. Despair flooded him, bringing with it bone-deep weariness. His knees started to give out, and he would've collapsed to the floor if Nicola hadn't grabbed hold of his arm to steady him. Given that she didn't seem to give a flying fuck about his daughter's death, he wanted to pull away from her. He didn't want the psycho bitch's help. But he was too drained to do more than stand there.

Ivory walked up to the Pig, her lips pursed in distaste.

"You know you're not welcome here," she said.

He attempted to smile, but the best he could do was part his swollen, blood-smeared lips to reveal a mouthful of cracked and broken teeth.

"I go where the job takes me," he said.

Ivory turned to Jayce. "The *Pig*" – she almost spat the word – "fancies himself as something of a low-rent Van Helsing. He views Shadow as a corruption of reality, and the beings who inhabit it as distorted, debased, and subhuman."

"That's about the size of it," he said. "Most of you fuckers are harmless enough, long as you keep to yourselves. But when you start messing with regular folks, that's when I go to work."

"Well, your work here is more than done." Ivory addressed the twin holding Ohio Pig. "Escort him off the premises – and you needn't bother being gentle about it. Make sure he doesn't return tonight. I'd like to finish my conversation with Mr. Lewis without further interruption."

What was there to talk about now? Emory was dead. And the piece of shit who'd killed her was standing right in front of him.

"You can't let him go," Jayce said. At first, speaking was an effort, but the longer he spoke, the more his strength returned. "He needs to pay for what he's done. We have to call the police."

"Those of us who live in Shadow police ourselves," Ivory said, a hint of frost in her tone. "But even if that weren't true, there would be no need to contact the authorities."

"You're insane," Jayce said.

"You don't understand," Nicola said. "Emory—"

Before she could finish whatever she intended to say, Trevor – the eyeless doorman – came running toward them, weaving between tables and people with a speed that belied his sightlessness.

"Madame!" he called out, his voice strained.

Ivory turned toward him as he approached. She frowned at first, as if irritated by this new interruption, but when she saw the look of sheer terror on his face, she became concerned.

"What's wrong?"

Trevor stopped when he reached her, and it took him a moment to catch his breath.

Too many damn cigarettes, Mother said.

When Trevor could speak again, his words burst out in explosive gasps.

"It's him! He's coming!"

"Who?" Ivory demanded.

Trevor fixed his shadow-filled eye sockets on her.

"The Harvest Man."

★　★　★

Jayce looked at Nicola.

"I thought you said he was an urban legend."

She looked confused – and more than a little worried.

"He is. At least, that's what I thought."

The people at the tables around them had been watching Jayce fight Ohio Pig with varying degrees of amusement and irritation. But now they began exchanging whispers and fearful looks. Several rose from their seats and began heading for the exit.

Ivory snapped at Trevor. "Don't be foolish! That's not possible!"

"I know what I smelled," Trevor said, unaffected by his employer's anger. "Cold moonlight, overturned soil, and rotting leaves." He then turned to Jayce. "It's what I smelled on you too. You have his stink on you."

Jayce had no idea what the man was talking about, but then he remembered the voice he'd heard behind Emory's apartment building, its single whispered word: *Soon.*

Jayce had smelled something there similar to what Trevor described. He'd also smelled it that day when he was thirteen and something had confronted him in the mall restroom. Had that something been the Harvest Man? And if so, what did the bastard want from him?

Before any of them could say more, shrieks arose from the far side of the club, near the elevator. People abandoned their tables and fled in panic, knocking over chairs and each other in their mad rush to escape. There were too many people in the way, and Jayce couldn't see what they were running from, but if Trevor was right, the Harvest Man – a being so monstrous that it terrified the jaded patrons of Crimson Splendor, men and women who lived in Shadow and had been transformed by it – was coming. Jayce supposed he should have been frightened as well, but he was too numbed by Emory's death to feel anything.

Ohio Pig had been quiet for the last several moments, but he spoke now, thrashing in Theron's arms as he did.

"Let me go! I don't want anything to do with that creepy fucker!"

"Some Van Helsing," Nicola muttered.

"Madame?" Theron said.

"Release him," she said.

Theron and his brother exchanged dubious looks. But Theron did as Ivory commanded and removed his hands from Ohio Pig. The Pig shot the guard a dark look, and Jayce thought the Pig was going to turn around and attack him, but he didn't. Instead, he turned toward Jayce.

"I'll see you later, asshole. Assuming you survive, that is."

And then the Pig turned and ran like hell, and Jayce lost sight of him in the burgeoning chaos.

Ivory turned to the twins.

"Go see what's happening," she ordered.

The twins lowered their heads, neither willing to meet her gaze.

"*Now*," she added.

Reluctantly, the twins started making their way toward the disturbance. They had to fight through fleeing patrons, and sometimes they were forced to knock someone aside or clout them on the jaw to get them out of their path. Jayce remembered something then. Ivory had referred to them as the *Therons* – plural. Did that mean something?

Jayce became aware of Nicola tugging on his arm.

"We should go," she said. Her grip was tight on his arm, and her voice held a note of fear. During their short acquaintance, he hadn't known her to be afraid of anything Shadow had to offer. Seeing her frightened drove home how serious the situation was.

But it didn't matter if the Harvest Man was real and was the most dangerous thing in the Cannery, a giant shark in a tank filled with sharp-toothed guppies. He couldn't leave, not without Emory – or at least her head.

Without saying anything to Nicola, he pulled free of her grip and rushed back to the table where they had been sitting when the Pig showed up. Like the twins, he had to battle the fleeing crowd to reach the table. He assumed they were heading for a back set of stairs or maybe a fire exit of some kind.

"Get the fuck out of my way!" Jayce shouted, but no one paid him any attention. He shoved, elbowed, shouldered, hit, and kicked his way back to the table, but aside from overturned glasses, it was empty. Then he remembered: Emory's head had fallen to the floor. He looked down, saw the bloodstained canvas bag the Pig had carried the head in, but there was no sign of the head itself. A horrible image flashed into his mind then – Emory's head being kicked around on the floor like some kind of grisly soccer ball as people fled from the Harvest Man. He imagined his daughter's features being pulped as dozens of feet struck her face, one after another. When the panic subsided, would there be anything left of her head, or would it be nothing more than scattered fragments of flesh, bone, hair, and brain tissue?

He stood at the table and looked around, trying to catch sight of Emory's head. As he did, he saw – on the far side of the room – a slender figure wearing only a pair of ragged jeans following in the wake of the fleeing crowd. The crimson lighting was too dim for Jayce to make out many details, but even from this distance he could feel the power emanating from the man, like rolling waves of thunder preceding a violent storm. The man moved with a slow, measured stride, so slow, in fact, that he almost seemed to be moving out of sync with normal time. It appeared at first as if the man was going to do nothing more than walk, but then his mouth – which looked *wrong*, even from this distance – yawned open, and a dark cloud emerged, expanding as it moved toward the club's fleeing patrons. The darkness engulfed a dozen of those at the rear of the crowd, and then the screaming began. These weren't screams of physical pain, although the agony in them was raw and piercing. These screams came from a place far deeper. It was as if their souls were being eaten away, dissolved by some kind of spiritual acid. A combination of smells filled the air, the autumn leaves and fresh soil that he was familiar with, along with the new smells of ashes and old rot. The dark cloud lingered for several moments and then retreated. Instead of dissipating, though, it flowed back into the mouth of its creator, as if the man were inhaling it back inside him. The men and women who'd been enveloped in the cloud no longer ran. They stood motionless now, their bodies blackened figures that held their shape for a handful of seconds before collapsing into small piles of dark residue.

They've been harvested, Mother said.

That word – *harvested* – hit Jayce like a gut punch, but what really got to him was a sense that he'd seen something like this before. Something to do with Emory in a basement....

During all the chaos, the singer – if that's what she could be called – sat on the stage, oblivious to what was happening, continuing to produce her strange inhuman sounds. The Harvest Man turned in her direction and, although he'd been moving slowly up to this point, he suddenly picked up speed, seeming to move forward in a series of fast-paced jump cuts, like a sped-up film, and within an instant he stood at the edge of the stage. At first the singer seemed unaware of his presence. The crone didn't look at him, and her body language continued to be relaxed. But after a moment her voice faltered, and then cut out altogether. She rolled forward and curled into a ball, as if lying this way would somehow protect her, or perhaps she was merely demonstrating silent acceptance of her fate. The Harvest Man exhaled a cloud of darkness onto her, and when he inhaled it, nothing remained of her except a mound of black dust shaped like the singer. An instant later, the mound lost cohesion and became a formless lump.

"Jayce!"

Nicola was at his side once more. She grabbed his hand and tried to pull him away from the table, but he resisted.

"I can't leave without Emory," he said, not taking his gaze from the Harvest Man, who'd turned away from the stage and was once again pursuing what remained of the crowd.

The Harvest Man breathed darkness – out, then in – and

another handful of people were reduced to nothing. The creature – because despite his name, he was only a man in the most general sense of the word – had come close enough now that Jayce could clearly make out his features. His skin looked crimson, of course, because of the lights, but Jayce knew it was really a mottled gray, like a lizard's. He was bald, bare-chested, and barefooted, the only clothes he wore an old pair of faded jeans, torn at the knees, cuffs ragged. His hands were twisted claws, the nails long and black, almost talons. His fingers curled and uncurled slowly as he walked, almost as if the action were somehow part of how he achieved locomotion. Jayce found this detail creepy as hell, but nowhere near as creepy as the creature's mouth. It was a circle of ringed flesh, like a lamprey's, and filled with several rows of tiny needle-like teeth.

The Harvest Man's eyes were glossy black orbs, like polished obsidian, and they never blinked. The sight of those eyes sent Jayce's head spinning. He felt as if the world tilted far to the right, and he was viewing everything from a wrong angle. He heard the sound of a bathroom stall lock clicking open of its own accord, followed by the slow metal creak of the door opening. He saw a face peering down at him, like a skull covered by tight, dry gray skin. And those eyes.... They'd been the ones that he was looking at now. Overlarge and bulging, black as the deepest recesses of the earth and cold as the airless void of space. He felt more memories threatening to rise from the muck of his subconscious, where he'd kept them locked away for so long. They crowded at the barrier hiding them from his full awareness, pushing and pounding, determined to break through once and for all. He sensed what those memories would reveal: what had happened to him between the time the Harvest Man had confronted him in the restroom and when he'd finally made it home, hours later. That missing time was the central mystery of his life, and he was closer to knowing the truth of what had happened during that time than he'd ever been before. The memories were there, knocking at the door of his conscious mind. All he would have to do was let them in.

He almost did it, but in the end he was too frightened by what he might discover, so he let the door remain closed. Besides, he had more important things to worry about right now – like surviving the next few minutes.

Despite their initial misgivings about confronting the Harvest Man, the twins – the *Therons* – moved toward him without hesitation, large hands balled into fists, ready to inflict serious damage. The Harvest Man appeared unaware of their approach. His attention had been caught by an obese naked man shackled to a brick wall close to the stage. The man was covered with glistening black leeches, huge swollen things a foot long. Jayce didn't know if the man was a patron, some sort of entertainment, a decoration, or some combination of the three. He struggled to pull free of the shackles as the Harvest Man came toward him, but they were too tight and all he could do was thrash uselessly, dislodging several of the overfed leeches, which fell to the concrete floor and hit it with wet smacking sounds. The man shook his head back and forth rapidly, saying, "No, no, no," over and over. The Harvest Man stopped in front of the leech lover and leaned close to the man, his nostrils flaring, as if drinking in his scent. He then pulled back and exhaled a dark cloud onto the man. The man shrieked as the darkness engulfed him, but his cry lasted only a few seconds, and when the Harvest Man inhaled the cloud once again, nothing remained of the naked man except an ashen replica of his body – including the leeches that had been affixed to it – which quickly collapsed into dust. The shackles fell loose and struck the wall with soft clanging sounds.

The Harvest Man was still facing the wall when the twins reached him. The first Theron who got there grabbed hold of the Harvest Man's right shoulder and spun him around. Theron drew back his fist, preparing to hit the Harvest Man in the face.

But before he could strike, the Harvest Man made a coughing sound and a small cloud chuffed out of his mouth to enclose Theron's head. Theron screamed for a half second, and then the Harvest Man inhaled the cloud back in. Theron's body remained unchanged below the neck, but his head had become black ash. When it flaked away, it didn't leave behind a bleeding stump. Instead, the top of the neck was covered with smooth, unmarked flesh, as if the head hadn't been destroyed so much as unmade. Now that his head was gone, Theron's body fell limp. But before it could strike the floor, his sibling rushed forward, tears streaming down his cheeks, and caught Theron's body. The brother — was he really also called Theron? — cradled his dead sibling in his arms and wept, his body racked with great heaving sobs.

The Harvest Man didn't bother exhaling a death cloud upon the second Theron. Perhaps he needed to recharge between exhalations, like a boiler that's released some of its steam and needs time to build up more. Whatever the case, the Harvest Man swung his claw-like hand in a swift vicious arc, and those sharp black nails sliced through this Theron's throat with ease, almost as if, for the Harvest Man, flesh wasn't any more substantial than air. Blood sprayed from the wound, splattering the Harvest Man's face and chest. The strike had been so deep that it nearly severed the second Theron's head, and the blow so strong that it knocked him — along with his brother's headless body — to the floor. He lay there, body twitching, gurgling noises bubbling up from his ravaged throat as he tried to breathe. The Harvest Man gazed down upon the twins — one dead, the other rapidly becoming so — for a moment before raising his head and turning his soulless black eyes toward Jayce.

The Harvest Man started forward again, moving in a rapid series of jump cuts. It was difficult to tell given the bizarre way the creature moved, but Jayce thought his body was absorbing Theron's blood, pulling it inward through his mottled gray skin until it was gone.

Looks like he has more than one way of harvesting, Mother said.
Instead of reacting with horror upon witnessing the twins die,
Ivory grew furious. Before either Jayce or Nicola could stop her,
she walked toward the Harvest Man, moving with sharp, angry
motions. The Harvest Man showed no reaction as she approached,
didn't even turn to face her, and Jayce wondered if the monster
was even aware of her.

"This is *my* club!" Ivory said. "I don't give a shit who or what
you are or how much power you possess. You can't just come in
here and—"

That's as far as she got before the Harvest Man's head swiveled
in her direction, his circular mouth opened wide, and he expelled
a mass of darkness at her. Ivory didn't cry out in fear, nor did she
raise her arms in front of her face to protect herself. She didn't even
take a reflexive step backward. She simply stood there, defiant, as
the cloud enveloped her. Jayce expected her to scream then, as all
of the others who'd been reduced to ash by the Harvest Man had.
But Ivory was silent. Jayce saw why when, a moment later, the
Harvest Man inhaled the cloud once again, and Ivory still stood
there, whole and unharmed. Seeing this, the Harvest Man cocked
his head slightly, as if puzzled. It was the most human gesture
Jayce had seen him make so far, but it only served to bring his
monstrousness into sharper relief.

"You can't harm me like that," Ivory said. "I haven't survived
two centuries without learning a few tricks on my own. Now, I
demand that you leave this place immediately and never return."

Her voice was strong and commanding. If she was afraid of
the Harvest Man, even a little, she was doing a damn good job of
concealing it.

Jayce wondered if the woman might actually pull it off,
if the Harvest Man would do as she demanded, turn and walk
away. He stood motionless as he regarded her, ebon eyes alien
and unreadable, lamprey mouth puckered like an oversized anus.

Then, without any warning, the Harvest Man did his jump-cut thing until he was standing almost nose to nose with Ivory. She looked startled, but she held her ground, and her stubborn pride proved to be her undoing. The Harvest Man jammed his clawed hands into the soft meat of her abdomen and blood gushed forth, splashing onto the Harvest Man and spilling onto the floor. Ivory gasped and her eyes went wide. She grabbed hold of the Harvest Man's wrists, as if she intended to try pulling his talons out of her, but all she did was hold on to them. The Harvest Man then lifted her into the air until her feet dangled several inches above the floor. Blood ran down her legs, dripped from her feet, and despite the agony she had to be suffering, she still didn't scream. Her eyes rolled back in her head and her body began twitching, as if her entire nervous system was shorting out. Then, with a pair of swift, savage motions, the Harvest Man swept his hands outward, eviscerating her. She fell to the floor amidst a shower of blood and shredded organs, and she did not rise again. Whatever strange abilities she might've possessed, they hadn't been enough to save her.

There's more than one way to skin a cat, Mother said.

The Harvest Man started walking toward Jayce and Nicola, blood-covered claws clenching and unclenching. When the Harvest Man was within ten feet of Jayce, Nicola screamed in his ear. "We've got to go – *now!*" She yanked on his arm so hard that a bolt of pain lanced through his shoulder and he stumbled backward several feet. He might've allowed Nicola to continue pulling him away, but he saw the Harvest Man stop, turn to his left, bend down, and reach for something on the floor. When the creature straightened once more, Jayce saw that the object he had picked up and was now examining like a curious artifact was Emory's head – or at least what was left of it after having been kicked around by the Crimson Splendor's patrons in their frenzied rush to escape.

Jayce pulled free from Nicola's grasp, intending to run toward the Harvest Man and claim his daughter's head, but even in his grief and anger, he realized doing so would be suicidal. He saw what had happened to the twins, but he *couldn't* leave without Emory's head. It was all that remained of her, all that he and Mackenzie might have to bury if the rest of her body couldn't be found. A memory came to him then, of when Nicola threatened the dog-eaters last night, how she'd told them she'd throw the vessel she'd bought at CrazyQwik at them if they didn't let him go. They'd been scared at the thought of what the vessel might do to them and had backed down. Jayce knew that not all vessels were dangerous – at least, not dangerous enough to be considered weapons. If they were, then people like Ivory wouldn't be able to use them safely as she had a while ago. And while Emory had become deeply involved with the world of Shadow and the beings that inhabited it, he couldn't believe she'd stock her refrigerator with the Shadow equivalent of live grenades. But some vessels had to be more volatile than others, or else Nicola's threat wouldn't have worked on the dog-eaters.

Jayce turned and ran toward the bar. Nyla was gone, no doubt having taken off with everyone else when the Harvest Man began reducing people to ash. He didn't blame her. If it hadn't been for Emory's head, he'd have been long gone too. He'd lost track of Trevor as well, but despite the man's lack of eyes, he seemed to get around fine, and Jayce hoped the man had made it out of the club safely.

He hauled ass behind the bar and stopped in front of the refrigerated cabinet where the club's supply of vessels was kept. The bandage on his wounded hand was dirty and starting to come apart, so he pulled it off and dropped it on the floor. He didn't bother checking his stitches. He had more important matters to deal with right then. He opened the cabinet's glass door and, since he couldn't interpret the strange markings carved into the jar's clay surfaces, he grabbed two at random – one for each hand – and ran back to where Nicola still stood. The vessels were so cold it hurt to hold them, but he didn't care. The Harvest Man hadn't moved while Jayce had been gone. He stood motionless, ebon-eyed gaze trained on Emory's head, which he held up before him as if he were some grotesque parody of Hamlet contemplating Yorick's skull. The Harvest Man brought Emory's ravaged head close to his face – Jayce saw dark patches of skin on the head now, almost like mold – and the creature inhaled deeply, like a goddamned gourmand testing a fine wine's bouquet.

Jayce ran past Nicola, his breath coming in ragged gasps, his heart pounding in his ears. The most exercise he got these days was an occasional walk around the neighborhood where he lived, and his middle-aged body was far too out of shape for him to keep on abusing it like this.

He stopped when he was within five feet of the Harvest Man. He was covered in sweat, and the sharp pain from his injured ribs made him grimace. If he hadn't known what the pain was, he might've been convinced he was having a heart attack. He intended to hurl the vessels at the Harvest Man – he didn't think a mere threat would have any effect on the creature – but before he could do so, he saw that poor Emory's battered head was beginning to… well, *dissolve* was the only word for it. Her flesh became darker and lumpier, as if it were riddled with mold, and then it sloughed off the skull in liquid strands that ran past the Harvest Man's clawed hand and fell to the floor with soft pattering sounds. The same thing happened to her hair, and within seconds the Harvest Man's obsidian eyes gazed upon Emory's naked skull. But then it too began to liquefy, and after only a few short seconds it had joined the gooey puddle on the floor, leaving behind nothing but a thin viscous layer of slime on the Harvest Man's palm. He regarded it for a moment, and then flicked it onto the floor with a couple of sharp gestures.

Jayce stared at the puddle that was all that remained of his Emmy. The Harvest Man had used yet another method to absorb her head, and although the rational part of Jayce's mind – what little of it still functioned at the moment – knew that Ohio Pig had been the one who'd killed his daughter, the Pig wasn't here. But the Harvest Man was. With a howl that was equal parts fury and despair, Jayce hurled the first vessel.

His aim was good, and the jar struck the Harvest Man's chest. It bounced off, and when it hit the concrete floor the seal cracked and the lid popped open. The Harvest Man seemed unaffected by the impact, or for that matter even aware that Jayce had thrown the vessel. He didn't take his gaze from the liquefied remains of Emory's head. Nothing emerged from the jar at first, and Jayce thought he'd grabbed a dud. But then a mass of beetles came scuttling out, far more than should have been able to fit inside the vessel. They swirled around the Harvest Man's bare feet and then began climbing onto him. They moved swiftly up his legs, onto his torso, down his arms, up over his neck and face until he was completely covered. Jayce allowed himself a few seconds of hope that the insects would strip the flesh from the Harvest Man's bones. But then the Harvest Man inhaled and sucked the beetles inside him as if he were some sort of monstrous vacuum cleaner. Within seconds, the last of the beetles disappeared down his throat and were gone. Jayce realized then that no matter how much the Harvest Man took into himself, he put on no weight, as if inside him were a gaping void that could never be filled, not even if he managed to harvest the entire world.

You got that right, kiddo, Mother said. *He's a direct link to the Gyre, and beyond that, to the Vast itself.*

He had no idea what she was talking about, which was weird since her voice was nothing more than a projection of his own personality, a manifestation of his self-doubt and fears. But he didn't care what the part of him that pretended to be his mother had to say. He only cared about taking vengeance for his poor dead Emmy, and so he threw the second vessel, putting all his strength into it.

The jar flew toward the Harvest Man's head, but this time the creature was ready. Without looking away from the viscous mass that had been Emory's head, he reached up lightning-quick and caught the vessel in one of his taloned hands. He made a fist and the jar shattered. Pieces fell to the floor, and as near as Jayce could tell, the vessel had been empty. But then the sound of soft laughter filled the air – dark, cruel, becoming louder by the second until it reached deafening volume. Wind accompanied the laughter, swirling around the Harvest Man, becoming stronger and more intense until he was trapped at the center of a small tornado. The wind buffeted the Harvest Man, knocking him off balance, although he did not fall. The laughter continued, so loud that it echoed through the club, so painful that Jayce clapped his hands over his ears. Beside him, Nicola did the same. Whatever the hell the second vessel had contained, it was clearly more powerful than the beetles, and Jayce was heartened upon seeing the Harvest Man being affected by both the laughter and the wind. He too pressed his hands against his ears, and the vortex lifted him several inches off the floor. The Harvest Man, as terrifying as he was, wasn't all powerful, and that gave Jayce the first true glimmer of hope he'd felt since the creature had walked into Crimson Splendor. He imagined the swirling wind growing stronger, becoming so violent that it would flay the meat off the Harvest Man's skeleton with scalpel-like precision.

But then the laughter began to die and the wind weakened. Whatever force had been contained within the vessel was spent, and the Harvest Man was lowered until his feet once again touched the floor, and he removed his hands from his ears as the laughter trailed to silence. The wind was nothing but a gentle breeze now, and then it too died.

The Harvest Man trained his glossy black eyes on Jayce, and Jayce expected the creature's lamprey mouth to widen and exhale a cloud of darkness that would engulf both him and Nicola, stealing their lives and reducing their bodies to ash and grit. But the Harvest Man's mouth remained closed. Even so, Jayce heard the creature's voice inside his head.

Soon.

Then the Harvest Man got down on his hands and knees. He lowered his head toward Emory's liquid remains, and a black appendage that looked more like a serpent than a tongue slithered out of his mouth, and he began lapping up the viscous mess. The fucking thing was eating what was left of Jayce's daughter.

Jayce started toward the monster, but Nicola grabbed hold of his wrist and pulled him backward. He didn't resist this time, didn't have the strength or the will, and he allowed Nicola to lead him away from the Harvest Man. As they fled, he heard the soft, wet sounds of the creature feeding on Emory, like a dog lapping water from a bowl.

CHAPTER NINE

Jayce knocks softly on Emory's bedroom door. She doesn't answer, but he can hear her crying inside. The sound is muffled, and he imagines her lying on her bed, her face buried in her pillow. He knocks again, a bit louder this time.

"Emory? Sweetie? Can I come in?"

Again, no answer. He tries the knob, finds it unlocked, so he turns it, opens the door, and steps inside. He debates whether to close it behind him, and he decides that Emory might feel more comfortable talking if the door's shut. And he doesn't want Mackenzie coming by, noticing them talking, and deciding to intrude on their conversation. He closes the door, almost locking it to keep Mackenzie from entering, but he doesn't. If she tries to enter and finds the door locked, she'll get angry, probably yell at him and pound on the door. Emory doesn't need that kind of stress right now, and honestly, neither does he.

Emory is thirteen, the same age he was when…when…. The memory refuses to coalesce and it fades before fully being born. He lets it go. Whatever it is, it isn't important right now. All that matters is Emory.

She is indeed lying facedown on her bed – the same one she's had since she was a little girl. She's tall enough now that her feet almost hang over the edge, and she marvels at how fast the time's gone. He knows this is a cliché, that all parents think the same thing as their children age, but that doesn't make what he feels any less powerful.

She's wearing a pair of purple pajama pants and a black T-shirt. He can't see it the way she's lying, but there's a cross-eyed cartoon monkey on the front, below it the words *I'm Bananas!* It's one of her favorite shirts. He wonders if she'll come to associate it with tonight, and if so, if she'll ever wear it again.

The walls and ceiling of her room are painted blue, and covering them are cute ocean creatures – an octopus, a stingray, a shark – all painted bright colors and sporting smiling faces. Jayce drew and painted them. He knows he's not an artist by any stretch of the imagination, but he thinks they turned out all right. Even though their expressions are unvaryingly pleasant, he imagines they're looking at him accusingly, as if they're thinking, *How could you do this to her?*

It's a question he's been asking himself.

Not all of the happy sea creatures he painted are visible now. Emory's taped up several posters of boy bands on the walls, covering some of her aquatic friends. More signs of how fast she's growing up. The boys all look somewhat feminine and harmless, but they're male and that makes them a threat, at least in Jayce's eyes. She has a bookshelf against one wall filled with her favorite series – Narnia, Oz, *Warriors*, *American Girl* – and next to it is an open chest filled with stuffed animals that she no longer sleeps with but which she can't bring herself to get rid of.

She doesn't look up as he crosses to her bed. It's a youth bed, low to the floor, and when he sits cross-legged next to it, the mattress comes up only to his waist. He could easily reach out and rub her back, just as he used to do when she was a toddler and needed his comforting touch to help her drift off to sleep. But he doesn't touch her now. He doesn't feel he has the right.

"How are you feeling, Emmy?"

He doesn't feel he has the right to speak with her, either, but he's her father. It's his job to take care of her, to try to heal her hurts, even those that he helped cause. Especially those.

She keeps her face pressed against the pillow, and her voice is muffled as she speaks – no, *wails*.

"I wish this was a dream!"

Me, too, he thinks.

He does reach out to touch her now, lays his hand on her back, and her body stiffens. Realizing he's made a mistake, he almost jerks his hand back, but he knows that would only compound his error, so he leaves his hand where it is.

Several minutes pass while Emory sobs into her pillow. He considers leaving the room to go get her some tissues, but he realizes the impulse is just an excuse to get away from his daughter – or more accurately, from the crushing guilt he feels. So he stays.

When he and Mackenzie married, he hadn't wanted children. Not because he wanted to be able to live life free from the responsibility, but because the world was a dangerous place, and how could he justify bringing an innocent life into it? How could he protect a child from all the hazards that came with living? He couldn't, of course. Bad things would happen to his child – some maybe *very* bad – and despite all his efforts, he wouldn't be able to prevent them. How could he then, in good conscience, help create a new life?

But he had other needs working in him as well, and one of the strongest was the need to be the kind of father he'd never had. He understood that it was, at least in some ways, a selfish desire, that he wanted to make up for this profound lack in his own childhood. Mackenzie wanted kids, and she worked on him, trying to convince him, and little by little she wore him down until finally he gave in. And now here he was, living his worst nightmare. Not only hadn't he been able to protect Emory from this hurt, he'd caused it. He and Mackenzie had sat Emory down on the couch and tried to explain to her what was going to happen in simple terms, each of them working hard to make it sound like divorce wasn't a tragedy but a transition. Halfway through their sales pitch, Emory had jumped off the couch and ran down the hall to her bedroom.

"Emmy, I know this is hard, but...." He trails off. But what? He can't find the words to comfort her, doesn't think there are any. Emory rolls onto her side and looks at him. Her eyes are red and puffy and her nose is running. She glares at him with anger so strong it strikes him like a physical blow.

"I'll never forgive you." Her voice is steely cold. *"Never."*

That makes two of us, kiddo, he thinks.

★   ★   ★

Jayce feels like he's burning up, but at the same time he can't stop shivering. He grips the steering wheel until his knuckles turn white, and he keeps blinking to clear his tear-filled vision. He felt crappy when he woke up that morning – achy, a bit lightheaded, stomach touchy – but not so bad that he thought he needed to stay home from work. But he kept feeling worse as the day went on, and after vomiting his lunch into a men's room toilet, he told his supervisor that he was going home, and after commenting that he looked like shit, she enthusiastically endorsed this idea. His condition worsened as he drove, and now that he approaches the house, he hopes that he can pull into the garage without hitting one of the sides. Fuck it. He'll park in the driveway and go in the front door.

It's a two-story house, white siding, black shutters, not much different than the others in this suburban neighborhood. There's a huge oak tree in the front yard which Mackenzie loves, but it's a pain in the ass in the autumn. All those damn leaves.... But it's not his problem anymore, is it?

He pulls his Nissan Altima – which received a high rating from the Insurance Institute for Highway Safety – into the driveway and parks at a lopsided angle. *Good enough for government work,* he thinks. He turns off the engine and sits for several moments, staring at the white garage door, brain enshrouded by flu fog. Mackenzie got the house in the divorce, naturally, and Emory lives here primarily, spending only alternate weekends with him in his cracker box of an apartment. Mackenzie's gone on a week-long trip to Vegas for her forty-fifth birthday with 'friends' – more likely a boyfriend she doesn't want to tell Jayce about – and she's asked Jayce to stay at the house to 'keep an eye on' Emory. Emory was upset by this, of course. What fifteen-year-old thinks she needs a babysitter, even if it is her dad? And it's weird to be staying in a place that used to be his home, but in which he's now a visitor. But he jumped at the opportunity to spend more time with Emory. Their relationship hasn't been great since the divorce, and he hoped that spending a week with her might help bring them closer, if only a little. And now he's sick. Wonderful.

He opens the door, steps out of the car, shuts the door, and immediately drops his keys. As he bends down to pick them up he experiences a wave of dizziness and almost falls over. He manages to retrieve his keys and straighten, and he figures that if any of the neighbors are watching, they probably think he's drunk. He wishes he was. It would be a hell of a lot better than how he feels right now.

It's only after he goes in through the front door that he realizes it's not locked. He left for work before Emory had to leave for school. Did she forget to lock it when she left? It's not like her, but then again, he no longer lives with her full-time. Who knows what she's really like these days? He locks the door now, and while in a situation like this he would normally go through the house and check to make sure that everything's okay, that no one entered while they were gone and stole anything, he's too sick to bother doing that today. Besides, all the stuff in here is Mackenzie's now. He doesn't give a damn if any of it is stolen.

He plans to head upstairs, undress, crawl into bed – trying not to think about how many lovers Mackenzie has fucked on it since their split – and hopefully sleep off whatever bug he's caught. With any luck, he'll feel at least a little better by the time Emory gets home from school. His hand's on the railing, right foot on the first carpeted step, when he hears music. The sound is muted, but a driving beat makes the wood beneath his hand vibrate, as well as the floor under his feet, and he realizes the music is coming from the basement.

A jolt of adrenaline disperses his brain fog, and his thoughts become clear and sharp. Mackenzie is in Vegas. Emory's in school. No one is supposed to be here. Did someone find the front door unlocked, enter the house, and...what? Go down to the basement and listen to some tunes? It doesn't make sense.

You came home, Mother says. *Maybe Emory did too. And maybe she's not alone.*

He tells himself it's a ridiculous thought, but it prompts him to turn away from the stairs and head for the kitchen, where the basement door is located. He puts his hand on the knob and hesitates. He can feel the pounding vibrations of the music through the metal. He turns the knob and opens the door. The basement light is on, and the music, without any barriers to muffle it, is louder now. The pounding beat reverberates through his body, and he feels his heart trying to match its rhythm. His head starts to throb in time with the beat as well, and as he descends the stairs, he grips the hand railing tight to steady himself. The last thing he wants to do is lose his balance, tumble down the stairs, and end up in a crumpled, broken heap on the floor.

The steps are carpeted and his footfalls make no sound. But given how loud the music is, he knows he could stomp as hard as he wants without being heard. He recognizes the music, although he can't remember the title of the song. It's an older tune, from a heavy metal group that was popular back when he was Emory's age called Slogeny. Their music is dark, even for the metal of the time, and he remembers it being linked to cult activity and a number of suicides. It's a far cry from the sort of weightless pop that Emory listens to. It's dissonant, grating, and unsettling, and overlying the pounding beat is a sound like a dozen whirring chainsaws. There's screaming too, or something like it, along with a mournful wailing that doesn't sound close to human. The basement serves as a rec room, and Jayce did it up right before he moved out. Flat-screen TV mounted on one of the paneled walls for watching movies or playing video games. Multi-game table that can be turned into a ping-pong, air hockey, or pool table. A leather couch and recliner, and in front of them a glass coffee table. And, of course, a kick-ass stereo system from which the pounding music is coming. He created the rec room to keep Emory at home, where she'd be safe. Why go to a friend's house when she had all this cool stuff at her place? Instead, her friends came here. When they were younger, they had sleepovers in the basement, but now that they are in their teens, they mostly hang out here after school and on weekends. And why not? It's a fun, comfortable place. But the sight that awaits him when he reaches the bottom of the stairs is about as far from comforting as it's possible to get.

Emory hangs naked in midair, her back arched, eyes closed, mouth wide open. Jayce hasn't seen her unclothed since he bathed her when she was a toddler, and her nakedness startles him almost as much as seeing her suspended in the air. Her breasts are larger than he'd realized, and her dark thatch of pubic hair seems obscene, a violation of the smooth pink skin she'd had down there when she was a child.

She's not levitating in the air, though. She's being *held* there. Purple-red tentacles extrude from the walls and ceiling, a dozen of them, each the thickness of a large snake, a boa or python. They're coiled around Emory's body – her wrists, ankles, torso – holding her aloft. That's not the worst part, though. Three of the tentacles have penetrated her body – one in the mouth, one in her vagina, and one in her ass. They slide in and out of her, blue-green surfaces pulsing and rippling. She makes *mmmmm* sounds as her body twists and undulates, and he wants to believe that she's being attacked, raped by whatever the hell these things are. But she's not resisting, and the sounds she makes are ones of pleasure, not pain.

Now that he's gotten a good look at the tentacles – which, now that he thinks of it, look more like large veins – he realizes they haven't emerged from the walls and ceiling as he originally thought. Their far ends protrude from blurry patches in the air *near* the walls and ceiling. He wonders what those blurry patches are. Portals of some kind? Openings that lead to somewhere else? Somewhere *bad*?

A memory hits him then. Those giraffes.... The things that emerged from the rock...cankerworms. These are like those, not exactly, but similar, he thinks. And although they don't seem to be hurting Emory – quite the opposite, in fact – he remembers what happened to the giraffe the cankerworms attacked. Panic sweeps aside his emotional paralysis and he runs toward his daughter, his illness forgotten.

The basement ceiling is high, fifteen feet from the floor, but Emory is being held – *Being fucked,* Mother's voice cuts in – about five feet below the ceiling. He can't reach her from a standing position, but the veins are holding her over the leather couch. He sees her clothes lying in a small pile between the couch and the coffee table, and he guesses that she was lying on the couch, naked, waiting for the veins to appear, slither downward through the air, encircle her in their rubbery coils, and bear her upward.

He doesn't have a weapon, doesn't know if he needs one. There's nothing nearby, not unless you count a goddamned ping-pong paddle. He's just going to have to use his hands.

He reaches the couch and jumps onto it, moving so fast he nearly loses his balance and falls off. Emory's eyes have been closed the entire time, and he's made so little noise up to this point that there is no way she could hear him over the music. But now something – instinct, perhaps – alerts her to his presence, and her eyes snap open and she looks toward him. Her eyes widen in surprise, which is followed almost instantly by shock and then by an anger so strong it feels like a slap across the face. He ignores her glare and grabs hold of her torso, his fingers brushing against several of the veins. Their surface is just as rubbery as it appears, but he's surprised by how cold they are. So cold that his skin feels like it's burning, and he wonders how Emory can stand to have the disgusting things touch her. Especially on the *inside*. He thrusts the thought away, ignores the sensation of his daughter's naked flesh beneath his hands, tightens his grip, and pulls downward as hard as he can.

The veins stretch but their hold on Emory doesn't slacken. The three that are fucking her begin thrusting frantically, as if desperate to finish the job before Jayce stops them. He realizes then that the things aren't fucking her, or if they are, that's not all they're doing. They're pumping some kind of substance into her. Cum or blood or something alien that he can't put a name to. With every pulse, Emory's skin reddens, as if she's blushing all over her body. The color quickly fades, only to return in an instant when the pulse comes. Emory's eyes blaze with fury at him, and she thrashes back and forth, as if trying to shrug him off. He doesn't let go, instead tightens his grip further, to the point where his fingernails are cutting into her skin. Her voice is still muffled by the vein she's fellating, but her volume rises and it's clear that she would be yelling at the top of her lungs if she could. Yelling at him.

Jayce pulls harder and the veins stretch thinner, their surfaces darkening from blue-green to deep purple. He can feel them straining to hold on to Emory, to pull her out of his hands, but he refuses to give in. Through gritted teeth, he says, "Let go of my daughter!"

A scent comes to his nostrils then — a blend of fresh soil, autumn leaves, and the sweet odor of rot. He feels a coldness deep inside him, roiling, seething as it rises upward.

"Let. Her. Go!"

As he shouts the last word, a black cloud gusts from his mouth. It spreads outward, engulfing both Emory and the throbbing purple veins that have penetrated her. He's so startled, so sickened by what has emerged from inside him, that he takes in a gasp of air without thinking. As if he has summoned the black cloud back to him, it reverses direction, rolling back into his mouth and going down deep inside him, returning to wherever it came. When it's gone, he feels no different than he did a moment ago, and he seems to be uninjured. The same can't be said, however, for the python-sized veins. They begin to shrivel and blacken, their surfaces becoming dry and brittle. As the veins weaken, so too does their hold on Emory. Jayce pulls her free easily now, and the two of them fall backward onto the couch. He doesn't care that his daughter is naked. He wraps his arms around her and holds her tight in case the veins recover and try to reclaim her. But they continue to wither, growing thinner, their substance beginning to peel away in small, black flakes that drift lazily to the floor like ash. A few moments later, and the things are gone, leaving nothing behind but black flakes which are also in the process of disintegrating. Soon there will be nothing left.

He reaches up to stroke Emory's hair.

"It's okay, Emmy. Whatever those fucking things were, they're gone now."

For a moment, all she does is lie in his arms, limp, scarcely breathing. But then she struggles and squirms, trying to free herself from his embrace.

"Let me go, you dumbass!"

He's so shocked to hear her call him this that he does as she asks. Once freed, Emory jumps off the couch, goes to the stereo to turn off the music, then turns back around to face him. She stands without the least hint of self-consciousness at her nakedness. Lines of reddish-white goo trickle down the insides of her thighs, and when she speaks, he sees the same substance smeared on the corners of her mouth. He saw her ass when she turned off the stereo, and he knows she's leaking from there too.

"Do you have any idea how hard it was to summon the Sanguinem Seminis? I studied and practiced for two whole months, and it *still* took me five tries!"

Jayce has no idea how to respond to her anger. Without realizing it, he presses himself back against the couch, as if he's trying to escape her.

"I know you don't want to have anything to do with this kind of stuff. Hell, you do everything you can to *forget* about it. That time with the giraffe at the zoo. The time you took me to the park and we watched a group of kids turn each other inside out. The day the sun never set, and you and I seemed to be the only two people who noticed it...."

Other than the giraffe, Jayce has no idea what she's talking about. And yet there's something, not memories exactly, but a sense that there are things in his head that he's better off keeping locked away.

"Well, I *do* remember, Daddy, and I'm interested in learning more. And in the future, I'd appreciate it if you'd stay the fuck out of my way."

She glares at him for a moment longer and then sighs.

"Why am I bothering? You're just going to forget this too, aren't you?"

She gives him a final look that's part exasperation, part pity. Then she picks up her clothes, walks toward the stairs, and starts climbing them. He hears the door open and then close. He expects her to slam it shut, but she closes it quietly, almost as if she doesn't want to disturb him any further.

He pushes himself into a sitting position and remains like that for several minutes, not thinking, not feeling, staring at the wall. Finally, he stands and starts walking toward the stairs. He wishes he could remember what he came down here for, but he supposes if it's important enough it'll come back to him eventually. As he mounts the stairs, he realizes that he feels better. Much better, like he never had the flu in the first place. *Must've been a twenty-four-hour thing,* he thinks. Or in his case, a six-hour thing. Still, he should probably take it easy the rest of the day. Work has been a bit stressful lately, and he could use a nice, quiet, boring day at home with his daughter.

★ ★ ★

After they'd managed to escape Crimson Splendor – and more important, the Harvest Man – Nicola led Jayce through the Cannery's streets until they reached a shithole bar called The Tears of Your Enemies. He now sat at a table, alone, while Nicola got drinks for the both of them.

As he'd waited, staring off into the distance, the memories had come flooding back, the images and sensations crashing into him like a tidal wave of information. For several moments he couldn't do anything other than let the recovered data settle in his mind. But as it did, he felt an increasingly strong mixture of rage and sorrow. The anger he felt was directed at himself. It was his fault that Emory had gotten caught up and eventually swallowed by the dark world of Shadow. After all, hadn't she inherited the Eye from him? He'd witnessed her corruption happening that afternoon in the basement of their home – his former home. He'd seen how Emory had given herself to the.... What had she called them? The Sanguinem Seminis. Yes, he'd freed her from them, but the memory had slipped away from him like quicksilver, and instead of trying to convince Emory that her fascination with Shadow and its creatures could only damage her, maybe even lead to her death, he had done nothing. And because he'd forgotten – just as he'd always done with any experience that threatened his fragile grasp on reality – he'd allowed the darkness inside Emory to grow. He was her father. He was supposed to guide her, teach her, and above all, *protect* her. And he had failed to do any of those things, just as he'd failed to keep his marriage together for her sake. And now she was dead.

You're forgetting something, Mother said. *When Emory was getting fucked by the cum-veins, you breathed a cloud of darkness to destroy them – just like You-Know-Who.*

"So what?" Jayce mumbled. He should've been horrified by that detail, should've worried that the Harvest Man had done something to change him that afternoon in the mall restroom when he'd been thirteen. But he couldn't bring himself to care. Emory was gone, and that was all that mattered.

"Here we go. Good for what ails you."

Jayce looked over at Nicola. He hadn't been aware of her sitting down opposite him, but she had, and she held a shot glass filled with multicolored liquid that reminded him of the way a puddle of gasoline looks when the light hits it just right. She had three more shots of the same stuff lined up on the table in front of her, and she'd gotten him four shots of the same iridescent booze. He hadn't noticed her put the glasses in front of him, and he made no move to touch any of them now.

Nicola downed the first shot, grimaced, then put the glass down gently with an unsteady hand. Whatever that shit was, Jayce thought, it must pack a hell of a kick. She drank the second shot, and this one must've gone down easier than the first, for she barely made a face this time.

His ribs still ached from his fight with Ohio Pig, and his hand hurt too, although the bleeding from the torn stitches had stopped. He picked up one of his shots and sniffed the alcohol suspiciously. It smelled like kerosene, only stronger.

You put a match to that crap, the explosion will take off your arm, Mother said.

He didn't bother replying, aloud or mentally. He was too exhausted – on all levels – to let her goad him.

He didn't trust whatever the hell was in his glass, and instead of drinking it, he looked around. When Nicola had brought him in, he'd expected to find another nightmarish collection of freaks, like in Crimson Splendor, but the bar – and the patrons – looked almost normal. Beer signs on the walls, along with a flat-screen TV playing a raunchy sex comedy, liquor bottles arranged on shelves – no vessels here – a couple of pool tables, a dartboard, a jukebox playing Seventies and Eighties rock, and wooden chairs and tables: scratched, scuffed, and old. He knew just how they must feel. Like any small funky bar where people went to sit alone and get drunk, the place smelled like a basement – musty and slightly damp. Normally, he would've found it depressing, but right now he found the smell a welcome one.

The people were a mix of ages and races, but none seemed particularly weird. Not until you took a closer look, that is. A young Asian guy at one of the pool tables had ears that were too small, and a slow trail of tears ran from his eyes without stopping. He didn't bother wiping the tears away, just let them fall wherever they would. Several people sat at the bar, and one of them – a heavyset middle-aged woman with short dark gray hair – quivered with full body tremors that came and went, some of them so strong they nearly knocked her off her seat. But no one had tentacles growing out of their shoulders or tusks jutting from their mouths, so that was a relief.

He wondered if this was the sort of bar his mother had come to when she'd been a Shadower. If this place was old enough, she might even have come here, maybe even sat at this table, in this very chair. He tried to imagine Valerie Lewis – the woman who'd become his obsessively overprotective mother – sitting here and doing shots that looked and smelled like gasoline. As hard as he tried, he just couldn't picture it.

When Nicola saw him looking around, she said, "This place is on the Outskirts, the edge of Shadow. Things are only slightly weird here. I thought you could use some normal right now."

"You thought right." He downed his drink in a single swallow. The liquid burned like fire going down, and he imagined it scouring flesh from his esophagus as it descended toward his stomach. As strong as the shit was, he wouldn't have been surprised if it ate its way through his body like industrial-strength acid and continued going through the chair, the floor, and then all the way to the center of the Earth. He put the empty down and reached for another. He didn't drink it right away, though. Too much of this stuff too soon and he'd end up unconscious on the floor. Although, considering everything that had happened tonight, that didn't sound like a bad idea.

He looked at Nicola. She was a bit blurry around the edges, but he was able to focus his gaze on her – more or less.

"We'll be safe from the Harvest Man here," she said. "He's a creature wholly of Shadow, and he won't venture this far from the heart of it."

Jayce hoped she was right, but how could she be certain? Before tonight, she'd believed the Harvest Man was only a dark fable. He glanced at the door, half-expecting the Harvest Man to enter at any moment and begin reducing the bar's patrons to mounds of ash.

"But we have more important things to deal with right now," Nicola said. "You know Emory isn't dead, right?"

Sudden anger cut through his numbness, and he whipped around to face Nicola.

"What the fuck are you talking about? We saw her goddamned *head*!"

His voice grew louder as he spoke until he was yelling. The other patrons in the bar turned to look at him for a moment, then turned away, as if his outburst wasn't interesting enough to hold their attention.

Nicola remained calm as she went on. "Do you remember what happened to the head after the Harvest Man picked it up?"

"I'll never forget it. He did something to it that made it liquefy." Once more he saw the Harvest Man get down on his hands and knees, saw the creature's long black tongue extend, heard the soft, wet sounds of it lapping at the viscous substance that had been his daughter's head.

"The Harvest Man didn't do that to her," Nicola said.

Jayce was so caught up in the horrible memory of the Harvest Man ingesting Emory's remains that it took him a moment to understand Nicola's words.

"It sure as hell wasn't a natural process!"

"A very *un*natural one," she said. "Both Ivory—" She stopped then, eyes glistening. She grabbed another shot glass, downed its contents, and then wiped tears from her eyes. "Sorry. Ivory and I weren't close, but I considered her a friend. At any rate, we both noticed patches of green skin on the head. Did you see them?"

He didn't want to revisit the image of Emory's severed head, but he forced himself to picture it anyway. He saw the Harvest Man holding it in his palm, saw the greenish patches on the flesh.

"Yeah."

"The head was already in the process of liquefying when Ohio Pig brought it into the club. It's a telltale sign of the Underborn. It's what happens when one of them dies."

Jayce almost stood, turned his back on Nicola, and walked away. He'd experienced so many bizarre things in the last day, been introduced to too many strange concepts and ideas, and he didn't think he could take any more. But he made himself remain seated and listened. For Emory.

"What are the Underborn?" he asked in a tired voice.

"I don't know much about them," Nicola confessed. "If Ivory were still alive...." She gave her head a single shake, as if to refocus her thoughts. "They show up in Shadow from time to time. They look like real people, walk and talk like them, but they're artificial. Robots made out of flesh and blood instead of metal and circuitry."

"So that *wasn't* Emory's head? It was the head of, what? Some kind of clone?"

Nicola nodded.

"Like I said, I don't know much about them. Mostly I've just heard rumors. They're supposed to act a little odd sometimes, as if they don't quite understand real people and aren't sure how to interact with them. Among Shadowers, if someone does or says something awkward, one of their friends might say, 'Don't be such an Underborn,' that kind of thing."

Jayce wondered what constituted *odd* behavior to a Shadower, but he decided not to ask.

"I don't know what the name means," Nicola said. "My best guess is it's a reference to them being less than human. They're *born* to be under *us*."

Jayce could feel himself starting to hope again, and that scared him as much, if not more, than anything that had happened to him in the Cannery so far. He wasn't sure he could take hoping that Emory was still alive, only to discover he was wrong again. The moment that Ohio Pig had tossed her head – a *duplicate's* head – onto the table had been the absolute worst moment of his life, and he didn't think he could go through another experience like that without it killing him. But he couldn't stop hope from rising within him. He was Emory's father. He loved her and he'd do anything to help her. Even if it meant his hope would turn on him and destroy him in the end.

"So you think one of these Underborn copied Emory somehow?"

"Yes. That's what they're supposed to do, at least according to the stories. But they're imperfect copies. That's why they dissolve shortly after they die. Whatever they're made of, it can't hold together without a lifeforce animating it."

"Where do you suppose Ohio Pig found Emory's doppelgänger? If we knew, it might give us a lead on where the real her is."

"He could've encountered the duplicate anywhere," Nicola said. "There's no way of knowing."

Jayce was sorry he'd attacked the man, not that the fucker hadn't deserved it for the way he'd tossed Emory's – no, the *Underborn's* – head onto the table in front of him, but because now the Pig wouldn't be motivated to help him anymore.

Jayce's anger had mostly left him now, and he felt a pleasant warmth from the shot he'd drank. It felt so good, in fact, that he took the opportunity to down his second. It didn't hit him as hard as the first, but the warmth inside him intensified, and he felt himself relax a little. Now that there was a possibility that Emory was still alive, his mind turned toward the memories that had come back to him while Nicola had been getting them drinks.

The first memory – the night he and Mackenzie had told Emory they were getting divorced – was the most painful memory he had. He sometimes thought that, if there was a Hell, for him it would be reliving that night over and over. The hurt he – and Mackenzie, too, of course – had done to that little girl could never be undone, not even in a realm like Shadow where dark miracles were not only possible but a common occurrence.

But the second memory, the one of coming home sick to find Emory in the basement engaging in some sort of occult sex act, that one had been hidden from him, and given how disturbing it was, he wished it had remained so. It was further evidence of Emory's seduction by Shadow – quite literally, in this case – but as bad as that was, the way he'd dealt with the Sanguinem Seminis was far more disturbing to him right now. He assumed the memory had been triggered by seeing the Harvest Man in Crimson Splendor, and more to the point, seeing the way he killed people – perhaps even *fed* on them – by breathing darkness. Jayce had done the same thing that day in the basement. He hadn't tried to, it had just happened. And then, as was usual with such experiences, he'd forgotten it almost immediately. He almost wished he could forget it again, forget everything that had happened since he'd set foot inside the CrazyQwik. But he needed to remember now, for Emory's sake, if no other reason.

Had the Harvest Man done something to him that day in the mall restroom, changed him somehow? Made him into a monster like him? Or at least kind of like him? Jayce had used the darkness inside him to help Emory, and as far as he knew, he'd never used it again. He had no way of knowing how many other memories he'd repressed over the years, and how many more might return to him when he least expected it.

The thought that he had the Harvest Man's darkness inside him terrified Jayce. It was like discovering his body was riddled with cancer. What would that darkness do to him, what had it *already* done? Nicola had told him that Shadow changed people. If he stayed in the Cannery searching for Emory, how much more would it change him?

"Something wrong?" Nicola asked.

"Hmm? Oh, nothing. Just thinking." He gave her a weak smile. "It's all a lot to process, you know?"

She nodded her understanding. Jayce didn't intend to tell her about what had happened in the basement or about what he feared lived inside him. He was afraid she wouldn't trust him if she knew, might even refuse to help him search for Emory anymore. He needed her help, and he didn't want to say anything that might scare her off. He knew that wasn't fair, that she deserved to know he could possibly be a threat to her. But finding Emory was his main – his only – responsibility, and he'd do whatever it took to fulfill it. So…he was a monster, at least partially. He decided to put that aside for now and concentrate on Emory. He'd had a lot of experience not thinking about uncomfortable things over the years, and if he wasn't going to forget that day in the basement again, he could at least do his best not to dwell on it. He had work to do.

"I can't believe the Harvest Man's real," Nicola said. She downed another shot, then she looked at him for a long moment before speaking again. "Do you think the Harvest Man showed up because of you? Trevor said you smelled like him." Her tone was casual, almost too much so, as if she were making a deliberate attempt not to sound suspicious.

"I think he might've been the being I encountered in the mall restroom when I was a kid. Maybe that's what Trevor smelled. Otherwise, I don't have any connection to him."

He thought of the single word the Harvest Man had 'spoken' to him.

Soon.

He thrust the thought from his mind and concentrated on keeping his expression neutral.

Leave it alone, Nicola, he mentally urged. *Please.*

She looked at him a few seconds longer, as if trying to gauge whether he was telling the truth. Finally, she smiled. "It was very brave of you to attack him like that. Suicidally stupid, but brave."

"Thanks – I think."

"Whatever the reason the Harvest Man appeared, I think we should keep an eye out for him – just in case for some reason he *is* following you."

"Agreed."

Who knows? Jayce thought. Maybe having some Shadow inside him might turn out to be an advantage. If it helped him find Emory, it would be worth it, even if it meant he would never be fully human again.

"Someone else we're going to have to watch out for is Ohio Pig," Nicola said.

"Why?" Jayce asked. "If what he killed was an Underborn masquerading as Emory, then he didn't hurt her, right? It was a real dick move of him to bring the head into Crimson Splendor, but...." He paused. "Oh. He's probably pissed that I broke his nose. And his teeth."

"You think? Right now, your name is at the top of his shit list, and I doubt it'll matter to him that you're not a Shadower. Sooner or later he's going to come looking for you, and when he does...."

"So I'll just have to hope for later," Jayce said. He wondered what the Pig would do if he knew of Jayce's connection to the Harvest Man. Scratch that. He didn't have to wonder. The lunatic would kill him without a moment's hesitation.

"What do we do next?" Jayce asked. "Ivory said she was going to ask around about Emory, but that's not going to happen now."

Nicola swallowed another shot. Her hands no longer shook and she was calmer than when they'd got here, but otherwise, she showed no sign that the alcohol affected her. How much was she used to drinking? Jayce had only had two shots of that stuff, and that was more than enough for him right now.

"We could try the bookstore," she said. And when Jayce gave her a blank look, she added, "Where Emory bought her copy of *The Book of Oblivion*."

Jayce remembered the bookmark folded in his wallet. He nodded.

"We can also try the place where she purchased the Pink Devil."

Jayce didn't like the sound of that, especially after what Emory's monstrous sex toy had done to him. But at this point he was willing to give almost anything a try. He nodded again, although this time with less enthusiasm.

"Let's go," he said.

Nicola finished the last of her shots, and then looked longingly at the ones Jayce hadn't drank. He thought for a moment that she might down those too, but she stood. Jayce did so as well, and the two of them headed for the door.

No one paid any attention to them as they left.

* ★ ★

As they stepped into the night, Nicola lost her balance. She grabbed hold of Jayce's arm to steady herself, smiled, and said, "Sorry," but she didn't let go of his arm. He didn't think too much of it. He figured the booze had caught up with her, that was all.

"I know a shortcut," she said, and before Jayce could react, she steered him into the alley next to the bar. After encountering the dog-eaters last night, Jayce was less than comfortable venturing into any of the Cannery's alleys. He started to tell Nicola this, but before he could speak, she turned and pushed him against the alley's brick wall.

At first, Jayce thought Nicola was attacking him, that she'd never really been interested in helping him find Emory, that she was just another predator hunting in Shadow, and she'd finally decided to take down her prey. But then she pressed her body against his, reached up to take hold of his head with both hands, leaned forward, and kissed him.

Jayce was caught off guard, and for several moments he did nothing. He didn't kiss her back, and he made no move to touch her. Her body felt hard against him, as if she worked out, and her hands held his head in a firm grip. Her woody acorn scent suffused his nostrils, along with the tang of sweat and arousal. Her lips were soft and moist, and she kissed him so gently it was like being touched by a cloud. Her tongue flicked out to gently brush his lips, but she didn't try to insert it into his mouth. His conscious mind might have been too shocked to respond to her, but his body had no difficulty doing so. His cock swelled and stiffened, achieving full erection faster than he had in years. He was still sore from the Pink Devil's ministrations, and the erection brought with it a dull ache that, in its own way, wasn't entirely unpleasant.

It had been so long since Jayce had kissed a woman that he'd almost forgotten what it was like, the simple but powerful feeling of closeness and connection. His hands moved to her waist, and he leaned into her and finally returned her kiss. It didn't go any further than that. He didn't move his hand to one of her breasts, and she didn't grab hold of his crotch and start kneading his swollen cock. They just kissed, and after several moments, Nicola gently pulled away, smiling.

"Shortcut, huh?" Jayce said.

Nicola's smile became a grin. "I lied."

She took his hand and led him back to the sidewalk, and they started walking north.

CHAPTER TEN

Nicola led him deeper into the Cannery, where the shadows became darker and seemed almost alive. As they walked, Jayce kept watch for both the Harvest Man and Ohio Pig. He saw no sign of either, though, and the two of them reached the bookstore without incident.

Tainted Pages had no sign or display window. Its name was painted on the door in simple black letters that were neat and precise. The door looked old, and Jayce expected it to creak when Nicola opened it, but it made no sound. They'd continued holding hands after leaving the alley, but now Nicola released his hand as she stepped inside the store. He felt a mild pang of disappointment and then chided himself for acting like a horny teenager. He followed Nicola inside.

The smell of decaying paper hit him first, so strong that he imagined he could feel particles of wood pulp scratching the inside of his nasal passages as he inhaled. The next thing that struck him was how cramped the place was. The shelves – all of which were crammed to overflowing with books, scrolls, and tablets made from paper, vellum, parchment, cloth, wax, and even stone – were set so close together that there was only room for one person at a time to move between them, and not a particularly big person at that. There were no signs to indicate separate sections, and no labels on the shelves, either. Many, if not most, of the works were written in languages other than English, but as near as Jayce could tell, none of them were alphabetized. The ceiling lights were uncovered low-watt bulbs that did little to illuminate the place, and he wondered how anyone was supposed to find books if there wasn't enough light to read by. Then again, he imagined the denizens of Shadow weren't overly fond of light anyway.

Nicola led the way through a twisting, turning maze of shelves, and although there were no stairs or obvious inclines or declines, Jayce had the sense that at times they were ascending or descending. They occasionally came across browsing customers, and they were forced to make their way awkwardly past them as best they could. As they walked, Jayce found himself thinking about the darkness that had emerged from the Harvest Man – the same darkness that had come from inside him when he'd discovered Emory in the basement being fucked by those *things*. What was it? Was it inside him right now, lying coiled somewhere deep within his being, quiescent, waiting patiently for when Jayce brought it forth again? And what if it decided to came out on its own? He hadn't willed it to emerge and attack the Sanguinem Seminis. It just *had*. The darkness hadn't made an appearance when the dog-eaters had hassled him or when he thought Ohio Pig had beheaded Emory. It hadn't even emerged when the Harvest Man showed up at Crimson Splendor. And if the darkness hadn't come forth any of those times, he figured the odds were good that it would remain sleeping inside him. Maybe the shock of seeing Emory being held in midair by the creatures she was fucking – coupled with how ill he had been – had lowered whatever defenses he had in place to keep the darkness from coming out. He needed to be careful, sure, but it wasn't as if he were a bomb ready to explode at any moment.

Keep telling yourself that, Mother said. *Repeat it often enough and you might even start to believe it.*

Jayce had no sense how long they traveled through the store, but eventually the space between the shelves began to widen, and they came to an open area containing a circular counter behind which a man stood. An old-fashioned cash register, the kind of thing with large keys to press down instead of buttons, rested on the counter next to him.

As Jayce and Nicola approached, the man gave them a smile and said, "Can I help you?"

"They call him the Bookman," Nicola whispered in Jayce's ear. "No one knows his real name."

The Bookman was in his forties, wore glasses, a light blue shirt with a blue striped tie, and sported a neatly groomed black mustache and goatee. He put Jayce in mind of a high school English teacher, the kind that all the kids liked, even if his class was boring.

"We're trying to find someone who's *lost*." Nicola put a slight emphasis on this last word, and the man nodded sagely. "We think she was a customer here. She purchased a copy of *The Book of Oblivion*."

The man chuckled. "Her and every other Shadower who's ever set foot in here."

The man's response irritated Jayce. There was nothing amusing about Emory being missing. But before he could say anything, he noticed something strange about the man's eyes. At first they were a normal brown — a *human* brown — but as Jayce watched they shifted to become cat's eyes, then lizard eyes, goat, fish, bird, insect.... They continued morphing every few seconds, running through the same sequence over and over. The effect was disquieting, and Jayce wondered if the man ran a store filled with mystic books because of his special eyes — *All the better to read you with, my dear* — or if his eyes were like that *because* of all the books he'd read, rare and dangerous as they were.

"What's her name?" the Bookman asked.

Nicola turned to Jayce to prompt him to answer, but he was transfixed by the man's ever-shifting eyes and didn't say anything at first. Nicola nudged him with her elbow, and he finally said, "Emory. Emory Lewis."

The Bookman thought for a moment. "Sorry. Doesn't ring a bell. You have a picture?"

Jayce showed the man Emory's picture on his phone, and he studied it for several seconds, eyes morphing from wolf to horse to fly. He looked away from the phone and shook his head.

"Sorry again, but I don't recognize her."

Jayce wanted to ask him to take another look at Emory's picture, but a customer had approached the counter and was standing behind them, waiting to be served. Jayce couldn't tell the person's gender. Whoever it was, they were short, almost child-sized, and wore a hoodie, jeans, and sneakers. The hood was up and the person kept his or her head down, so Jayce couldn't see any features. The customer held a large book that looked as if it were bound in uneven patches of tanned hide that had been stitched together.

Hide? Mother said. *Or skin?*

Written on the cover, or perhaps tattooed there, was the title: *The Insanirarium.* Jayce could feel wrongness coming off the book in waves, and he couldn't keep from shivering. Only then did he notice that the hands that held the book had very long fingers with twice the number of joints they should have.

"Thanks anyway," Nicola said to the Bookman, and then she turned to Jayce and said, "Let's go."

He didn't need any further encouragement.

They wended their way through the maze of shelves once more – Jayce trying not to think about how there would be no room to run, or defend themselves, if either the Harvest Man or Ohio Pig attacked them here. Soon, they were back outside on the sidewalk. A light rain had begun to fall while they'd been inside, but it wasn't much more than a sprinkle and was easily ignored.

Nicola looked at him and grinned.

"Next stop, sex shop."

She took his hand and they started walking. Jayce tried not to read anything into the way she'd grinned at him before they set off, but he couldn't help it after their kiss in the alley.

They walked two blocks before the rain began to pick up, and by the time they drew near the sex shop they were running. It was absurd, but Jayce almost felt like laughing. Here he was, searching for his daughter in a place like a madman's nightmare, *after* discovering that he'd been transformed by a darkness-breathing monster when he was thirteen, and he was happy – even if only for this moment – to be holding hands with a beautiful woman in the rain. Was he truly so lonely that this actually seemed *romantic* to him? Or was he crazier than he realized? Maybe both, he decided, but right then he didn't give a damn.

The sex shop was far less nondescript than Tainted Pages. A large neon sign jutted from the building's brick façade, spelling out the establishment's name in blazing vertical letters.

"The Hole Thing?" Jayce said aloud. He turned to look at Nicola. "Seriously?"

Without answering, she led him to the entrance – a glass door with iron bars covering it – and pushed it open. A bell jingled as they entered, and the door swung slowly shut behind them. They stood there for a moment, clothes sodden, both of them dripping onto the floor. Unlike Tainted Pages, this place was brightly lit by fluorescent light panels in the ceiling, and while there were numerous display shelves, the entire floor was a single open space, and there was plenty of room to walk around and browse. The separate sections were clearly labeled, with large signs with big red letters. *Lubes, Dildos, Vibrators, Sex Dolls, BDSM, Assplay, Watersports, Whips, Restraints, Leatherwear, Rubberwear,* and an extra-large section labeled *Fetish World!* complete with exclamation point.

Jayce wasn't the most worldly of men when it came to sex, but he didn't consider himself a prude by any means. Still, there were several section labels for sexual proclivities he was unfamiliar with: *Autopsychotic Degradation, Molecular Bestiality, Genital Deconstruction....* But worst of all were the smaller signs attached to the shelves, each of which contained a different, but equally terrible, pun. *Urine for a treat! I wouldn't wish that on my worst enema! Dildon't miss out on this deal!*

Everything in the store – aside from the products on display – was white. Ceiling, walls, floor, shelves.... It reminded Jayce of how the future was portrayed in Seventies films: large empty spaces where everything was white, white, white, and there wasn't a single scuff mark or speck of dirt to be found anywhere. The smell of the place was far different from the rank miasma of sweat, semen, and desperation he'd expected. It smelled like a hospital, as if every surface had recently been scrubbed with bleach and antiseptic. He could already feel his sinuses beginning to burn from the chemicals in the air.

The Hole Thing was busier than Tainted Pages, which given its wares was only to be expected. A dozen people walked around or stood in front of displays, some alone, some in pairs, some in groups of three or more. Some were quiet and serious, giving off a definite creeper vibe, while others laughed with lighthearted amusement or awkward embarrassment at whatever products they were checking out. Men and women were represented in more or less equal numbers, and their ages ranged from early twenties to a foot-and-a-half in the grave. They all had hints of what Jayce had started to think of as being Shadow-touched. Altered features, distorted bodies, strange behavioral tics.... But as near as he could tell, none of the people were dangerous. He wondered if that was merely wishful thinking on his part, or if he was actually beginning to learn his way around Shadow, at least a little.

"What do we do now?" Jayce asked. "Start going up to people and asking if they've seen Emory?"

"It would make more sense to check with the owners first," Nicola said. "They don't sell Pink Devils to just anyone. The things are *way* too dangerous."

Jayce looked around, but he didn't see any signs indicating

Pink Devils were sold here. Nicola must've guessed what he was thinking, for she said, "They keep the *really* hardcore stuff downstairs, on the pro level."

"And how do you know that?" Jayce asked.

Nicola gave him a gentle hip bump. "How do you think?"

He smiled and tried not to think about all the things Emory must've done to qualify for the 'pro level'. If she'd summoned the Sanguinem Seminis when she was fifteen, how much more – and worse – had she done in the years since? She was an adult and he knew her sex life wasn't any of his business and that it wasn't his place to judge her, but he feared what her exposure to the people and things of Shadow – and beyond – might have done to her.

But before they could begin their search for an employee, one approached them. He wore gray coveralls and black shoes, and he carried a plastic bucket in one hand and a mop in the other.

Nicola glanced down at the puddles of water around their feet, then looked up and smiled apologetically. "Sorry about that."

"No problem. Rainwater's not the worst thing I clean up around here, believe me."

Jayce and Nicola stepped aside to give the man room to work. Jayce tried not to stare as he put the bucket on the floor and started mopping up the puddles. He was medium height, on the stocky side, with black stubble on his head. No facial hair, not even a hint. His lips, nose, and ears were small, almost underdeveloped, and his skin color was strangely indeterminate, sometimes looking lighter, sometimes darker, depending on how the light hit him as he moved. His voice was soft and higher-pitched, like a boy who hadn't been through puberty yet, and he spoke without any particular tone or inflection. Taken together, these characteristics made it difficult to guess his age. He could've been anywhere from mid-teens to mid-fifties. *Maybe he's a eunuch,* Jayce thought. He'd always had the impression that eunuchs were something that had gone out with the Middle Ages, but maybe not. And even if they were a thing of the past, that didn't mean anything in the Cannery. This place ran by its own set of demented rules.

"You might be able to help us, Ronnie," Nicola said.

Jayce looked at her, and he was surprised to see how unattractive she appeared in this garish light. She was pale, hair wet and scraggly from the rain, features boyish, figure all straight lines and hard angles. He thought of how she'd kissed him in the alley, and the memory sent a shudder of revulsion through him, accompanied by a twist of nausea. How could he have ever let her do that to him?

Nicola looked at him then, and her lips pursed in distaste. She averted her gaze quickly, as if she couldn't stand the sight of him. The feeling was mutual, Jayce thought.

He was so caught up in the disgust he felt toward Nicola that he almost forgot why they had come here. He took his phone from his pocket, brought up the picture of Emory, and held the device out for Ronnie to look at it.

"My daughter's been missing for two weeks," Jayce said. "I know she…was a customer. Do you remember seeing her?"

The man stopped mopping and leaned in close to get a good look at Emory's picture. He stared at the image for several moments, the soft, almost girlish skin of his brow furrowed in concentration.

"She *does* look familiar," he said after a time. "But we get a lot of customers in here." He looked away from the phone and met Jayce's gaze. "Do you know what she was into?"

Before Jayce could answer, Nicola said, "Pink Devil."

Ronnie's eyes widened.

"Not everyone can handle one of those babies. We keep that kind of thing downstairs, but I don't have much to do with any of that stuff. My wife's in charge down there. She might be able to help you."

"Thanks," Jayce said. He pocketed his phone and he and Nicola moved off. Their clothes were still wet, but at least they weren't dripping as much now. As soon as they'd put some distance between themselves and Ronnie, Jayce felt a warm flush come over him. He looked at Nicola, and she was beautiful once more, and the way her wet dress clung to her body made her look sexy as hell.

Nicola saw him staring at her and laughed.

"It felt weird, didn't it? Ronnie is antisexual. He projects some kind of energy that suppresses other people's sex drives, to the point where they begin to find the very idea of sex, or anything related to it, repulsive."

Jayce glanced back over his shoulder at Ronnie. It *had* felt strange, like for a brief time a fundamental part of himself had ceased to exist. It was as if, in an emotional sense, the world had lost all its color and become dull, gray, and cold.

"Seems a quality like that wouldn't be good for business."

"Once he's no longer near you, your sex drive returns full force, making you more horny than you were before. You're even more inclined then to buy stuff and rush home to try it out." She smiled. "I'm feeling it right now, and I bet you are too."

Jayce gave her a strained smile. "No comment."

They walked through the store until they reached an unmarked door in the back. It was painted black and had a highly polished chrome knob. Before Jayce could ask, Nicola said, "It doesn't need a sign. When people are ready for this level, they find it."

Jayce reached for the knob, but Nicola put her hand on his wrist to stop him before he could open the door. Her touch was electric, and he felt his cock stiffen. He told himself the response was an aftereffect of whatever strange ability Ronnie possessed, but that didn't make his reaction feel any less powerful.

"Ronnie's wife Sela is his exact opposite," Nicola said. "He suppresses sex drives, but she *enhances* them. The effect can be overwhelming if you're not used to it."

"I'll keep thinking about cold showers," he said.

Nicola let her hand linger on his wrist a moment longer. Then she removed it, he opened the door, and they began heading down a flight of creaky wooden stairs.

★   ★   ★

Nicola closed the door behind her just as someone entered the shop. The bells rang softly, and as the man stepped inside, Ronnie looked up from his mopping.

"Can I help you?" he asked in his toneless voice.

The man – nose bent and swollen, chunk of flesh gouged from his cheek, eyes blazing with hatred – smiled, displaying a mouthful of broken and missing teeth.

"Thanks, but I plan on helping myself."

★   ★   ★

Jayce could feel it before they were halfway down the poorly lit stairs. A pressure in the back of his head, beads of sweat appearing on his skin, a tingling in his balls. Next came the odor, a thick, rank smell, like something that would waft forth from the lion enclosure at the zoo. His cock didn't so much harden as become instantly engorged, tight flesh throbbing in concert with his pulse.

"You weren't kidding, were you?" he said, voice low and husky.

"Nope." Nicola's voice sounded normal enough, if a bit strained, and Jayce wondered if that was because she'd had experience resisting Sela's power or because – despite their earlier kiss – she wasn't really attracted to him.

He pictured himself grabbing hold of her, hiking up her skirt, tearing off her panties – assuming she wore any – unzipping his pants to free his cock and fucking her from behind right here on the stairs. He'd pound her so hard that by the time he was finished, she wouldn't be able to walk straight for a week. *That* would show her.

A different image flashed through his mind then, two of the Pink Devil's tendrils wrapped around his wrists while a third slithered into his pants. He recalled how trapped he'd felt, how helpless and violated, and those memories blunted his heightened state of sexual arousal. More, they made him feel guilty for his fantasy about Nicola. Not guilty for imagining having sex with her, but for the anger bordering on rage that had accompanied the fantasy.

He gave Nicola a sideways glance, as if afraid she was somehow aware of what he'd imagined and the emotions that had come along with it. But she looked straight ahead, not meeting his gaze. He realized then that she was concentrating, doing her best to manage the feelings Sela's power stirred in her. He thought again of the rage he had felt a moment ago. Had it been entirely an effect of Sela's influence, or had her power only intensified something that was already inside him and brought it closer to the surface? The Harvest Man's darkness – or at least some measure of it – dwelled within him, and it had emerged once. Once he remembered, that was. Maybe the rage he'd experienced was a precursor to the darkness emerging again. By going down to the store's lower level to talk with Sela, he might be putting her, her customers, and most of all Nicola, in danger.

Oh, for Degradation's sake! Mother said. *You might be a monster, but you're a goddamn wishy-washy one. If you want to find Emory, quit being so fucking sensitive and get on with it!*

For the first time in his life, Valerie had actually given him some good advice. Even more shocking, he decided to take it.

The stairs ended at another door exactly like the one on the upper level. Jayce opened it – finding the knob warm and a bit sticky – and he and Nicola stepped through. The atmosphere on the other side of the door was so sexually charged that for an instant Jayce experienced a wave of vertigo and his vision blurred. The worst of the dizziness passed after several seconds, and when his vision cleared, he got his first good look at The Hole Thing's lower level.

He'd expected something dark, dim, and dungeon-like, but it was as brightly lit as the upper level. The walls were mirrored, intensifying the light to the point where Jayce had to squint to keep his eyes from hurting. The walls formed a large curved circle, and in the center was a round structure that rose all the way to the ceiling. It was made of highly polished dark wood, and there were curved doors spaced at regular intervals. Mounted on the wall next to the doors were various devices, none of which Jayce recognized, but it didn't take a genius to intuit their purpose. These were sex toys, but they were as far removed from simple dildos and vibrators as a laptop computer was from a child's first book of numbers. The devices were fashioned from different substances – plastic, metal, wood, leather, and what looked to Jayce like actual flesh. They were shaped in enigmatic, even alien configurations that made their specific functions impossible to guess at, but they all shared the same basic purpose: to take their users to the highest level of sexual fulfillment that was physically possible without killing them. And who knows? Maybe even past that point and back again.

Fewer people browsed down here than upstairs, and while Jayce expected them to be more obviously into kink than those on the upper level, they didn't look all that different from other people he'd seen in the Cannery. To be sure, several of the customers were tatted and pierced and wore their share of leather, but most were more nondescript and wore T-shirts, light jackets over dress shirts or blouses, along with jeans or slacks. A few were alone, but most were couples or trios, mixed gender or same gender, talking about the devices' different features and their pros and cons without bothering to keep their voices low. These people obviously felt no embarrassment or shame about being here and didn't give a damn if anyone heard their conversations.

He tried to imagine Emory walking down the stairs and entering this level, slowly circling the displays and pondering the devices for sale. Had she come here on her own or with a lover? What had it been about the Pink Devil that made her say to herself, *This is the one. Definitely.*

Jayce became aware of muffled sounds then. Buzzes, whirrs, and clicks mingled with soft moans and sharp cries. He realized the sounds were coming from behind the doors. He looked at Nicola and she said, "Those are demonstration rooms. Here, you get to try it before you buy it."

Knowing people were right now behind those doors – less than a dozen feet from where he and Nicola stood – having sex with one or more of the sinister-looking devices on display was disturbing enough, but the realization brought with it the memory of what it had felt like to be violated by the Pink Devil. Nausea gripped his stomach, and his body started trembling. He still felt the effect of Sela's power, and his highly charged libido clashed with the sensations brought on by the flashback to his rape earlier that evening. He found himself caught between two intensities – a nearly overwhelming desire for sex and an utter revulsion of it.

Nicola took his hand then, maybe because she sensed how he was feeling or maybe due to Sela's influence. Either way, he was grateful for the contact. It helped calm him and focus his thoughts. And while his feelings of revulsion and helplessness didn't vanish, they became more manageable. He squeezed Nicola's hand and gave her a grateful smile, and she smiled back.

"Welcome to the Funhouse."

A woman approached them, and Jayce knew it was Sela even before he had a clear impression of what she looked like. He felt her power precede her as a tidal wave of pure lust that overwhelmed everything in its path. The energy she projected, however, didn't match her appearance. He had expected her to be some sort of exaggerated sexual goddess – tall, long-legged, wasp-waisted, big-breasted...an imposing presence, part sex-kitten, part dominatrix. But there was nothing overtly sexual about her. She wore a white sweater over a floral-print dress, with brown open-toed shoes that had modest heels. She was barely five feet tall, round-faced, with curly black hair. She wore no makeup or jewelry, and her nails were short and ragged, as if she chewed them. She flashed them a smile as she drew near, and while her upper row of teeth was straight, the bottom was slightly crooked. Like her husband, her race was impossible to guess. She seemed a combination of them all, as if she came from a future where humanity had blended to the point where race no longer mattered. She was on the plain side of pretty, but Jayce had never wanted to fuck anyone more in his life. He felt a sudden surge of resentment toward Nicola for holding his hand, for claiming him as hers in front of Sela. Jayce wanted the woman to know he was single and more than available. He almost jerked his hand from Nicola's grasp, but Sela stopped, took a couple steps backward, and the urge diminished. It was still present, but Jayce could resist it now.

Sela smiled at him. "I'm not psychic, but I saw you tense up, so I figured it would be best if I kept some distance between us." Her voice was soft and throaty, and it felt like warm honey in his ears.

"Thanks," Jayce said, the word coming out as a hesitant croak.

Sela's smile took on a teasing edge. "I take it this is your first time here?"

Jayce didn't trust himself to speak, so he nodded.

He wondered why two people as different as Ronnie and Sela would marry. Given their opposite energies, it was like they were batteries, one which ran on AC and one on DC. But then he realized their different energies didn't clash so much as leaven one another. Ronnie's anti-sex energy brought Sela's ultra-sex energy down to normal, manageable levels, and her power gave Ronnie an actual sex drive. Only with each other could they have a normal sexual relationship.

"There's no sales pressure here," Sela said. "Look around, and if there's something you'd like to take for a spin, let me know and I'll open a demonstration room for you."

"We didn't come here to buy," Nicola said. "We're looking for someone."

Jayce took that as his cue. He showed Emory's picture to Sela, careful to hold his phone out as far as he could so she wouldn't have to come any closer to him than necessary.

"Her name's Emory—"

Sela interrupted him before he could go any further.

"Pink Devil!" she said. "She bought one a month ago. I remember because she insisted I show her the most extreme product we carry, and they don't come more extreme than Pink Devils."

Jayce felt a surge of hope, but he reminded himself not to get carried away just yet.

"She's my daughter. I'd appreciate anything you could tell me that might give me an idea where to look for her. Anything at all."

"I don't know that it'll be of much use, but I can tell you that she returned here a couple weeks ago to ask me advice on how to get the most out of her Pink Devil. They can be sensitive and somewhat volatile devices, and operating them is often more art than science."

Sela's words seemed too good to be true. He'd finally found someone who'd actually *seen* Emory – and from the sound of it, not long before she'd disappeared. He was so excited that he forgot about Sela's powerful aura of sexuality and stepped closer to her.

"Can you tell me what you talked about with her? Did she say anything else that wasn't connected to the Pink Devil? How did she act? Did she seem worried or in distress?"

The questions poured out before he could stop them. But before Sela could begin answering, someone shouted from the stairwell, the voice muffled but still audible from behind the closed door.

"I'm coming for you, Jayce! And this time no goddamn boogeyman is going to save you!"

Jayce recognized Ohio Pig's voice. He exchanged a look with Nicola, as if to ask her, *What do we do now?*

You should've killed that asshole when you had the chance, Mother said.

Jayce couldn't argue with that.

Nicola turned to Sela. "Put us in one of the rooms – please!"

Sela didn't hesitate. She led them around the Funhouse until she came to a particular door. There was no outer sign that it was unoccupied, but Sela removed a set of keys from her sweater pocket and quickly unlocked the door. Inside was a small space not much larger than a department store dressing room. The walls and ceiling were painted black, and a leather upholstered bench was the only item inside. The floor was concrete and had a slight depression, in the center of which was a drain. There were sprinklers on the ceiling – four of them – and from the astringent smell in the room, Jayce knew that the sprinklers didn't release water, but rather some kind of cleaning chemical used to sanitize the room – and likely the device being tested as well as the customers themselves – before its next use.

"How romantic," he muttered.

Nicola quickly stepped inside and pulled him after her.

"Please don't tell him we're here," she said to Sela.

The woman pressed an index finger to her lips, winked, and then closed and locked the door. There was no lock on the inside, and Jayce didn't like it. It made him feel trapped. But he liked the idea of Ohio Pig opening the door to find him inside even less.

Jayce and Nicola stood behind the door, listening. They heard the sound of the door to the lower level slamming open, almost as if Ohio Pig had kicked it in.

"Jayce? Jayce Lewis! Where the fuck are you? Come on out and face me like a man!"

The Pig's voice was thick, almost as if he had a cold, and Jayce put this down to the man's broken nose. His missing teeth created a slight whistle when he spoke, but neither of these factors made him sound any less intimidating. If anything, he sounded more crazy and dangerous than ever.

"Can I be of assistance?" Sela asked, and Jayce pictured the woman walking up to Ohio Pig, bringing him into her sexually charged aura. How would the man react? Would he be overwhelmed and thrown off guard, or was he so filled with fury and hate that her power would have no sway over him?

"You can help me by staying out of my fucking way," the Pig snapped. There was a rustle of cloth and a soft *oomph,* and Jayce guessed that the Pig had shoved Sela to the side.

"Hey, you can't do that to her!"

Jayce assumed this was one of the customers. The voice was male, and he sounded pissed. Jayce heard the sound of boots clomping, but he didn't know if Ohio Pig was charging the man who'd shouted at him or if it was the other way around. Either way, some shit was about to go down. But as he was listening closely, trying to picture what was happening outside, Nicola stepped up behind him, pressed her body against his, reached around and began massaging his cock. With the arrival of Ohio Pig, his dick had softened – nothing sexy about *that* maniac's appearance – but as soon as Nicola started working it, it swelled and hardened almost instantly. He knew his body's response had more to do with being near Sela than any real desire on his part, and now was definitely *not* the time to give in to sexual urges that, while having a basis in reality, had been artificially enhanced. He knew this intellectually, but he couldn't stop himself from turning around, taking Nicola in his arms and kissing her.

After that it was like a dam had broken. The two of them began pawing each other like animals, kissing, sucking, biting…. They tore at each other's clothes, desperate to get at the flesh beneath but so caught up in animalistic passion that they couldn't remember how to properly disrobe. Cloth tore, buttons popped off and clattered to the floor. The next thing Jayce knew, Nicola was lying naked on the leather bench, legs spread wide and awaiting him. As if coming to him across a great distance, he heard shouting, punches being thrown, cries of pain and anger. A nearly dormant part of his mind worried that he couldn't afford to ignore those sounds because they meant danger was near. But he was unable to stop himself, and he stepped forward then plunged his ramrod-stiff cock into Nicola's warm wetness, and then everything in the world ceased to exist except the overpowering need to pound himself into Nicola again and again.

An image came to Jayce's mind then, a pair of insects copulating like mindless machines, oblivious to the gigantic foot that was coming toward them from above, ready to flatten them into paste. But instead of making him pause, the image only made him thrust faster, as if he were determined to finish before the giant foot could descend upon them.

Nicola's eyes were closed, her lips parted, head thrown back. She squeezed her right breast with one hand while she worked her clit with the other. Her legs were in the air, and Jayce gripped her ankles to support them as well as give him more leverage for thrusting.

I understand it's been a long time since you had sex, Mother said, *but if you two keep on going like this, there's a good chance you'll end up fucking yourselves to death.*

Valerie's mental voice hit him like a splash of cold water, and while it wasn't enough to make him stop thrusting into Nicola, he did slow down.

"We. Have. To. Stop." He grunted out these words in time with his thrusts.

Nicola didn't open her eyes, didn't take her hands from her body as she replied, "I know."

Still they kept going. Jayce's body picked up the tempo once more until he was thrusting as fast and hard as he could. Sweat coated both their bodies, and their breaths came in sharp gasps.

Outside, the situation was getting worse. The shouts had become louder, and Jayce could hear the sound of scuffling footsteps, as if two or more people were struggling to knock each other down. There was a loud thud, and Jayce knew someone – Ohio Pig or one of the people trying to stop him – had been slammed against one of the demonstration room doors. Judging by how loud the sound was and the way the impact made their own door rattle, Jayce guessed whoever it was had hit close by, maybe only a couple doors away.

There wasn't much time left.

Nicola had been making little *uh-uh-uh* sounds as they pushed against each other, but now these became higher-pitched cries. The sound of them excited Jayce even more, and he began thrusting furiously. He heard a noise that was half growling, half groaning, and he realized it was coming from his own throat.

This isn't much different than what happened to you with the Pink Devil, Mother said. *You're not doing this because you chose to. You're doing it because you're being compelled.*

Jayce ignored her. At that moment, it didn't matter to him why this was happening. He was caught in a force he couldn't resist, and all he could do was ride it out to the end.

He felt a hot tingling spread throughout his lower abdomen as he began to build toward orgasm. That's when he heard the first gunshot. His body didn't react to it – at that point he doubted anything short of a nuclear blast could have made him stop fucking. He heard another shot, then a third, followed by the sound of people running. Doors slammed open, and Jayce knew the other demonstration rooms were emptying out, their occupants perhaps more accustomed to Sela's power and thus able to resist it better. Was anyone hurt? Or dead? How many more seconds would it be before Ohio Pig kicked in this door and starting shooting at them? Would they finally stop fucking at that point, or would they keep at it, blood spurting from gunshot wounds like red cum?

Nicola orgasmed first. Jayce felt her spasm around his cock, grip it like a fist, and the sensation brought him to climax. They cried out their release in unison, and Jayce's own orgasm was so intense that for an instant his vision went black and his legs threatened to give out. He was on the verge of losing consciousness, but he managed to hold on. His exertions slowed, but he continued thrusting, determined to give Nicola every spurt of his semen.

He wasn't surprised when he heard the sound of a boot slamming into the door. Neither of them had been quiet as they fucked, and the sounds of their passion had led Ohio Pig right to them. The lock broke and the door burst open on the second kick, and Jayce pulled out of Nicola and turned around, his cock shooting one last ejaculation into the air. Ohio Pig stood in the doorway, holding a 9 mm Glock and grinning as best he could with his damaged mouth.

"Looks like you two are going to get to go out with a bang – literally *and* figuratively!"

He raised his gun and aimed it point blank at Jayce's chest. His lust spent – not to mention a weapon being pointed at him – Jayce's mind cleared instantly. He knew there was no way he could rush forward and try to grab the 9 mm from the Pig before the man could shoot him. He could stand between the Pig and Nicola and shield her, but as soon as the Pig dropped him, Nicola would be vulnerable. The best Jayce could do was delay her death by a few more seconds. There was nothing he could do except stand there and wait to feel bullets tear through his flesh.

Not true, Mother said. *There's one thing you could do.*

He thought back to that day in the basement, when he'd discovered Emory having sex with the Sanguinem Seminis. He'd brought forth the Harvest Man's darkness that day, although it had come to him unbidden. Could he call it now, on purpose? He had no idea how he might accomplish this – or what consequence summoning the power might have – but he had no choice. He had to try.

He pictured what the cloud of darkness had looked like as he'd breathed it out on that long-ago day, and as he did so, he tried to remember what it had felt like inside him. He remembered a cold stirring deep in his being, as if a mass of serpents coiled around each other. He remembered that writhing cold rising upward, moving from his stomach into his throat, over his tongue and past his teeth to be released into the open air. In his mind, he saw the Harvest Man's obsidian eyes gazing into his, and he heard a whispered word.

Soon.

He felt nothing inside, and he knew that this time – for whatever reason – he was unable to summon the darkness that lived inside him, and because of this failure, he and Nicola were going to die.

Ohio Pig lowered his gaze to Jayce's cock.

"Looks like you got yourself a drooper there. I wonder if I can hit it before it goes all the way soft."

He lowered the barrel of his gun until it pointed at Jayce's rapidly deflating dick. Jayce felt a sudden wave of sexual energy then, and despite the situation, his cock stiffened once more. The Pig must have felt the same energy, for he turned around, but he was too slow. Sela jammed a stun gun to the side of his neck and released a charge. There was a crackling sound, and Ohio Pig's body bucked and seized. Sela kept the charge going, and the Pig's hand sprung open and the Glock dropped to the floor. He collapsed, and Sela followed him down, keeping the stun gun in constant contact with his flesh until he lay on the ground, eyes closed and body twitching. She deactivated the stun gun then and straightened.

Nicola had remained lying on the leather bench this whole time, Jayce's cum dripping out of her, but now she stood and walked to Jayce's side.

"Thank you *so* much, Sela!" she said. "I thought for sure he was going to kill us."

Sela gazed down upon the Pig's semi-conscious body with disgust. "I *know* he would have. He killed two of my customers on his way to you."

"I'm so sorry," Nicola said.

Jayce felt self-conscious and exposed standing naked before Sela with a raging hard-on, but Nicola seemed perfectly comfortable in her nakedness.

"It's not your fault," Sela said. "But on the bright side, having the Pig means we can make an extra delivery now."

Jayce had no idea what the woman was talking about. He looked at Nicola, but it was clear from her expression that she was as confused as he was.

His cock began to soften once more, and he felt the sexual pressure Sela exuded ease. A moment later he understood why, when Ronnie appeared behind his wife. Their two powers were balancing each other.

"It's a hell of a mess down here, babe," he said. His voice was deeper now, more masculine.

Sela smiled and touched his cheek. "It's *always* a mess of one kind or another down here."

He smiled back. "True. Let's take care of these two so I can start mopping up."

Jayce saw that Ronnie also held a stun gun. He raised it now and the two of them stepped into the demonstration room.

CHAPTER ELEVEN

Jayce wakes abruptly, fully aware, as if he's a machine and someone has pushed his ON button. One instant he's not conscious, the next he's almost hyper-conscious. Sometime during the night he kicked off his covers and since he sleeps in a T-shirt and underwear, he feels chilled. It's mid-July, but his mother likes to keep the air at sixty degrees during the summertime, which means he's always cold. He'll be heading to college next month, and one of the things – the many things – he's looking forward to about living on campus is that he'll be able to control the temperature in his dorm room. No longer will he have to bake in winter and freeze in summer.

Faint light filters between the slight gap in his curtains, and he knows it's nearly dawn. He guesses it's around five a.m., and the dim early morning light has transformed his room into a hazy collection of shadowy forms – dresser, bookcase, study desk with typewriter, stereo and speakers, laundry hamper with a mound of clean clothes on the floor next to it that he hasn't gotten around to putting away yet. But these ordinary objects are only indistinct shapes at the moment, and he supposes they could be anything, really. Anything at all.

There's an odd combination of smells in the air – sour-sweet mixed with the faint scent of strawberries, and the stale odor of coffee breath and cigarettes. He recognizes the strawberries as the shampoo his mother uses, and before she can speak, he turns his head and sees her shadowy form sitting at his bedside. She's moved the chair from his desk, he realizes, and seeing her there surprises him and makes him acutely aware that he doesn't have any pants on. She's his mother, but he's eighteen – long past the point of being unselfconscious about nudity, even partial nudity – and he sits up quickly, reaches down to grab the covers bunched at the foot of the bed, and draws them up to his waist.

"You don't have to hide from me, Jayce. You can't even if you want to, so there's no point in trying."

Her voice is flat and toneless. The early morning light doesn't penetrate far enough into his room to reveal her features. She's a smear of shadow, an outline filled with darkness. Something is wrong, *seriously* wrong, but he can't bring himself to ask her what it is. He's too afraid to speak.

"You never knew your father, but I'm not sorry about that. It was a mistake for me to be with him." A dry rasp of a chuckle. "Mistake. *That's* an understatement, huh?"

Jayce wonders if she's drunk. She enjoyed an occasional glass of wine at night, but lately she's been drinking more than that. One glass became two, then three, then the entire bottle. But he doesn't smell any alcohol on her, and that scares him even more. He would understand if she's drunk. But if she's acting like this while she's sober, that's really fucked up.

"I was different back when I met your father. I liked danger back then. Or at least what I thought was danger. Couldn't get enough of it. Booze, drugs, sex – the kinkier, the better – vandalism, shoplifting, minor arson a couple times.... Penny-ante shit, but I thought I was one hardcore bitch." She pauses, sighs. "But I didn't know dick."

He's heard his mother cuss before – usually when she's really upset – but nothing like this. It's like she's become a different person. Or maybe she's stopped concealing a part of herself that she usually keeps hidden from him.

"I'd always been able to see things...things that no one else could see. Strange, dark things. I didn't talk to anyone about what I saw. Even as a child, I knew people would think I was crazy if I said anything. Mostly I did my best to ignore the weird stuff. But when I was in my twenties and running wild, I started seeing more things, more often. And I met people who could see the same things. And then I discovered a whole new dark playground to run around in."

He's starting to worry that his mother's mind has snapped. The things she's saying don't make any sense. And yet, there's something strangely familiar about her words.

"Once you were born, I decided to change my ways. I gave up my life in the shadows, got a job working the cash register at a car parts place, and decided I was going to be the best mother to you that I could. I wanted to raise you right, so you wouldn't make the same mistakes I did. And I prayed that you wouldn't see the dark things of the world like I could. And as the years went by and you started to grow up, you seemed like a normal little boy, and I was so relieved. I wanted to keep you safe, wanted to make sure you weren't exposed to anything bad – anything dangerous or traumatic that might trigger your ability, if you had it. I guess I went a little overboard in that department. Maybe a lot. But all I wanted to do was protect you. And I thought I'd succeeded. But now I know I was wrong. You saw things, but you were able to make yourself forget them. Shit, that's a skill I wished I'd developed. If I had...." She shakes her head, dismissing that line of thought. "Do you remember going with me to the doctor yesterday?"

The sudden shift in topic catches him by surprise.

"Huh?"

"My plantar fasciitis was acting up, and the doctor wanted to give me a steroid shot. Because it was in my right foot, you drove me."

"Yeah, I remember."

And he does. Kind of. The details are fuzzy, though. He knows he took her, but he can't summon up any specific memories of the trip. No sights or sounds, nothing that either of them might have said. He can't recall any of the businesses or landmarks they drove past.

His mother is silent for several moments before she speaks again. More light has filtered into his room now, and he's able to see her face. She looks sad, deeply so, as if her soul is filled with sorrow. Her eyes glisten as if she might cry, but she gives him a small smile.

"After we got to the doctor's and were sitting in the waiting room, do you remember what was crawling in the corner of the ceiling?"

He has a flash of memory then, an image of something dark with far too many legs and eyes that glimmered with emerald light. Then it's gone, as quickly as it came, and he begins to forget it almost as fast. Before the memory, such as it is, can leave him entirely, his mother's left hand lashes out and strikes him hard across the face.

"Do you *remember*?" she says, her voice little more than a hiss.

"Yes." He reaches up to rub his stinging cheek. He's afraid, yes, but he's angry too.

Her hand moves back to her lap again, and she nods slowly, as if he just confirmed something important. "It was nasty-looking, wasn't it? Of course, I've seen worse in my time." She pauses, then adds in a whisper so soft he can barely hear, "Lots worse."

She doesn't speak for a while after that, and while the two of them sit there in silence, full dawn arrives. Enough light now comes through the gap in Jayce's curtains to reveal that his mother's left hand — the one that struck him so hard across the face — is empty. But her right hand, which hangs at her side past the seat of the chair, is not. She holds a large kitchen knife, gripping it so tight that her knuckles are white and her hand trembles.

The memory of the thing in the corner of the doctor's ceiling is mostly gone once again, but the emotions that accompanied it linger. Confusion and fear, primarily, but the fear he experienced while gazing upon the thing that only he and his mother could see is nothing compared to the terror of seeing that knife in his mother's hand.

"Mom? Are you going to hurt me?" His voice is small, higher-pitched than usual. A little boy's voice. No, a *baby's*. Jayce feels ashamed, but that's nothing next to his fear.

His mother speaks as if she hasn't heard him.

"I'd hoped you wouldn't be like me. Wouldn't be like *him*. But you are, aren't you? And you're only going to get worse." She gazes at the strip of sunlight between the curtains as she says this, and then she turns to look at him and frowns. "Did you say something?"

His mouth feels dry as sunbaked earth. He has to swallow a couple times before he can make his voice work again.

"I asked if you're going to hurt me."

Valerie's face breaks into a wide, amused grin, and the sight of it causes him to relax a little. *Maybe this is just some kind of weird joke*, he thinks. Or maybe his mother was sleepwalking or something and is finally starting to wake up.

"I'm not going to hurt you, sweetheart." Her grin remains firmly in place as she gets to her feet and raises the knife above her head. "I'm going to kill you."

Her grin never falters as she brings the knife down in a swift, vicious arc. Instinctively, Jayce rolls away from the strike, and the blade strikes his mattress and sinks in all the way to the handle. Jayce sleeps in a small twin bed, the same one he's had since he was little. There's not much room on it, and he rolls away from the knife strike so fast that he falls off the mattress and onto the floor. He lands on his back, the impact knocking the breath out of him. He senses more than hears his mother rush around the bed toward him, and although he knows it's foolish, he can't help hoping that the shock of trying to murder her only child has snapped Valerie out of whatever spell she's under. She'll be filled with horror and remorse, he thinks, and she'll cast aside the knife, kneel, sweep him up in her arms and, crying, apologize for scaring him so badly. But that doesn't happen. Instead, she straddles him and raises her knife, using both hands this time. Tears begin sliding down the sides of his face, and he knows that whatever has gone wrong with his mother, there's nothing he can do to stop it.

Her hands come down, knife a silver blur as it streaks toward his chest. He doesn't wonder if it will hurt. He's sure it will, but how *long* will it hurt? Will it be over in an eye blink, or will he take his time dying? The latter, he fears. Again, his body acts on instinct, and he reaches up and grabs hold of her wrists to stop the knife's descent.

Her grin gives way to gritted teeth, and she puts every ounce of strength she has into pushing the blade down and into his chest. He grits his teeth as well and squeezes her wrists tight, not only to keep the knife from descending any further, but in the hope that he'll squeeze hard enough to make her hand spring open. Once that happens, he can take the knife, and when he has it, he can fend off his lunatic mother, get out of the house, and run for help.

As the two of them struggle, Valerie begins to cry at last.

"You *have* to die, Jayce. It's the only way to save you. You have to see that!"

Jayce opens his mouth. Maybe he intends to deny his mother's words, or maybe beg for his life. But what comes out of his mouth instead is a black cloud, and just before it envelops Valerie in darkness, Jayce sees the expression on her face. She isn't scared or angry. She looks resigned, as if she expected this to happen.

And soon after that, she's gone.

★   ★   ★

Some hours later, Jayce wakes up. He has no idea what he's doing on the floor. Did he fall out of bed sometime during the night? His back feels a little sore, but if he hit hard enough to hurt himself, why didn't he wake up?

He gets to his feet, still groggy, and staggers to the bathroom to piss. By the time he reaches the kitchen, he's more or less awake. And when he sees the time on the wall clock – 11:17 – he's jolted fully awake. He must've slept through his alarm. He has stuff he needs to do to get ready for his classes in the fall, and he doesn't have time to be sleeping in. A thought occurs to him then. Why didn't his mother get him up? She doesn't like the idea of him going away to college, but she wouldn't do something petty like let him sleep in to show she doesn't intend to help him with his plans to leave her – would she?

Then, for the first time, he hears his mother's voice in his mind. *I can't do anything,* she says. *I'm gone.*

★   ★   ★

When Jayce realized his mother wasn't coming back, he figured she decided to abandon him before he could abandon her. As the years passed, his memories altered, and he came to believe she'd died of a sudden massive heart attack. He was fuzzy on the details, though. And when he heard his mother speak inside him, he put it down to stress and the aftereffects of having been raised by a crazy person. It might not have been *the* truth, but it was *his* truth, and that was just as good as the real thing. Better, in fact. So Jayce continued living his life, such as it was, until the day he decided to go in search of his missing daughter.

★   ★   ★

Jayce's first thought on waking was *I killed my mother.*

You did more than that, Valerie said. *You absorbed my spirit and you've held it prisoner all these years. You're more than a son to me, Jayce. You're also my own personal Hell.*

She had been trying to kill him at the time, but that didn't keep Jayce from feeling guilty and more than a little sickened by what he'd done. Valerie – the actual, honest-to-God woman herself – was still alive, after a fashion, and she dwelled within the body of her only child. The voice that he'd heard in his head for decades – warning, nagging, and mocking him – wasn't merely an extension of his own personality. It was his mother's…he supposed *ghost* was as good a word as any, but it didn't feel quite right. But terminology didn't matter right now. He finally had proof of something he'd suspected for a while. He truly was a monster.

He became aware of two things simultaneously then: his head was pounding and his eyes were closed. The lids were stuck together, and it took an effort to open them. When he did, he saw that he sat in the backseat of a moving vehicle. There were two people in the front seat – Ronnie and Sela – the latter behind the wheel. The windshield wipers weren't moving, and Jayce realized it had stopped raining. He was naked, his hands bound in front of him with plastic zip ties. He looked to his right and saw Nicola and Ohio Pig also occupied the backseat. Nicola was naked, but the Pig was fully clothed. Both of them were asleep or unconscious, Nicola slumped against the Pig's shoulder. Groggy as he was, Jayce knew Nicola wouldn't want to be sleeping on the motherfucker, so he turned, got hold of her left wrist as best he could, and pulled until she slumped over against him. The action took more effort than he'd expected. His muscles were sore and he felt kitten-weak.

Nicola remained unconscious, but the movement of her body attracted Sela's attention. The woman glanced in the rearview mirror.

"Looks like you're the first one awake. Congratulations," she said.

"Too bad we don't have a prize for you," Ronnie said, and both he and Sela laughed.

Jayce turned to look out the window and saw they were riding higher off the road than he'd expected. They were in a van, he realized. He remembered Nicola telling him that she'd been abducted by a black van when she was a girl – along with another girl named Gretchen – and she had no memory of what had happened after that. This probably wasn't the same van. Both Sela and Ronnie were too young to have been driving the vehicle that Nicola had seen as a child. But he believed it was a *similar* van, with a similar purpose.

He continued looking out the window, trying to determine where they were. It looked like they were still in the Cannery, but he didn't know the area well enough to guess their exact location. He opened his mouth to speak, but his tongue felt like a lifeless lump of meat, and his throat was raw, as if someone had reached inside him and scoured it with sandpaper. The best he could do was make a raspy coughing sound.

"Try to take it slow," Sela said. "After we stunned you, we injected you with a delightful cocktail of sedatives. It'll take a while for the drugs to wear off completely."

"Which is the point," Ronnie said, and the couple laughed again.

They drove in silence for several minutes after that. Jayce was glad Ronnie was present to ameliorate the effect of Sela's sex aura. He might have been a prisoner, but at least he didn't have to ride with a full erection bobbing up and down every time they hit a bump in the road.

"I'm sure you want to know why we captured you and where we're going," Sela said. "You'll find out soon enough. But one thing I *can* tell you. You'll find your daughter there."

After what she and her husband had done, Jayce had no reason to trust the woman. And even if she was telling the truth, there was no guarantee he'd find Emory unharmed – or even alive. And given the transformations Shadow could work on people, she might no longer be human. Hell, *he* wasn't anymore. So he had no reason to hope for a good outcome, and every reason to expect a bad one. Still, he couldn't help feeling a tiny kernel of hope deep inside. One way or another, it looked like he was finally going to find out what had happened to his Emmy.

He relaxed against the seat, and although his body urged him to close his eyes and get more rest, he fought to stay awake. He would keep watch, for Nicola, if no other reason. And if a chance came to fuck up either Ronnie or Sela, he'd take it.

★   ★   ★

Jayce supposed he should've been surprised when Sela pulled the van into the alley behind Crimson Splendor, but he wasn't. He didn't think anything about the Cannery and the people who dwelled there could surprise him anymore. Sela parked behind a metal door with the word *Deliveries* painted on it. Jayce had no idea what time it was, but the sky was still full dark, with no hint of a coming dawn.

Very symbolic, Valerie said.

"Thanks," he whispered. His voice was better, but not much.

Nicola was awake, more or less, and she and Jayce held hands as best they could. Ohio Pig was still out of it, and Jayce wondered if Sela and Ronnie had given him a stronger dose of sedative, considering that he'd shot up the Funhouse and killed a couple of their customers. It was what he would've done.

Neither Sela nor Ronnie got out of the vehicle. Jayce thought Sela might honk the horn, but instead she took out her phone and sent a quick text. A few moments passed, and then the door opened and the twins – Theron and Theron – stepped into the alley.

Jayce had been wrong. The Cannery still held surprises for him.

One of the twins slid open the van's side door, unbuckled Ohio

Pig's seatbelt, and pulled him out of the van as if he weighed no more than a jumbo-sized package of extra-soft toilet paper. Theron slung the Pig over his shoulder and walked away. The other Theron reached in then, and he undid Nicola's and Jayce's belts, took them out of the van, and slung each over a shoulder, lifting them without any more effort than his brother had lifted Ohio Pig. Although Jayce and Nicola were awake, both of them were still quite weak, and they were unable to put up a fight as Theron carried them around the front of the van, following his brother. Jayce squinted in the glare of the van's headlights, but when they were past them, he caught a glimpse of Sela and Ronnie through the windshield. They smiled and waved, and then Sela put the van in gear and pulled away.

The alley was unlit, but the headlights had allowed Jayce to see the van's color as Theron carried them. It was a glossy, bright red.

The twins carried them to the building and closed and locked the door behind them. They were in a small, dimly lit room with a set of stairs leading downward. The first twin descended, carrying the Pig, and the second followed with Jayce and Nicola.

"Where are you taking us?" Jayce's voice was thick and slow, as if he were still partially drugged, but at least he could get the words out.

Theron didn't answer.

Jayce caught Nicola's eye, but she shook her head. It seemed she had no more idea about what was happening than he did. He assumed this was the rear exit for Crimson Splendor – or at least, one of them – and he imagined people fleeing up these stairs earlier during the Harvest Man's attack. The twins continued down for a time until they came to another metal door. One of the twins opened it, and he and his brother walked through, carrying Jayce, Nicola, and Ohio Pig with them.

Crimson Splendor was empty, the red lights turned off in favor of bright fluorescents. The lighting made the place look stark and shabby, no longer a scene of dark wonder. Now it was just another shitty club after closing time. No effort had been made to clean up the mess that had been left when the club's patrons had panicked and fled. Chairs and tables were overturned, and broken glass was scattered everywhere. As the twins carried them past the bar and farther into the club, Jayce had the sense that they were not as alone as he'd thought. He couldn't see forward the way Theron carried him, but he heard the soft sound of ice cubes clinking against the inside of a glass. The twins stopped at a table, and Theron put Jayce and Nicola into seats. Both were still weak, but they were able to keep themselves propped up by resting their arms on the tabletop. The other twin made no move to put Ohio Pig down.

Ivory, still dressed in her tuxedo, alabaster skin virtually gleaming, sat across the table from Jayce and Nicola. She held a glass of amber liquid with ice cubes floating in it.

"Gave up huffing vessels?" Jayce asked.

Ivory raised her glass. "Vessels are for the young. I only drink brandy, the more sinfully expensive, the better."

Ohio Pig stirred then, and Ivory looked at the twin holding him.

"Take him on down, and give him a stimulant to wake him up. I'll bring these two when I'm finished speaking with them."

The twin nodded to acknowledge her words and then bore the Pig off in the direction of the elevator.

"Down where?" Jayce asked, but Ivory ignored his question and took a sip of brandy.

Nicola was taking longer to shake off her drug-induced haze than Jayce had, and she stared at Ivory with bleary eyes, blinking to clear her vision.

"You're...alive," she whispered.

Ivory smiled at her. "And I intend to stay that way for a very long time. Forever, if I can manage it."

"You're a duplicate," Jayce said. "One of the Underborn."

"Close, but no cigar," she said. "I'm the real deal. The Ivory you saw the Harvest Man destroy was *my* duplicate. I didn't survive as long as I have by taking chances. I spend most of my time below, and my duplicate runs – I mean *ran* – things up here. I'll need to make a new one now." She sipped her brandy once more. "I dislike the process. It's messy and uncomfortable, but I suppose you can say that about actual birth too. At least creating an Underborn doesn't leave stretch marks."

Jayce glanced at the remaining twin, who stood close to the table. "They're Underborn too, aren't they?"

"Yes, but they're not twins. They're created from a single individual, a very strong and extremely loyal servant of mine who volunteered to be the raw material from which my luscious-looking guards are created. I make sure only two of them are seen in public at any given time. Even in the Cannery, it would cause questions if a dozen copies of the same person were running around at once."

"And they're all called Theron," Jayce said.

Ivory shrugged. "It's too much work to come up with separate names for all of them. Besides, there's no way to tell them apart, so why bother?"

Nicola's eyes looked clearer now, and she sat up straight, more or less.

"Have I ever...." Nicola's voice was breathy. She paused, swallowed once, and when she resumed her voice was firmer. "Have I ever spoken to the real you?"

"A few times," Ivory said. "But most of your interactions were with my duplicate. Sorry, but you and I aren't really besties."

"You – the other you – didn't have any intention of helping me find my daughter," Jayce said. "Because *you're* responsible for what happened to her."

"Not directly, but yes, I am ultimately responsible. A place like the Cannery, where Shadow is so strong, is very much an ecosystem. And like any ecosystem, it requires balance to remain healthy. If this balance becomes upset, if it tips one way more than another, the result is chaos. For the last two hundred years – almost from the founding of Oakmont – I've worked to maintain the balance between Shadow and 'normal' reality in this town. The denizens of Shadow have…*appetites* that need to be sated, and all too often their satisfaction comes at the cost of ordinary humans, people to whom Shadow is, at most, only a partially glimpsed nightmare, easily dismissed and more easily forgotten. If Shadow's influence was allowed to spread unchecked, it would eventually mean the end of Oakmont. The town – and everyone in it – would die, and the denizens of Shadow, bereft of prey, would move on to other towns and begin to spread their corruption there.

"I realized long ago that what the Shadowers in this town needed wasn't free-range prey, but rather a reliable, steady, and above all *cultivated* supply. So I brought the Primogenitor to Oakmont, installed it in the Creche, and began duplicating a select number of townsfolk, people handpicked for certain desired qualities. A particularly ear-piercing scream, for example, or extra-succulent flesh. Or, in the case of your daughter, exceptional sexual intensity. These chosen are given to the Primogenitor, who then produces duplicates – whom we call the Underborn – that can survive Shadowers' attentions again and again. And when a duplicate reaches a point where it can no longer fulfill its function—"

"You mean when it's dead," Jayce interrupted.

"—we simply replace it. Of course, the originals eventually wear out after several decades, so we're always on the lookout for fresh supplies. That's the true purpose of Crimson Splendor and The Hole Thing, along with many of the other establishments in the Cannery – almost all of which I own, by the way. My servants continually keep watch for extraordinary individuals who will satisfy even the most jaded Shadower."

"That's how you found Emory, isn't it?" Jayce said. "She shopped at The Hole Thing, bought a Pink Devil, probably even tried it out in one of the demonstration rooms. Sela was so impressed by her sexual 'intensity' that the next time she visited the shop, Sela and Ronnie abducted her and brought her here."

"Yes. And I understand how you must feel about that. But your daughter's sacrifice – along with that of the others who are bound to the Primogenitor – is a meaningful, even necessary one. Because the most dangerous Shadowers are able to do what they must with a virtually endless supply of Underborn, the citizens of Oakmont are spared." She paused. "Most of them, anyway."

"Is that what you're going to do with us?" Jayce asked. "Give us to this Primogenitor and use us to make life-sized, living, breathing action figures for your customers' entertainment?"

"Oh, no. I have something *much* more fun in mind for you two." She finished the rest of her brandy in a single gulp, then put the empty glass down on the table. "We're going downstairs now. You can walk on your own if you behave yourselves. But if you do anything you shouldn't, Theron will be right behind you to remind you of your manners."

Ivory rose then and headed for the elevator, without a backward glance to see if they followed.

Jayce was able to stand without help, although his legs felt a little wobbly. Nicola started to rise, but then her legs gave out. Even with his hands bound, Jayce was able to grab hold of her arm and keep her from falling. She gave him a weak but grateful smile, and after a couple seconds, she nodded. Jayce let go of her arm, and she was able to remain standing on her own.

"Get moving," the Theron said. There was no gruffness in his voice, no animosity. He might as well have been reminding them of an appointment they didn't want to be late for instead of giving prisoners an order.

Jayce and Nicola started walking side by side. Nicola's gait became stronger and more sure with every step, but Jayce wanted to stay close to her in case she needed his help again. Theron traveled close behind.

Ivory was halfway to the elevator, and she spoke without looking back at them. "I must say, the appearance of the Harvest Man was a surprise, and one I could have very much done without. Customers will avoid the club like it's a plague zone for weeks. Trevor managed to get out before the worst of it, and he told me he could smell the Harvest Man on you, Jayce. Did *you* bring him here?"

She tried to make the last question sound casual, but Jayce picked up on the undercurrent of tension in her voice.

"I'd never heard of the Harvest Man before tonight." Technically, he was telling the truth. He hadn't heard the *name* before. "And I have no clue why his scent was on me." This was at least a partial lie. He didn't actually know, although he guessed it was due to their encounter at the mall when he was young.

He wanted to tell Ivory that if the Harvest Man had entered Crimson Splendor because of him, his only regret was that the monster hadn't killed the real her. But he restrained himself. He didn't want to piss her off any more than she already was. He didn't care what happened to him, but he didn't want Nicola to be hurt because he mouthed off. And although their situation was bad, he was closer to finding Emory than ever before, and he didn't want to jeopardize his chances of being reunited with her.

Ivory didn't reply, didn't so much as slow her pace toward the elevator. She seemed content to let the matter go for now, and that was good enough for him.

When Ivory reached the elevator, she pressed a button and the door opened. She went inside, then pressed another button on the car's control panel to hold the door for the rest of them.

"Do you know what's below this level?" Jayce asked Nicola.

She shook her head. "I didn't know there *was* a level deeper than the club. I knew about the Underborn, but I had no idea exactly where they came from."

They joined Ivory in the elevator and Theron came after. Ivory took her finger off the hold button and the door slid closed. The elevator began descending then, but when Jayce looked at the control panel, he saw only one button for a lower level, the one that took people to the club. He didn't know how Ivory had signaled the elevator to go lower, but it was.

They rode for only a short time before the elevator stopped and the door slid open again. Theron put his hands on Jayce's and Nicola's shoulders to keep them from exiting. Ivory once more pressed the hold button to keep the door open.

"This is the level immediately below the club," she said. "Here, Shadowers can sate their most debased and disgusting sexual desires. I call it Carnality."

Beds, couches, and rugs were everywhere, along with free-standing shower stalls and bathtubs. There were chairs and tables with built-in leather restraints, and the walls were covered with manacles for both wrists and ankles. The lighting was blue here, and the music – industrial metal with a pounding beat – was deafening. The level was filled with people fucking and being fucked in every combination and configuration imaginable. People made liberal use of sex toys and strap-ons, whips and riding crops, paddles and rods, and all manner of devices mundane and exotic. Jayce recognized some of the more sinister-looking toys from the Funhouse at The Hole Thing, including more than a few Pink Devils, although in this light they looked more like Blue Devils. As loud as the music was, Jayce could hear a chorus of moans, groans, grunts, and screams, and the air stank of sweat, semen, vaginal juices, piss, and shit. A number of Therons – all naked – walked among the revelers, keeping an eye on them and, when necessary, pitching in to lend a hand, or any other body part, as required. Evidently Ivory's prohibition against more than one Theron being seen in public didn't extend to Crimson Splendor's lower levels.

Jayce noticed something else about the people taking their pleasures in Carnality. Half of them looked like normal humans, but the rest were distorted or deformed in various ways, some of which were quite monstrous. He remembered then what Ivory had said about how the levels below the Club were designed to cater to those beings who had been most changed by Shadow and had the most extreme appetites. He also noticed something else: a number of the regular humans resembled each other, as if they were clones. No, he told himself. Underborn created by the Primogenitor.

Ivory spoke then. "This is where Emory – or rather, her duplicates – work. If you wandered around, I'm sure you could find at least half a dozen of them out there right now, giving as good as they're getting." She gave Jayce a sly sideways glance. "And if you ever had any father-daughter fantasies, I'd be happy to pause on this level for a while and give you a chance to act them out. Provided, of course, that you let us watch."

Jayce gritted his teeth in anger, but he refused to let her bait him. "No thanks."

There was nothing even remotely erotic about the spectacle before them. There was no love, no tenderness, not even the simple joy of engaging in a highly pleasurable physical activity with another. This was mindless satiation, the exploitation of flesh for its own sake, taking without any thought of giving in return. And even if Emory herself wasn't present, the thought that her image was out there being used like disposable tissues to ejaculate into sickened him.

"Too bad," Ivory said. She released the hold button, the door closed, and the elevator began to descend once more. Again, they didn't travel far before they stopped and the door opened.

This level was green, and screams of agony filled the air, along with loud classical music. In some ways, this level was laid out like Carnality. There were tables and chairs, both with restraints, and manacles were affixed to brick walls. Duplicates of Theron – these fully clothed – were present as well, some walking the level as they did above, others standing by to assist customers with their needs. And while those needs still related to the flesh, they were less about its sexual pleasures and more about finding as many different – and bloody – ways to ravage it as possible. The stench here was even worse than in Carnality. The level stank of coppery blood and raw meat, and the air fairly vibrated with the agony of those whose flesh was being violated. The tables and chairs were metal with built-in gutters to catch and channel blood into floor drains. Each 'station' had a table with an assortment of equipment laid out: surgical tools, knives, hammers, screwdrivers, hatchets, axes, electric carving knives, blowtorches, barbed wire, chainsaws, handguns, shotguns, rifles, and compound bows. There were also glass and plastic containers of chemicals which Jayce assumed held bleach, acid, kerosene, gasoline, and all manner of poisons, from those that killed instantly to those that took their time. The patrons here were even more monstrous than those above, and the beings they played with were all Underborn. Some of the Shadowers wore surgical gowns, masks, and rubber gloves. Others wore industrial coveralls and boots. Some wore plastic ponchos, while others were naked so they could feel the blood spatter on their skin. The Therons acted like surgical assistants, handing patrons tools of torture and death as needed.

Jayce was surprised to recognize one of the sadists. It was the Napkin Eater. He wore a gore-smeared leather apron, and his metal case lay open on the equipment table next to him, displaying a staggering variety of knives. The Napkin Eater stood before the body of a naked toddler – boy or girl, it was impossible to tell – whose chest was being held open by rib spreaders. As if aware he was being watched, the Napkin Eater turned toward the elevator, and when he saw Jayce and Nicola, he grinned and waved, blood flying from an object gripped in his green-gloved hand. That's when Jayce realized the sonofabitch was holding a small heart in his hand.

"This level is called Snuff," Ivory said. "For obvious reasons. There's also a special café in the back for those who like to eat what they kill. My chefs can prepare meat any way you like, and if you prefer to do it yourself, there are open cooking stations."

She removed her finger from the hold button, the elevator door closed, and they continued their downward journey.

Jayce began to shake, his trembling having nothing to do with being naked. He'd experienced so many awful things since setting foot in the CrazyQwik last night, and he'd remembered even more. But none of them were as mind-numbingly horrible as what he'd just seen, not even the memory of killing his own mother.

Speak for yourself, Valerie said.

"The Underborn work especially well on that level," Ivory said. "They're stronger than the humans from which they're created. Hardier. They can take a lot more punishment before dying. The longer they last, the more damage my customers can inflict, and the happier they are. And when they're happy, fewer humans are slaughtered aboveground."

"You're just a fucking saint, aren't you?" Jayce's voice shook with anger. "Selflessly protecting John and Jane Normal, not to mention all their little Normals, from the big, bad monsters of Shadow."

"Hardly selfless," Ivory said. "My customers pay *very* well for access to the more specialized levels of Crimson Splendor. But yes, I do care about what happens to the citizens of Oakmont, even if to me they're little more than animals." She smiled. "I suppose you could say I'm a conservationist at heart."

Jayce glared at the woman, and he wondered what the odds were that he could loop his bound wrists over the back of Ivory's head and choke her to death before Theron could snap his neck.

Not too good, he decided. Too bad. If there was ever anyone who needed killing, it was her.

The elevator came to a stop once more, and the door slid open.

"And this is our destination," Ivory said. "The *final* destination for you two, I'm afraid. I call it the Pit."

CHAPTER TWELVE

Ivory stepped out of the elevator, and Theron prodded Jayce and Nicola to follow her. Jayce heard crowd noises – shouting, cheering, clapping, and stomping. The lights were bright here, forcing him to squint. No music and no color theme this time. Whatever took place in the Pit, it seemed Ivory wanted to make sure that every detail was clearly visible. This level was far more unfinished than the others. The floor was smooth stone, but the walls and ceiling remained corrugated and craggy. Floodlights were attached to a metal framework which hung from the ceiling above a large circular depression. Wooden bleachers had been erected on the edge of the Pit in a U shape, the open end of which pointed toward the elevator. The bleachers were filled with Shadowers, but none turned to look as they approached. Their attention was focused entirely on whatever was happening in the Pit. Their eyes shone with hunger, their features twisted with cruel excitement. Some pumped their fists in the air, while others cupped hands to their mouths and shouted things like, "Kill the fucker!" or, "Do it NOW!"

What's the first rule of Fight Club? Valerie thought.

You died before the book came out, Jayce replied.

I read it when you did, she countered. *You've been my eyes for the last thirty years.*

Like that's not creepy.

Ivory led them to the edge of the Pit. A metal railing bordered it, and in front of the railing was a chair, an overstuffed, antique-looking thing that seemed as if it had been shipped directly from the nineteenth century. Jayce didn't have to ask who it belonged to.

Ivory moved past the chair, stepped to the railing, gripped the top bar, and leaned forward to get a better look. Jayce saw his chance. He didn't know how deep the Pit was, but he figured that if it required a railing, it was probably deep enough to cause some damage if someone was unlucky enough to fall into it – or be pushed. He took a single step forward, but then Theron's hand clamped down on his shoulder like a vise.

So much for that idea, Valerie thought.

Theron kept his hand on Jayce as he urged him and Nicola forward. When they reached the railing, Jayce could see that the Pit's floor lay twenty feet below the level of the bleachers, deep enough that anyone inside couldn't escape, but not so deep as to decrease the quality of the view. The walls had been made smooth – so there would be no hand or footholds, Jayce guessed – but the floor was rough and uneven. Probably to make fighting more difficult for the combatants, and therefore more exciting for the audience. There were two people in the Pit, and one of them was Ohio Pig. He wore the same clothes he'd had on when he was captured, only now they were torn and even more bloodstained than before. He was covered with cuts, some of which looked bad enough to qualify as serious wounds. His body was slick with sweat, and his chest heaved as if he were on the verge of exhaustion and was having trouble catching his breath. He gripped a machete in his right hand, his only weapon from what Jayce could see, the blade coated with blood.

His opponent was one of the Therons, presumably the same one that had brought him down here while Ivory had chatted with Jayce and Nicola. The duplicate's body was covered with machete cuts, and he was bleeding quite a bit more than the Pig. His left ear was missing, and a strike to his face had sliced open his right cheek, which hung from his face in a slick red flap, revealing the teeth underneath. The Theron had no weapon, and when Jayce looked at Ivory, she said, "As strong as the Therons are, it evens the odds when they enter the Pit barehanded." She patted the cheek of the Theron gripping Jayce's shoulder, and he smiled as if she'd given him a personal compliment.

The Pig looked as if he could barely hold up the machete, and despite how badly the Theron was bleeding, the duplicate looked alert and full of energy. The two men circled each other, Theron crouched over, arms spread out as if this were a wrestling match, Ohio Pig with his machete pointed at the other man's chest. Then, without warning, Theron let out a roar and charged. The Pig stood his ground and waited, and at the last moment, instead of stabbing the machete into Theron's chest, he spun to the left and away from the other man's charge. The Pig's momentum brought his machete arm around, and as Theron stumbled forward, the Pig struck a solid blow to the man's back. The blade cut into flesh and muscle, and blood gushed forth from the wound. The impact of the blow, coupled with the uneven ground, caused Theron to lose his balance and he fell forward. The Pig yanked the machete free from the man's back as he fell, and when he hit the ground belly-first, the Pig jumped forward and swung the machete at the back of Theron's neck. The blade hit just below the base of the skull with a nauseating *chuk!* sound, and the Pig pulled it out and struck three more times in rapid succession. *Chuk-chuk-chuk!*

The Pig straightened, gasping for air, arms hanging limply at his sides. The machete slipped from his blood-slick fingers and clanged to the stone floor. Theron lay motionless, his head partially severed, a widening pool of blood spreading around his head like a dark red halo.

The crowd fell silent, watching, listening. When Theron didn't move after several moments, they broke into thunderous cheers and applause. The Pig, weary and bleeding from his injuries, raised a hand and gave the crowd the finger, turning slowly around all the way to make sure everyone saw it. The gesture only served to make them cheer harder, though.

Ivory clapped softly.

"I have to admit, I'm impressed," she said, speaking loudly to be heard over the crowd. "There aren't many who can survive going a few rounds with a Theron, let alone kill one. The Pig does look somewhat the worse for wear, though. I'll be interested to see how he fares against his next opponent." She smiled at Jayce and Nicola. "I'll be even *more* interested to see how you two perform. You're both fresh and uninjured" − she paused as she glanced at the stitches on Jayce's hand − "for the most part, so hopefully you'll be able to help him." She turned to the Theron who still gripped Jayce's shoulder. "Take them down to the staging area and get them ready. I'll signal when it's time to begin."

"Yes, ma'am," the Theron said, and then − still holding on to Jayce's shoulder − he led them to an open doorway carved into the wall on their right, where a set of curving stone stairs descended into darkness. There were no lights or handrails, and with their wrists bound, Jayce and Nicola couldn't put a hand on the wall to steady themselves as they went down. The stone steps were damp and he feared they might slip and tumble down the stairs. It didn't help that they were both barefoot.

Yeah, it would be a real shame if you two got banged up before you were tossed into the Pit to get slaughtered, Valerie said.

Don't be such a bitch, Jayce thought back. *Remember, if I go, you go.*

His mother had nothing to say to that.

Jayce saw light as they neared the bottom of the stairs, and soon they entered a chamber with a domed ceiling. The chamber opened onto the Pit, and the opening was where the light came from. There were several wooden benches here, and Ohio Pig sat on one of them, slumped forward, head hanging down, mingled sweat and blood dripping from his body to patter on the stone floor. A Theron stood behind him, tending to his wounds with supplies from an open medical kit sitting on the bench next to the Pig. The Pig held a half-empty water bottle in his right hand, the plastic surface smeared with blood. As the Theron worked, the Pig raised his head, drank the remaining water, and then slumped forward once more, the bottle slipping from his fingers to hit the floor, bouncing and rolling before it came to a stop.

"Wait here," said the Theron who'd escorted Jayce and Nicola down. There was a wooden armoire set against the far wall, and the Theron walked over to it, pulled the doors open, and reached inside. He drew forth a pair of folded white garments, carried them over to Jayce and Nicola, and dropped them on the floor in front of them.

"Hold out your hands," he said.

They did so, and the Theron drew a knife from his belt and cut them free from their zip ties. The plastic strips fell to the ground, and the Theron sheathed his knife, picked up the ties – along with the empty water bottle the Pig had discarded – and carried them with him as he returned to the armoire. A metal waste can sat next to the armoire, and Theron dropped the severed ties and the bottle into it, then returned his attention to the armoire.

As Jayce and Nicola massaged their sore wrists, the Pig looked up at them, the Theron continuing to work on him as he spoke.

"So nice of you to join me," he said.

Jayce saw no sign of the man's machete. He figured he'd been forced to leave it in the Pit. No way the Therons would allow him to remain armed between matches.

The Pig nodded toward the clothes the Theron had dropped before them.

"I think you're supposed to put those on." He leered at Nicola. "Although in your case, it would be a shame to cover up that body." He looked at Jayce. "Too bad I can't say the same about you. By the way, what's that shriveled thing dangling between your legs? It looks like a penis, only smaller."

Jayce and Nicola ignored him as they picked up the garments, unfolded and examined them. They were white coveralls with a zipper down the front. One pair was larger than the other, and Jayce took that one since he was taller – not to mention wider around the middle – than Nicola. The coveralls' fabric was thin and scratchy, and Jayce didn't think it would provide any more protection from a weapon than a piece of wet paper. Jayce wondered why Ivory bothered to have him and Nicola dress. Wouldn't it be more exciting for the crowd – and more demeaning for them – if they were forced to fight naked? But then he realized the coveralls would allow for a kind of mutilation striptease as the cloth was cut from their bodies. And as for the white color? It would make the blood stand out more dramatically.

It's all about the theatrics, Valerie said. *I hated watching these damn shows when I was alive. I think I'm going to hate participating in one even more.*

After Jayce and Nicola were dressed, Ohio Pig snorted. "I'm glad I was already wearing clothes when they grabbed me. You two look dumb as hell in those things."

The Theron that had brought them their clothes now brought them a pair of weapons that he'd selected from the armoire. One was a large hunting knife – the kind the dog-eaters had carried, Jayce thought – and the other was a three-ball flail with spikes.

"Choose," the Theron said.

"I won't fight either of them," Jayce said. Now that he knew the Pig hadn't killed Emory, he had no reason to hate the man. Sure, he was crazy as fuck, but that was par for the course when it came to Shadowers. He had no desire to hurt the man any further than he'd already been. And as for Nicola – he couldn't say he loved her, but he felt close to her after everything they'd been through, especially in the Funhouse. But more than that, she'd offered to help him search for Emory when no one else would, and what had it gotten her? Captured by Ivory and brought to her private Coliseum to take part in a Shadow version of Christians versus Lions. Nicola didn't deserve this, and not only wouldn't he fight her for the amusement of Ivory and her 'customers', he'd do everything he could to protect her.

"You're not supposed to fight each other," the Theron said. "You're supposed to fight *together*."

"No guns?" Nicola asked.

The Theron grinned. "Guns are too easy – and too fast. The crowd likes it when we draw out the fun as long as possible."

And then, as if he could no longer be bothered to wait, he carried the knife and flail to the Pit opening and tossed them through. He then took up a position in the opening, standing sideways so he could keep one eye on them and another on his mistress above. He folded his arms and waited for Ivory's promised signal.

The crowd had been talking amongst themselves since the Pig's battle with the Theron had finished, but now some of them began chanting Ivory's name, only a few at first, but then more picked up the chant until the crowd seemed to be speaking in a single deafening voice. The chanting soon died away, and Jayce imagined that Ivory had raised her hands for quiet.

"Good evening, ladies and gentlemen," she said. Her voice didn't sound as if it were miked, and she didn't shout, and yet Jayce could hear her as clearly as if she were standing next to him. "I trust you've all been enjoying yourselves this evening?"

Cheers, shouts, applause.

"Glad to hear it. Our next match will begin shortly. Ohio Pig will be back—"

Some cheers at this, but just as many boos.

"—and this time he'll be joined by two others. Together, they're going to face three *very* special opponents, so get ready. You'll be talking about this one for years!"

The crowd went crazy at that, clapping, cheering, hooting, whistling, and stomping.

Jayce, however, was far less excited. Once he'd learned that he, Nicola, and the Pig wouldn't have to fight each other, he'd assumed they would fight more Therons. But from what Ivory said, it sounded as if she had something different – and no doubt worse – in mind.

Jayce looked at the Pig. The Theron tending to his injuries had moved in front of him and was applying some kind of thick goo to the cuts on his arms and chest.

"Look," Jayce said, "about what happened in the club—"

"Forget about it," the Pig said. "I can be kind of an asshole sometimes."

"Kind of?" Nicola said.

"How did you know the Underborn you killed wasn't Emory?" he asked.

"I didn't at first," the Pig said. "After I left you at your daughter's apartment, I drove around the Cannery, checking with my usual sources to see if anyone had heard anything about a woman named Emory. I didn't have any luck at first, but after a while someone told me she knew an Emory who was turning tricks on a certain street corner. I hauled ass over there and sure enough, there she was. I talked to her a couple minutes, let her think I was just another horny John looking for some action. When I was convinced it was her, I tried to grab her, but she took hold of me and slammed me up against the side of a building. She was so damn strong that I knew something had been done to change her, and since I've dealt with plenty of Underborn in my time, I figured she was one. We fought for a while, and she was tough, but in the end I was too fast and too smart for her, and I was able to take her head off. I tossed the body in an alley, where I knew it would liquefy soon enough, but I decided to bring the head to show you. I didn't think you'd believe the Underborn were real unless you saw the head dissolve. It takes about thirty minutes or so for one of them to go gloppy, so I knew I needed to find you fast. I tried calling, but I didn't get you. That's when I decided to gamble that you were in Crimson Splendor. The cell reception is shit in the club. The rest you know."

"Why Ohio Pig?" Jayce asked, curious.

The man frowned. "What do you mean?"

"Your nickname. Why did you choose Ohio Pig?"

"That's what my license plate says. I put it on there because I like to make barbecue. I guess you could say it's kind of my hobby. I go to festivals and compete in competitions, that kind of thing. But my *name* is Owen."

The Theron stepped away from the Pig, examined his handiwork, nodded once, then closed the first aid kit, picked it up, and headed for the armoire. He put the kit away, closed the armoire's doors, locked it, and then walked to the Pit opening to stand opposite his 'brother', folding his arms in exactly the same way, so that they looked like mirror images of each other. Which, Jayce supposed, in a way they were.

He thought of what the Pig had told them. Maybe the version of Emory he'd killed had been a simple prostitute, but more likely she had been a lure to capture more people so Ivory could bring them to the Primogenitor and use them to make more Underborn. He now understood why Ivory had brought the three of them here. By searching for Emory, they'd discovered the truth of what the Underborn were and more, what they were used for. To keep her secret, Ivory needed them dead, but simply killing them would be no good. Where was the fun in that? Instead, she would make them fight – and die – in the Pit, for her amusement and that of her patrons. He tried to think of some way out of this situation, but he didn't see any. No way they could escape from the Therons, and even if by some miracle they did, where could they go? They would still be trapped in an underground chamber with several hundred Shadowers, as well as who knew how many Therons. One way or another, the three of them were going to die here. It was only a matter of how quickly and by what means.

We who are about to die salute you, Jayce thought bitterly.

Maybe he deserved to die for what he'd done to his mother, even if it had been instinctive and in defense of his own life. And Ohio Pig had killed who knew how many Shadowers. Maybe none of his victims had been completely innocent, but that didn't mean they had deserved to be killed by a lunatic, either. He didn't know Nicola well enough to determine how much, if any, blood she had on her hands, but he didn't think she deserved this fate. But the one real regret Jayce had was that he would die before he could find and free Emory. Once he was dead, there would be no one to help her, and she'd remain a prisoner of the Primogenitor, used as raw material to create Underborn for as long as her body lasted.

Ivory began speaking once again.

"Is everyone ready?"

The two Therons guarding them give their mistress thumbs up, and the crowd roared its approval.

"Then let's begin!" she shouted.

The Therons turned to face them. "You're on," they said in unison.

Ohio Pig – or rather Owen – rose from the bench with a sigh, wincing as his injuries protested.

"I don't care which weapons you two use, but hands off the machete. It's mine. And don't get in my way. I don't want to hurt you, but I won't lose any sleep if I accidentally cut either one of you."

"Good luck to you too," Jayce muttered.

The Pig trudged past the Therons and out into the Pit to a chorus of cheers, boos, hisses, and shouted profanities.

Jayce turned to Nicola. "I don't know what to say. If you hadn't helped me with the dog-eaters...."

She smiled. "Don't get maudlin. We aren't dead yet."

She gave him a quick kiss and headed toward the Pit.

Figuring he was as ready as he was ever going to be, Jayce followed.

He stepped into the Pit and gazed upon the Shadowers seated in the bleachers. As on the other lower levels of Crimson Splendor, the beings were more monstrous and distorted than 'normal' Shadowers. He imagined them – as well as those currently engaging in the dark delights of Carnality and Snuff – out in the streets instead of in here, free to sate their foul appetites however, and with whoever, they wished, and for a moment – just a moment – he wondered if Ivory really was fulfilling the role of a conservationist, protecting the herd of humanity from the predators that lurked unseen in their midst.

Ivory was seated in her chair, a new pair of Therons standing on either side of her. The two who had brought them down remained standing by the opening, no doubt to prevent them attempting to escape that way. There was another opening on the opposite side of the Pit, guarded by yet another pair of Therons. Jayce wondered how many of them there were in total. A hundred? Two hundred? It was as if Ivory had her own private army.

Neither Jayce nor Nicola had been given shoes to protect their feet from the rough stone floor of the Pit. He thought that both of them would end up with torn, bloody soles before this was over, and then he almost laughed. As if *that* was the worst of their problems right now. Aside from a lot of blood on the ground, there was no sign of the Theron that Ohio Pig had killed. He assumed other Therons had removed the body, perhaps even carted if off to Snuff where it would become the nightly special in the café. The weapons lay on the ground near the opening, and Ohio Pig had already retrieved his machete. Nicola bent down and picked up the flail. That left the big-ass knife for Jayce, and he bent down, took hold of its handle, and stood. The weapon felt good in his hand. Solid. Strong. He'd never used any kind of weapon against anyone in his life, and he wondered if he'd be able to when the time came.

You beat the shit out of the Pig in the club, Valerie said. *You'll be fine. After all, you've got some monster in you, right? Time to let it out to play.*

The Therons guarding the opposite entrance made no movement, gave no signal, but three figures stepped past them, entered the Pit, and stopped. Jayce's breath caught in his throat when he saw who they were. All three of them were Emory.

"Surprised, Jayce?" Ivory called out. She rose from her seat and gripped the railing as she addressed the crowd. "Ladies and gentlemen, the three lovely women who just entered the Pit are Underborn. What's more, all are duplicates of *that* man's daughter." Here she pointed at Jayce. "The daughter he came to the Cannery to find! Well, he's found her now, hasn't he?"

The crowd burst out in cruel, mocking laughter. Ivory then held up her hands for silence, and they quieted.

"Actually, I should correct myself." She paused and a wide grin split her face. "Only two of these women are Underborn. One is the *original!*"

The crowd went wild, and Ivory held up her hands once more to silence them.

"And to make things even more fun, the women have been given a special pharmaceutical cocktail to send them into a homicidal rage. So all three – *including* the original – are going to do their damnedest to gut their father like a fucking fish. So let the bloodbath begin!"

Ivory had whipped the crowd into a frenzy, and the Shadowers shrieked with dark delight. And as if that were their cue, the Emorys started running toward Jayce and the others, teeth bared, eyes wild and filled with hate.

Each was dressed the same – black tank top, black yoga pants, and athletic shoes – and their long brown hair was pulled back in three identical ponytails. They carried different weapons, though. One held a meat cleaver, one a hatchet, and one wore a leather glove from which a single sharp blade protruded. Jayce's gaze darted from one to the other as he searched for some sign that would tell him which of these women was the real Emory. But at that moment, none of them looked like his daughter. They were drug-crazed beasts whose only desire was to spill as much blood as possible.

"Don't hurt them!" Jayce shouted, but neither Nicola nor the Pig listened. The Pig raised his machete and ran forward to meet the Emorys' charge. He no longer looked tired or weakened from his injuries, and he let out an enthusiastic cry that was part shout, part whoop. If Jayce had any doubt that the man had been driven insane by his exposure to Shadow, it vanished in that instant.

Nicola didn't move to engage the Emorys, but she spread her feet apart in a battle stance, raised her flail, and began spinning it in preparation to strike.

Jayce held his knife at his side, unable to do anything more than stare, paralyzed, as three separate but equally murderous versions of his daughter attacked.

Cleaver Emory headed for Ohio Pig. She raised her weapon over her head and screamed as she drew near him. Jayce could see how bloodshot her eyes were, and her face was flushed nearly beet-red. Whatever sort of drugs Ivory had used to turn the Emorys into crazed killers, it was taking its toll on their bodies. It also seemed to have speeded up their reflexes, for when the Pig swiped his machete toward Cleaver Emory's midsection, she jumped back and the Pig's blade swished through empty air. When he was off balance, she brought her cleaver down on the man's right shoulder. The metal *thunked* into meat, blood spurted, and the Pig howled in pain.

The crowd roared its approval.

Hatchet Emory made for Nicola, and just as she was about to take a swing at the other woman, Nicola sidestepped and swung her flail around to strike Emory's back. Three spiked balls slammed against her shoulder blades, tearing cloth and flesh as if both were no more substantial than tissue paper. Emory cried out in pain, stumbled, and fell to the ground, her back a scarlet ruin.

"No!" Jayce shouted, but his voice was drowned out by a fresh chorus of cheers from the crowd.

He started running forward to help Emory, not caring if she was the real one or not, only knowing that she looked like his daughter and that was all that mattered. But before he could reach her, the third Emory – the one with the knife-glove – came at him. Her hand was curled into a fist, and the blade projected forward a good nine inches, maybe more. It was more like a dagger, Jayce thought, or maybe a short sword. She thrust it toward his abdomen and he stood there, thinking that if this was *his* Emory, there was no way she'd hurt him, no matter how drugged she was. She would turn aside the blade at the last moment, then she'd pause, confused, and her eyes would clear. She'd look at him hesitantly, and in a soft voice say, *Daddy?*

But Knife-Glove Emory didn't slow down, didn't pull her strike, and with a maniacal grin she jammed her blade into him.

He didn't feel any pain at first, which surprised him. He felt the impact of the blade, actually felt the sharp metal slide into his body, but it didn't hurt. Emory grabbed hold of his shoulder to keep him from moving, and she shoved the blade all the way in. She held it there for a moment and looked into his eyes, her forehead pressed against his, their noses touching. He could feel how hot she was, as if gripped by a high fever. Another symptom of Ivory's drugs, he assumed. Her furnace breath panted into his face, and he searched her eyes for any hint of the little girl he'd read bedtime stories to before tucking her in at night, but all he saw was cold, dark glee.

"I'm sorry," he whispered. Sorry that he hadn't been a better father, sorry that he hadn't been able to protect her from a world that had turned out to be every bit as dangerous as Valerie had always warned.

For an instant, he saw a flicker of doubt in her gaze, but then it vanished and she sneered as she yanked her blade free, giving it a twist as she did so. And that's when the pain finally hit him.

Fire exploded in his gut, and he dropped his knife and grabbed hold of his belly in an instinctive attempt to stop the flow of blood fountaining from his wound. But he might as well have tried to hold back Niagara Falls, for all the good it did. Blood gushed past his fingers, making them instantly slippery. He tried to keep pressure on the wound – wasn't that what you were supposed to do? – but there was so much blood, and his hands were now so slick that he couldn't maintain his grip.

Sorry to tell you this, kiddo, Valerie said, *but you are well and truly fucked.*

No shit, he thought.

Emory let go of his shoulder and stepped back. She grinned as she watched blood pouring past his fingers and splattering onto the Pit's stone floor. The crowd – which had gone silent the instant the blade had entered Jayce's body – now went insane, clapping, cheering, stomping, and shouting things like, "Do it!" and "Cut off his fucking head!" and "Slice off his balls and feed them to him!"

Jayce could already feel himself becoming lightheaded and weak, and he didn't think he could hold on to consciousness much longer. But if he was going to die – and with each passing second it seemed more like a done deal – at least he would enter the darkness knowing that if Knife-Glove Emory was his true daughter, he hadn't hurt her.

Then Nicola was there, and she swung her flail toward Knife-Glove Emory's face. The spiked balls rent flesh and crushed bone with sickening wet sounds, and the impact spun Emory around and she fell to the ground, motionless. Before Jayce could react – although, really, he was too busy dying to say or do anything – Nicola stepped forward and swung her flail at the back of Emory's head, pulping it.

The crowd went ape-shit.

Horrified, Jayce looked to see if the other two Emorys were okay. The one Nicola had originally fought lay on the ground several yards away. Her head was also a shattered wet ruin, and Jayce guessed Nicola had performed the same maneuver on her as she had on Knife-Glove Emory. He looked for Ohio Pig and saw that he lay with Cleaver Emory on top of him. Neither was moving and both were covered with deep, bloody cuts, the ground around them splashed with crimson.

All three Emorys were dead. Two of them had been Underborn, but one had been his daughter, his *Emmy*. Now she was gone, and in a few short moments, he would be joining her.

Jayce.... Valerie began.

Not now, he thought. *Just let me die in silence. Please.*

Tears streamed down his face and he went down on his knees, barely feeling them crack against the rough stone floor. Nicola stepped toward him, blood, hair, and bits of brain matter stuck to the balls of her flail. She reached out toward him, but he waved her off with a bloody hand. He slumped onto his side, no longer bothering to attempt to staunch the blood flowing from his stomach wound. At this point, the faster he bled out, the better.

Even though Nicola was on his side, the crowd chanted, "Finish him, finish him!" But she let her flail fall to the ground and gazed sadly down at him.

From where Jayce lay, he could see Ivory. She stood, hands gripping the railing, grinning with delight. *Glad we put on a good show for you, bitch,* he thought. His vision began to dim then, and he wondered what, if anything, would come next for him. Whatever it was, he doubted it could be much worse than what he'd already experienced. He could still see Ivory, although her image was blurry now, but Nicola was closer and more clear to him. He saw both women step backward at the same instant, and although he could no longer make out Ivory's expression, he could see Nicola's well enough. Her eyes were wide and her mouth hung open.

He realized then that the crowd had gone deathly silent. When he smelled rotting leaves and overturned soil, he knew why.

He turned his head, the effort requiring almost all of his remaining strength, and he saw the Harvest Man standing there, gazing down at him with his inhuman obsidian eyes, lamprey mouth a puckered ring.

And then he remembered.

★   ★   ★

The stall door opens and something – some kind of *monster* – stands there, looking at Jayce with large, shiny eyes filled with darkness. The creature's skin looks something like a lizard's, or maybe a rhino's, and its mouth is a circular nightmare, like an anus filled with small sharp teeth. The creature raises one of its clawed hands and steps into the stall.

Jayce is terrified beyond measure, his heart pounding so fast that he thinks it might explode any second. *This is it,* he thinks. This monster, whatever the hell it is and wherever it came from, is going to tear out his throat and drink his blood. Maybe it will feast on his flesh as well, devour his organs, slurp down his skin, crunch his bones and suck out the marrow. After all, that's the sort of thing monsters do, right?

But instead, the creature puts its hand on top of Jayce's head, the gesture a gentle, even tender one. The moment the gray hide comes in contact with his body, Jayce's fear vanishes, and he becomes instantly, completely, utterly calm. He looks up at the creature's grotesquely inhuman face, but he no longer sees ugliness there. He sees beauty.

"I know what you are," Jayce says, voice barely a whisper.

And I know you. I have something for you. Something that belongs to you. Will you accept it?

Jayce answers without hesitation.

"Yes."

The Harvest Man's round mouth irises wide and he breathes forth a stream of darkness. Jayce opens his own mouth, and the darkness flows toward and into him. He inhales its coldness, and he can feel it settling into him, changing him, and it feels good. No, more than that.

It feels wonderful.

★   ★   ★

Jayce's mind returned to the present and he looked up at the Harvest Man.

"I remember," he said.

Then it is time, the Harvest Man replied.

CHAPTER THIRTEEN

Then the Harvest Man's body shimmered, like waves of heat rising from a summer road, and he was gone.

Jayce, still bleeding, but no longer weak, rose to his feet, the front of his coveralls soaked with dark blood from his stomach wound. The audience, still stunned by the Harvest Man's appearance, watched him with silent awe and perhaps more than a little fear.

"Jayce? Are you all right?"

Nicola looked afraid of him too, but she held her ground and didn't move away from him.

He gave her a grim smile. "Never better," he said, blood still leaking from his ravaged gut and pattering onto the stone floor.

Ivory had been as stunned as everyone else, but she was quick to recover.

"Kill him!" she shouted.

Therons ran forth from the entrances on both sides of the Pit, the four that had been watching the match joined by a dozen more, some of them carrying weapons, some of them armed only with their bare hands. Jayce didn't care. Armed or unarmed, it was all the same to him.

He remembered the feeling of the darkness entering him for the first time, and with this memory came the knowledge of how to bring it forth again. He opened his mouth and an ebon cloud shot forth to engulf one half of the attacking Therons, and without waiting to see the results, he turned toward the second group and did the same thing. Two streams of darkness trailed from his mouth, and he inhaled, drawing them both back into him with silent ease. The Therons were all motionless ash figures now, and they quickly lost cohesion and collapsed to piles of black dust.

The crowd sat in horrified silence for several seconds, and then pandemonium broke out. Shadowers screamed, wailed, shouted, and sobbed, and everyone tried to flee at once, pushing, shoving, hitting, kicking, clawing, and biting. If they had weapons, they used them, and if they didn't, they improvised. If they were strong enough, they tore lengths of wood from the bleachers to use as clubs, and if they lacked strength, they employed their intelligence, pushing people down toward the Pit, using gravity as their weapon. Shadowers fell, rolled, slammed into the railing. Others weren't so lucky and were trampled in the crowd's mad panic to escape.

Jayce watched the chaos for several moments, coldly amused, and then he spread his arms outward and began slowly spinning in a circle. Darkness gusted forth from inside him, pouring into the air and racing toward the fleeing Shadowers. More darkness emerged, vast clouds of it, far more than a single human body should have been capable of containing. But then Jayce wasn't human and hadn't been for some time. Maybe not ever. He just hadn't known it until now. Valerie had, though. It was why she'd given up her life as a Shadower, left the Cannery, and never returned. Why she'd been so overprotective of her only child, why she'd worked so hard to convince him the world was a dangerous place. She didn't want to risk anything waking the monster inside him.

And I failed, Valerie said. *Lords of Blight, how I failed.*

As he rotated, Jayce saw Ivory running, not toward the elevator, though. In a different direction. It stood to reason that there would be other ways in and out of Crimson Splendor's lower levels besides the elevator, even if those ways were only known to Ivory herself. Jayce wasn't worried that she'd get away. He knew he could find her any time he wished.

Nicola remained where she'd been when the Harvest Man appeared, only now she crouched low to the ground, as if she were trying to make herself as small as possible so she might go unnoticed by him. She watched Jayce, but she didn't look afraid of him now. If anything, she looked happy, almost joyful. Her reaction struck Jayce as odd, but he was too caught up in what was happening at the moment to worry about it.

His darkness rolled over the bleachers in billowing waves, and wherever it went, another voice was silenced, then another, and another. Until, more swiftly than would've seemed possible to him only a short while before, the Pit was silent. He paused for a moment, relishing the stillness, before breathing in once more. The darkness rushed back toward him, moving even faster as it returned home. As it flowed back into him, it brought with it the minds and spirits of everyone it had touched. No longer was Valerie alone inside him. Joining her were the dozen Therons he'd gathered – no, *harvested* – along with hundreds of Shadowers, and he could feel all of them, each and every one, could hear their weeping and moaning, their voices a tumult inside him.

I contain multitudes, he thought, and he knew he could hold more, infinitely so. This was only the beginning.

"Hush," he said softly, and the legion inside him fell silent at his command.

He closed his eyes and searched inside for Ivory, but he was not surprised that she wasn't there. She'd made her escape – for the time being.

Clouds of black dust rose into the air as the ashen remains of the Shadowers collapsed, and the particles began drifting down into the Pit like black snow. Jayce thought he'd never seen anything more beautiful.

Nicola straightened. Blood splatter marred the white of her coveralls, but she didn't appear to be wounded. She walked up to him, smiling, then bowed her head and knelt before him.

"I won't hurt you," he said.

She looked up at him, beaming. "I know."

He held out his hand, and she allowed him to help her rise.

"Did Ivory—" she began.

"She remains free, but I know where to find her." He paused, then added, "I know many things now."

He glanced at the bodies of the three Emorys lying on the stone floor of the Pit.

"It's time to finish this," he said, his voice like the mournful wind of an October twilight.

★　★　★

He led Nicola to an opening in the wall behind one of the bleachers. He presumed it was a secret door, one that Ivory had opened and, in her haste, failed to close. A set of stairs led down, and while they were unlit, Jayce didn't hesitate to take them. He didn't need light to find his way anymore. He didn't want to drip blood on the steps and risk Nicola slipping and getting hurt, so he concentrated and the flow from his stomach wound stopped. He didn't bother to close the wound itself. There was no need.

Nicola followed at a respectful distance.

The air grew warmer and more humid the farther they descended, and the atmosphere quickly became stifling. It felt like he was breathing through a throat full of wet cotton, and runnels of sweat flowed down his body. He smiled. It seemed he had some human left in him after all. A rank miasma of body odor filled the stairwell, and Jayce imagined hundreds of bodies jammed together, sweating in the heat. Once, the smell would have turned his stomach and made his gorge rise, but now it did nothing to him. It was merely a detail to be noted, nothing more. There was a different scent in the mix, a combination of stagnant water and rotting fish. Jayce didn't need his new abilities to tell him what the smell belonged to. It was easy enough to guess: the Primogenitor.

They reached the bottom of the stairs and stepped into a cavern, what Ivory had referred to as the Creche. There was no source of light, but Jayce could make out the details of the place as clearly as if they were on the surface and the sun was shining bright. The cavern appeared to be a natural structure, with no reshaping by human – or inhuman – hands. The walls, ceiling, and floor were unhewn rock, and stalactites and stalagmites projected from its surfaces. A huge fungus-like mass grew on the ceiling, and it had used the stalactites to anchor itself, growing around them to the point where it appeared they had pierced it like spears. The ceiling wasn't very high, maybe twenty feet, Jayce guessed, but the greenish fungus was so thick that it cut that height in half. The mass was covered in a thick viscous layer that resembled clear gelatin, and embedded in this substance, hanging facedown and arms stretched wide as if they'd been frozen in the act of flying, were the naked bodies of men, women, and children, eyes closed and faces expressionless. They ranged in age from infants to seniors, and different races and body types were represented. It made sense. Ivory would want a wide selection to offer her customers. Did she bring some of them down here – only the most wealthy and esteemed among them, naturally – and allow them to choose from her stock, like a high-class restauranteur showing off the quality of her wine cellar? Probably.

The cavern wasn't high, but it was wide, and the fungus – the Primogenitor – covered the entire ceiling. Dozens of bodies were held in its substance, so many that Jayce had difficulty estimating their number. One hundred? Two hundred? More? And until recently, Emory had been among their number. If only he'd come into his power sooner, he might have been able to save her. It was too late for that, but it wasn't too late to take vengeance in her name.

Ivory stood in the center of the chamber, surrounded by a number of robed figures holding long metal rods like they were staves. The figures made no apparent move, but the top ends of their staves began to glow with baleful yellow light. Nicola, now able to see their surroundings, looked up at the Primogenitor and gasped. Jayce kept his attention focused on Ivory. She struggled to maintain control of her emotions, but even from a distance, Jayce could see the fear in her eyes. But she was a creature that had endured for two centuries or more, and she hadn't survived that long by giving up easily.

She stretched her hand toward them and pointed. She gave no verbal command, but the robed figures lowered their staves as if they were weapons and charged. Some of their hoods fell back as they ran, and Jayce could see that the Primogenitor's attendants were more Therons. He waited until they were within ten feet, breathed out, breathed in, and they were gone, their ashen forms falling apart an instant later. With no hands to hold them, the staves clattered to the floor, glowing tips still providing light.

Ivory stood alone now.

Jayce walked toward the old woman, not hurrying. He knew she had nowhere else to go. Nicola trailed after him, but he was barely aware of her presence. His attention was focused entirely on Ivory.

"Stay back," the woman said. She raised her hands above her head, fingers twisted into strange configurations. "I am far from defenseless."

"If you possess magic, use it," Jayce said as he kept walking.

"I'll harvest it the same way I harvested your servants."

Ivory began to tremble and a quaver entered her voice.

"You know that I come down here from time to time to make duplicates of myself, but you have no way of knowing how *many* duplicates of me there are, or even if I'm the *real* Ivory. I might not even know which is the real me by this point."

Jayce continued toward her. He closed most of the distance until only two feet separated them. He stopped, so close now he could reach out and touch her. But instead of drawing back, Ivory lowered her arms, and a sly smile spread across her face.

"I brought the Primogenitor here, although it was much smaller then, of course. It obeys me, and if I tell it to, it will crush all of those it holds within its substance. Including your daughter."

Jayce had a sudden realization. "You lied in the Pit. None of the Emorys were real."

Ivory laughed. "Of *course* I lied! You think I would waste an original when I can have the Primogenitor make as many duplicates of her as I wish? The Emorys who died in the Pit were all Underborn. The real Emory is still here" – she gestured toward the Primogenitor and the naked forms trapped in its substance – "somewhere."

"And if I let you go, you'll return her to me, is that it?"

From behind him, Nicola said, "Don't trust her, Jayce."

"Not exactly," Ivory said, ignoring Nicola. "You let me leave and I won't tell the Primogenitor to crush everyone. Once I'm gone, you'll be free to search for her. When you find her, I'm sure you'll be able to figure out a way to free her – especially given your new...*talents*."

Jayce considered her words. "You could be lying now. The real Emory might be one of the three lying dead on the level above us, and you're just hoping to save your own skin."

"I admit, I *have* become rather fond of it over the centuries.

Well, if your abilities don't extend to determining whether someone is lying – and it appears they don't – then I suppose you'll just have to take a chance, won't you? And you know better than to try to breathe your darkness on me. It didn't affect my duplicate in the club when the Harvest Man tried it, so you know it damn well won't affect me."

Now that she was negotiating, Ivory was less fearful and more confident. She was once again in her natural element, and no matter what Jayce had become or what powers he'd gained, he was just another mark that she could manipulate.

"By bringing the Primogenitor to Oakmont and using it the way you have, you've thrown Shadow out of balance. The imbalance worsened as the years passed, and now it has reached the point where it can no longer be tolerated."

"I've saved lives!" Ivory insisted. "I've made Oakmont a *better* place, a *safer* one!"

Jayce gave her a grim smile. "Shadow isn't supposed to be safe."

And then, before she could say or do anything more, his hand shot out, his fingers wrapped around her throat, and he gave her neck a single, sharp twist. A loud *crack* sounded in the humid air, and Ivory's eyes went wide for an instant before they glazed over and her body went limp. Jayce released her, and she fell to the floor and lay still.

Nicola stepped forward and gazed upon Ivory's corpse. She looked at the woman for a long moment before spitting on her face. Afterward, she turned to face Jayce.

"You were helping him all along, weren't you?" Jayce didn't have to speak the Harvest Man's name. They both knew who he was referring to.

She gazed at Jayce with undisguised adoration.

"Yes. Remember when I told you that I was lost in Shadow for a time when I was younger, and I couldn't remember what happened to me? Well, I lied about not remembering. *He* came to me. He told me things – awful, *wonderful* things – and he showed me foul glories beyond anything human minds can imagine. He said that there would come a day when he would need a successor. I hoped he meant me, but he said that was not my destiny, but another's. My task was to help the successor, to guide him until he was ready to take on the dark mantle of the Harvest Man. And now that I have done as I was bidden, I have only one request of you, my new lord."

Jayce smiled and reached out to gently touch her cheek.

"You have been a good and faithful servant, and you shall have your reward."

He leaned forward to kiss her, and as she opened her mouth, he breathed his darkness into her. She sighed, then fell silent as he inhaled. When he stepped back, a face of ash stared at him and then, bit by bit, it collapsed into a pile of black dust. He felt Nicola inside him, heard her shout for joy. Jayce looked upon Nicola's remains for several moments before turning his attention to the Primogenitor.

Ivory should never have brought the thing to Oakmont from whatever dark corner of the world she'd found it in, but she had. It could no longer be allowed to exist, that much was clear, but the question was what to do about all the people who'd been abducted and forced to serve as raw material to create the Underborn? If he released them, several hundred missing people – some of them missing for decades – would be free to return home. And once they did, attention would be drawn to the Cannery. National, and maybe even international, attention. He could see the headlines now: *Hundreds of Prisoners Held Captive Beneath Ohio Town. Naked Abductees Used in Sinister Cult Rites. Crazed Cave Cult Captures Citizens!* He doubted the people would remember much, if anything, about what had happened to them, but even with humans' ability to ignore the strange things happening in their midst, there would simply be too many people returning to ignore. He knew instinctively that it was now his purpose to preserve the balance between Shadow and the rest of existence. But what was the best way to do that in this case?

In the end, he didn't see he really had a choice. He took in a deep breath – deeper than any he'd ever taken before – held it for several seconds, and then exhaled.

★ ★ ★

When it was over, the Creche's ceiling was clear, the stalactites free of any encumbrance, and the cavern's floor was covered with black dust. The Primogenitor, along with the bodies it held, was gone. But Jayce wasn't alone. Lying on a bare spot on the floor several feet from him, curled into a fetal position, naked body glistening with slime, was Emory. He allowed her to wake up in her own time, and as she slowly stirred, he removed Ivory's tuxedo so she would have something to wear. He shook black dust from the clothing, and when he was finished, he folded Ivory's shirt, jacket, and pants, and along with the shoes, placed them on the clean floor next to Emory. He then knelt at his daughter's side. She was still half asleep, so he spent the next few minutes licking the slime from her with his new elongated black tongue. Not long after he'd finished cleaning her, she opened her eyes. She looked around for a moment, confused, and then she focused on him.

"Dad? Is that you?"

Jayce smiled.

"More or less."

★ ★ ★

Jayce didn't bother destroying those Underborn on Snuff or Carnality. They would be used up soon enough, and no replacements would ever be made. Sometimes, the best way to achieve balance was to let events run their natural – or in this case, unnatural – course.

The sky was a pale blue when Jayce and Emory stepped out of the building and onto the sidewalk. Dawn was near.

Emory, dressed in Ivory's tuxedo, turned to him. The outfit was a bit snug on her, but it would do until she got home. He thought she looked rather cute in it, actually. Her hair was a matted, tangled mess, but he'd only been able to clean it so well with his tongue. She'd need a shower and *lots* of shampoo and conditioner.

She gazed at the bloodstains and black smudges on his once-white coveralls. When she'd first noticed them in the Creche, she'd feared he'd been injured and needed help. He'd assured her he was fine, and while she'd seemed skeptical, she hadn't challenged him. Now she looked like she wanted to say something about the blood again, but instead she said, "I'm not sure how I got down there. The last thing I remember was...." She broke off, as if suddenly embarrassed.

"Being in The Hole Thing. I know. It's okay. It's your life to live, and all you need to know is that I love you, no matter what. Just try to be careful, huh? Shadow is a dangerous place."

She nodded, eyes glistening. Did she sense this was goodbye? Maybe.

"Why don't you go home, get cleaned up, and get some rest? I'll see you later."

She looked at him for several seconds, and he thought she was going to say something, but in the end she nodded and gave him a quick kiss on the cheek – being careful not to brush up against his filthy coveralls – and then she turned and walked away. As he watched her go, he knew that while he'd never have regular contact with her again, he would keep his promise. He *would* see her again. He would watch over her, and if she ever needed his help, he would be there. He might be a monster now, but he was still her father. And when it came to his daughter, balance be damned.

When Emory turned at the corner of the block and was lost to his sight, he started walking. He had one last stop to make before this was all over. It looked like it was going to be a nice day, and he decided to travel on foot instead of taking his Altima. He'd never need the vehicle again, anyway. He passed pedestrians on the sidewalk, and commuters drove by on their way to work. Most of them didn't see him, and those that did, did a double-take, frowned, shook their heads, and promptly forgot about him.

CHAPTER FOURTEEN

The two-note electronic tone sounded as he pushed open the door to CrazyQwik. *Bee-baw*. He stepped inside and saw Virgil standing behind the counter. The store was empty, aside from the two of them, but this didn't surprise Jayce. They had private business to conduct.

Virgil smiled as Jayce approached the counter.

"Hello, Jayce."

Jayce smiled back. "Hello, Dad."

Virgil's smile widened into a grin. "Figured it out, huh?"

"Yeah. Not that it was any great trick, now that I know Mom's inside me. She can't hide anything from me anymore."

"Want a beer?" Virgil asked. "I know it's early, but I sure could use one."

Without waiting for Jayce to reply, he came out from behind the counter, walked to one of the coolers – *not* the one containing the vessels – grabbed a couple Sam Adams, and returned. He held the bottles up to his mouth and breathed a small cloud of darkness onto the caps. He breathed in again, and the caps dissolved. He blew the black dust away from their mouths and then handed a bottle to Jayce. Jayce took it, pressed the cold glass rim to his lips, and drank. Nothing had ever tasted this good to him before. And it was emotionally satisfying, too. After all, what boy didn't want to one day share a beer with his father?

"You were the man my mother slept with back when she was a Shadower. Except you weren't a man, were you?"

Virgil took a long sip of his beer, and when he finished, he smacked his lips.

"Valerie was a good woman." He frowned. "At least, I think she was. I'm not very good at judging that sort of thing. I appeared to her as human at first, in a different form than this one. But I soon revealed my true face to her, and when I did, she pledged her devotion to me, and I became like a god to her."

"Just like with Nicola."

"Except I never had sex with her. There was no need, since I'd already procreated. Valerie turned against me after you were born, though. She tried to protect you from me." He snorted. "As if that were possible."

"You were the one who drove the black van that picked up Nicola and her friend when they were kids, weren't you? Why the van? Get tired of appearing and disappearing at will?"

"I use whatever methods – and guises – my work requires." He gestured toward the face he currently wore. "Case in point."

"What happened to the girl who was with Nicola?" He paused as he reached for her name. "Gretchen?"

"I only needed one of them, and Nicola was the stronger of the two."

Jayce didn't have to ask what had happened to Gretchen. He had a good idea.

"You posed as Virgil so you could meet Emory, right? Hell, you probably created this damn place just so she could get a job here. Maybe you steered her toward Crimson Splendor and The Hole Thing too, so she would be captured and I'd come looking for her."

"I posed as the manager of Emory's apartment complex as well. I needed to make absolutely certain that everything happened according to plan."

"But why involve her?" Jayce demanded.

"Something changed in your mother after you were born. Once she held you, gazed into your wide, wondering eyes, fed you at her breast, she could no longer bear the thought of you one day taking my place. And so she left the Cannery and never returned."

"If she wanted to keep me away from you so bad, why didn't she move to a different town?"

"There was nowhere for her to go. Shadow is everywhere, to one degree or another. And wherever Shadow is, I am. She worked hard to keep you away from Shadow, and you were a big help to her. When, despite her best efforts, you caught a glimpse of Shadow, you were so damn *good* at forgetting it. Practically a genius, really. I knew you could never embrace your heritage on your own. You needed…encouragement. A push in the right direction. And so I gave it to you." He smiled. "To help prepare you to take over the family business."

"And Emory was that push."

"Yes."

"Was Ohio Pig part of your plan too? Was he one of your followers, like Nicola?"

Virgil shook his head. "No, but he did prove useful in the end, didn't he? For his amusement factor, if nothing else."

They drank in silence for several moments after that. Jayce was still human enough to hate his father for manipulating him all these years, and he hated him even more for what he'd done to Nicola, and *especially* for how he'd used Emory. But his emotions weren't as strong as they should've been, and in fact, they didn't seem altogether genuine. More like echoes of emotions he knew he *should* feel, but couldn't quite. He'd changed too much, he realized. He wasn't really Jayce Lewis anymore, only a walking ghost of that man.

Jayce finished his beer and sat the empty on the counter.

"Why do you need a successor?" he asked.

"Entropy," Virgil said. "If we're to keep the balance, we're subject to it like anything else in existence. We might be able to put death off a little longer than most, but it catches up to us in the end. I knew my time would come one day, just as it did for my mother and for her father before her, all the way back to the screaming chaos that in its madness and agony birthed the universe. There have been Harvest Men and Women since this planet was only a ball of magma hurtling through space, and they will be here long after it's nothing but a cold, empty rock continuing to spin out of blind habit." He shrugged. "It is the way of things. You too will need a successor one day."

"No offense, but I don't know if I can bring myself to create a child knowing its only purpose is to become a monster."

For an instant, Virgil's eyes became large and glossy black, but they quickly became human once more.

"Good thing you already had a child then, isn't it?" He finished the last of his beer and set the empty down. "Good talk, but it's time I was moving on. And you've got a lot of work ahead of you. A good harvest to you, my son."

Jayce's only reply was to nod. Then he breathed upon his father, and when he inhaled again, Virgil was gone, without even an ash figure to mark where he'd been. He lived inside his son now, as did all the Harvest Men and Women who had come before him. Jayce was like an infinitely receding collection of nesting dolls, one inside the other, and every being the Harvesters had collected since before the beginning of time dwelled within him as well.

It was magnificent.

Jayce – now bald, skin a mottled gray, eyes large black orbs, mouth a tooth-filled ring, hands cruel-looking claws – turned away from the counter and moved in a series of rapid jump-cuts to the door. He stepped outside and into the sunshine of a new day.